SECRETS OF RUIN

THE SHADOW REALMS
BOOK 11

BRENDA K DAVIES

Brenda K Davies

CHAPTER ONE

LIGHT DIDN'T OFTEN COME to the bowels of the pyramid; when it did, it never brought relief or joy. In this dark pit of despair, light meant the return of their captors and pain.

After their arrival, when the first torches lining the walls burnt out, they remained that way until the ophidians returned to reignite them. And when they came back, it meant only one thing... they'd returned to have fun... or at least it was fun for *them.*

For the prisoners trapped in this endless loop of suffering, filth, and misery, it meant only agony.

Everything here brought discomfort from the captors who so loved to torture them, even the dirt floor that dug into Kaylia's increasingly protruding bones while she tried to sleep. The bucket in the corner held her waste and cast a foul smell, but this whole place consisted of awful smells she'd somehow adjusted to; however, it was adapt or go insane in this place.

They were in Hell, but instead of burning in that fiery place, a chill encompassed the damp air of the dungeon. It had crept into her bones until she was permanently cold, and the ophidians didn't provide blankets or warmer clothes to ease the ice inside her.

Kaylia had no idea how much time had passed since the ophidians confined them—time meant nothing here. It was endless but steady as it ebbed and flowed like the ocean's waves that she feared she'd never see again.

Without the sun or moon to mark the passing days, there was no way to track them, and she wouldn't if she could. Why did she want to know how much of her life was wasted here?

The only thing that gave her hope and kept her sane was holding Brokk's hand. Lying on her side and reaching through the bars of their cell, she could stretch her hand far enough into his cage to clasp his.

Night after night and day after day, she sought Brokk's solid presence in this place that reeked of waste, anxiety, sweat, and death. And *so much* death had occurred since their arrival; far too many of their group had perished in this pit.

More would soon follow; she did not doubt that, as the ophidians enjoyed their demise. They loved their torment, too, so they drew out their deaths, but it was only a matter of time before those monsters destroyed them all.

As time passed, Brokk became a shell of the man he used to be. The ophidians brought them shitty food, and she supplied him with blood, but it had been….

Well, she had no idea how much time had passed since they were last together and he'd nourished the dark fae part of himself. It could have been a month or a year.

Now, in the dim glow of the torches the ophidians left behind after their last visit, she studied Brokk as he lay, staring at her, his hand encasing hers. They were all weakening in this place, but the toll of their inadequate nourishment had been toughest on him.

Dirt marred cheekbones that were far more prominent than

before he entered this place. His once lively, aqua-blue eyes were duller, and their twinkle had vanished.

The ophidians sometimes brought in buckets of water and soap for them to wash, probably when they could no longer stand the smell of them, but it had been a while, and grime had turned his dark blond hair brown. A thick, brown beard obscured his handsome features and grew an inch or two past his chin.

Sometimes, the twinkle in his eyes would return when he looked at her, but not today. It hadn't been there since they watched the ophidians torture and kill another amsirah.

That man's death wasn't too long ago, as the torches remained lit. They'd soon go out and plunge them back into darkness. Until then, she planned to savor seeing Brokk again.

Kaylia turned her hand over and lifted her wrist toward Brokk. He shook his head as his thumb traced the two puncture marks there. A matching set marked her other wrist.

Sometimes, he'd feed on her, but he never took enough. Her blood helped keep the vampire part of him nourished. However, the dark fae part of him was starving as, without sex, he grew weaker.

At first, dozens filled the dungeon cells; now, only a fraction of that number remained. Hopelessness swelled amongst the survivors; it permeated the air and came out in muffled sobs or whimpers.

No one looked at those who broke down in tears; they all required their moments in this place. So far, no one had completely cracked and slipped into madness, but Kaylia suspected it was only a matter of time… if any of them lived that long.

Eventually, the ophidians would destroy what remained of them. Until then, the hideous monsters would continue torturing them until their spirits broke.

To her right, Ryker shifted in his cell. His movement drew

her attention from Brokk to the large man standing in the center of his small cell.

Before coming here, he'd been bulkier with thickly corded muscle on his arms and chest; he'd shriveled in size while here. He hadn't lost as much as Brokk, but he was barely recognizable as the man he once was.

Fresh marks from a whip marred his chest and back; while the ophidians had flayed him open, he hadn't made a sound. He'd stood there and took it while they tore away his skin.

Beneath the fresh marks lay faded white scars. Some of those scars had come from his time at war, but judging by the shape and size of them, Kaylia suspected many of his scars came from other beatings. Those beatings must have been brutal if he still bore their marks.

Ryker stared relentlessly ahead; his beard-covered jaw moved back and forth as he ground his teeth together. His hands fisted at his sides while he glowered at the locked door where the ophidians entered and exited.

He'd barely moved since the ophidians left after killing another amsirah. During their time here, his dark brown hair had grown past his shoulders, and his silver eyes shone with a coldness that wasn't present before his imprisonment.

Beyond him, more of Ryker's men remained in the other cells stretching into the shadows until Kaylia couldn't see the ones at the end. Most of those cells used to be full, but not anymore.

Only two witches who'd helped the amsirah in Doomed Valley remained. The others had succumbed to the ophidians' endless torture. Kaylia shuddered as she recalled what it was like to suffer at the hands of those monsters.

CHAPTER TWO

SENSING HER DISTRESS, Brokk squeezed her hand. A smile curved his mouth when she shifted her attention back to him. That smile didn't reach his eyes, but it revealed the tips of his retracted fangs. They were still more visible when not extended.

Despite his weight loss and the dirt and blood marring him, he was still gorgeous. Kaylia's heart beat faster, and her breath caught as she basked in his smile.

Before being tossed into this dungeon, her feelings for him had grown to the point where guilt and uncertainty over her emotions battered her daily. She'd pledged to spend the rest of her life with Fabian, a man taken from her by the senseless act of a vampire; she shouldn't be experiencing anything for another man... but she was.

To deal with Fabian's loss, she'd locked herself away in the crone realm as she tried to come to terms with losing the only man she'd ever loved. Free of that realm, and in Doomed Valley, she'd discovered a sexual reawakening with Brokk, but more, she'd developed feelings for him... something she'd believed impossible.

Immortals only ever loved once; it was the way of things.

They didn't give their hearts easily, but when they did, they never gave them again.

Over their time in Doomed Valley and inside these bars, she couldn't deny that she'd come to care deeply for Brokk. If she ever got the chance to escape this place and destroy these monsters, she'd gladly make the ophidians pay for what they'd done to him.

Never had she enjoyed taking a life; she killed when it was necessary, but she would *relish* slaughtering these reptile pricks who'd stolen the twinkle from Brokk's eyes and their freedom.

"Everything okay, beautiful?" Brokk inquired.

His voice was far raspier than before they entered here, but it still made her heart beat faster. A small shiver ran down her spine as her hand tightened on his.

She doubted she looked beautiful right now, but when he said it, she *felt* it and believed he meant it. No matter how she looked, he found her beautiful.

"Just another day in paradise," she whispered.

He smiled as he traced his thumb across her palm. The bars were so close together that he couldn't fit his hand through them, but she could get hers through without touching the ensorcelled metal.

If they accidentally touched the bars, the metal could shoot them across their cell. She'd made the mistake of touching one once; she wouldn't make it again.

"What's your idea of paradise?" Brokk asked.

They'd spent countless hours discussing different things, asking each other random questions, and learning more about one another. Sometimes, they would lie silently, holding onto each other, but she enjoyed learning about him.

"I'm not sure," she answered.

At one time, her answer would have been easy. Paradise was anywhere with Fabian.

That answer didn't come to her now. And neither did the

guilt that once accompanied the realization her dead fiancé, the man she'd loved more than any other, was becoming less of a once-in-a-lifetime love to her.

She should have remained in love with Fabian and loyal to him until the end of her days, but Brokk changed that. She still loved Fabian and always would, but he'd ceased being her idea of paradise.

Someone else was steadily replacing him as that man. Guilt flared but faded when she met Brokk's eyes again.

"Anywhere outside of here and…." Her words trailed off as they lodged in her throat.

He kissed the tips of her fingers. "And?"

"Somewhere warm but *not* humid."

He chuckled as his smile widened. After their time in Doomed Valley, neither wanted to experience the oppressive humidity of the jungle again.

"Somewhere with friends who have become family." As she spoke, her words came out more broken as a sob lodged in her throat. "Somewhere… outside of… here."

He rested his forehead against her palm. She shouldn't say it, but he deserved to know how much he meant to her; they might never leave this place, and she couldn't hold the words back.

"Somewhere with *you*."

Brokk lifted his head, and when their gazes locked, the steely gleam in his eyes rattled her. *Did I say something wrong?*

"I'm going to get you out of here," he vowed. "I don't know how I'll do it, but I promise you will *not* die here, Kaylia."

Kaylia closed her eyes. "You can't die here either."

Her heart couldn't take the loss of another man she loved.

"I won't let these fuckers kill me," he said.

And she believed him. She didn't know how they'd break out of this place when they'd already failed to, but he'd find a way.

"What's your idea of paradise?" she asked.

"Being back in Dragonia with my family, friends, and *you*. It sounds so simple, but it's all I want."

"Me too. I hope my familiar will finally find me when we return."

"I've never seen your familiar."

"Her name is Ursula; she was a white cat in her last incarnation. She passed before you and Sahira found me in the crone realm. I've been waiting for her to return, but she hasn't yet... or maybe she has, and I'm trapped here."

"Could she find you here?"

"Maybe, but I doubt it. Our familiars are attracted to our energy; it's how they find us throughout their different incarnations. I doubt I'm giving off much energy this far below the earth." And this emaciated, but she kept that to herself; it would only upset him.

"You'll find her again."

"I know."

Before they could say anything more, the scrape of a key turning in a lock alerted them the ophidians had returned. Things were about to get a *lot* worse.

CHAPTER THREE

BROKK TENSED before releasing Kaylia's hand. He'd meant what he said; he had no idea how, but he *would* get her out of here if it was the last thing he did.

The others shifted in their cells as the tension in the dungeon rose. He almost reclaimed Kaylia's hand, but these creatures didn't know about their growing relationship... whatever it was.

If they knew about it, they would have already used it against them in the most awful ways possible. Brokk couldn't load that gun and hand it over to these monsters.

As the ophidians entered, they carried the rack Brokk had become all too familiar with seeing. Flashes of memories ran across his mind as phantom pains stabbed his arms and legs.

It was easy to recall the feeling of his muscles, bones, and joints being pulled too far in directions they shouldn't go. On two occasions, the snakelike beasts who had captured and imprisoned them got a little too carried away with their stretching and ripped apart two of the amsirah.

He was not looking forward to what would come as a participant or a watcher. Sometimes, he didn't know if it was worse to be the one they tortured or the one helplessly looking on while others suffered.

The feeling of vulnerability that had gripped him ever since his cell door slammed shut was one he despised, but he couldn't shake it. He was useless in this place, something he'd never been before, and he didn't know how to come to terms with it.

Brokk pushed himself into a seated position and bit back a groan as his bones protested the movement. Every part of him pulsed with misery and hunger, and it was about to get worse.

He was so ravenous that it had become an incessant, clawing monster that tore at his gut, ripped through his veins, and shriveled his insides. Kaylia's blood and the meager rations the ophidians provided helped to soothe some of his starvation, but not enough of it.

He didn't dare take more blood from Kaylia. She always offered him more, but while she wasn't as starved as him, she was also suffering.

She'd lost a lot of weight, her cheeks had hollowed out, and her collarbone stood out against the tattered clothing she'd worn since arriving here. The worst part of all was that some of the radiance had gone out of her.

She used to shine with vitality, but that had dulled. She was still beautiful; nothing could take that from her, but she was dying in this place of darkness and suffering.

Witches thrived on the sun, the earth, and the moon. They thrived on all things nature and absorbed the world's strength. There was nothing but suffering to absorb here.

He hated this place and these monsters but was helpless to change anything. And that was what pissed him off the most.

There had to be a way out of here, but the ophidians had never shown any signs of weakness or made any mistakes with their prisoners. He didn't hold out hope someone would rescue them.

He had no doubt his family was looking for him, but the

chances of finding this pyramid in Doomed Valley were slim to none. It was a possibility but not one he counted on. They had to make their own opportunities here... somehow.

Slithering forward on their tails, the bottom half of the ophidians was that of a snake, while the top half was of a man or woman. When one of them rose on his tail, his head nearly touched the ten-foot-high ceiling.

Their yellow eyes, with elliptical pupils, surveyed what remained of those trapped in the cells. Some forked tongues flicked in and out, but most remained unmoving.

Their hair flowed to their waists, and neither the men nor the women wore any clothing. All of them clutched the silver sticks they used to immobilize their prey.

Brokk could easily recall being jolted by one of those things, and his body tensed in preparation. If they came for him today, he'd feel the torment of that thing, but worse, Kaylia would have to endure it if they decided it was her turn.

He glanced at her as his fangs tingled and his compressed lips twitched toward a snarl. When it came to her, it was far worse to watch as they beat and tortured her than it was to be the one enduring the abuse.

Nothing in his life had ever been worse than that, including this cell, these creatures, and the suffering they unleashed. She'd come to mean so much to him; he loved her, and the idea of losing her caused something primitive to unravel within him.

If given the chance, he'd gladly destroy every ophidian with his bare hands. He'd tear them apart piece by tiny piece for what they'd done to her.

She was his heart, but more, while trapped here, he'd grown to suspect she might also be his consort. Unlike the dark fae, vampires had fated loves they bonded with. All immortals could love another, but a vampire's consort was something rare and special, like a lycan with their mate.

Kaylia being his consort would explain his intense reaction

to her, but so could the fact he'd fallen in love with her. Either way, he couldn't stand the ophidians focusing on her today.

Brokk's heart sank when another ophidian slithered through the door. The man's black hair flowed past his waist and down his tail almost to the ground. His yellow eyes shone in the glow of the torches on the walls.

A golden nemes headdress flecked with emeralds and rubies was perched on the emperor's head. Brokk had never learned the man's name, but this creature ruled the ophidians and had imprisoned Ryker's king.

Where the amsirah king was, Brokk didn't know, but he doubted Leonidas was dead as he was far too valuable to the ophidians. However, he wasn't in this dungeon with them, meaning they had hidden him somewhere else in Doomed Valley or another realm.

Gritting his teeth, Brokk kept his displeasure over seeing this man concealed. The emperor didn't come every time the ophidians doled out their torture, but when he did arrive, someone usually died.

CHAPTER FOUR

BEHIND THE EMPEROR, another table rolled in; foot-long spikes covered this one. Much like the rack, thick, metal manacles hung where the head and feet of their victim would go.

Not good. Not fucking good.

Brokk glanced down through the row of those who remained. He didn't want to see any more of them die, especially not so soon after the last amsirah. The ophidians were upping their game, or the emperor was unusually bloodthirsty this week.

Brokk couldn't stand to lose another one already. They'd all grown closer while trapped here; he knew their names, histories, and about the families waiting for them.

But while he didn't want to see any of them die, he'd far prefer it was one of them instead of Kaylia. If they went for her, he'd tear this place apart.

As he pondered it, helplessness overwhelmed him. If they decided to go for her, he couldn't do anything to stop them.

He couldn't touch the bars of his cell, let alone stop them from killing her. A bellow of frustration lodged in his chest, but he'd never let these monsters know how upset he was.

The emperor's attention shifted to his cell, the last one in the row. As he met the man's callous gaze, Brokk's eyes narrowed.

The corner of the emperor's mouth quirked into a smile. "What are you? You're not an amsirah or a witch, not with those fangs, but you were out in the day when we captured you."

It was the first time the man had spoken to him or any of them. He usually pointed out the poor souls he wanted and watched as his followers removed them from their cells, brought them forth, and tortured them.

Brokk would prefer not to have a conversation with this beast, but maybe if he spoke with the emperor, he could somehow stop the horror about to unfold. He doubted it, but at least it would delay this freak a little.

"I am half dark fae and half vampire," Brokk replied.

"Interesting," the emperor murmured. "*Who* are you?"

"Brokk of the house of the dark fae, and *who* are you?"

The man's lips twitched toward a smile again. "Ah, so you are Brokk. Your family is in *my* valley looking for you."

Brokk didn't respond as he pushed down the excitement trying to rise in his chest. He'd known his family was looking for him, but they hadn't found him yet.

"From what I've heard, you're a prince," the emperor continued.

"So I've been told."

"And a funny prince, too. I like a sense of humor."

Brokk seriously doubted that.

"They've sent dragons into my realm," the emperor continued.

Brokk remained emotionless, but along the line of cells, some others shifted. For most immortals, the mention of dragons sparked terror, but with Lexi in control of them, the dragons wouldn't level the realm unless ordered to do so, and she wouldn't do that.

But if dragons were here and not unleashing destruction on

Doomed Valley, then Lexi had to be awake again. No one else could control the dragons enough to send them here and keep them from devastating the realm.

Unless the dragons were also here looking for crudue vine, but none had entered the realm with him and Kaylia. Things might have changed, but when they left, the dragons remained in Dragonia to watch over Lexi.

If they were moving around, it meant she was okay, that *someone* had found crudue vine and rescued her. Or at least that was the hope he clung to; it was the only one he had in this place.

"Do you know why there are dragons in my realm, Brokk of the dark fae?" the emperor asked.

"To find me."

And Kaylia, but he kept that to himself. He didn't know if such a revelation would keep her safer or put her in more danger, but Lexi and his brothers would be searching for her, too. She'd helped them too much against the Lord to abandon her here without answers, and she and Lexi had become good friends.

"My followers have captured and questioned some of these intruders; we don't like interlopers in our realm."

Considering the ophidians were interlopers in this realm and the mandarus were now all dead because of *their* intrusion here, that was a ballsy statement to make.

"Do you know what all those we've captured have to say about why they're here when we ask them?"

"They're searching for me."

The emperor flashed his teeth, but his eyes remained cold and calculating. "Yes, they're looking for you and... a witch."

When the emperor's gaze shifted to Kaylia, Brokk stiffened, and his breath exhaled harshly through his nostrils. *Shit.*

"You know some powerful people, Brokk of the house of the dark fae," the emperor murmured.

"I do, and they'll search for me until they get the answers they seek."

It wasn't much of a threat, considering he was behind bars and those searchers hadn't found them, but it was true.

The emperor chuckled. "The dragons have gone home. It's been days since we last saw one, and none of the searchers went with them. We made sure of that. They may send more to look for you, but will they find you?"

"My brothers won't give up until they know what happened to me. They'll keep coming, and eventually, they'll find answers. I can guarantee it."

The emperor didn't look at all impressed by his words. "Maybe I'll give them a body to make them happy… or a witch's body."

So that's why they rolled in two torture devices. They may not intend to use them both, but the implication was there.

When the emperor's gaze shifted to Kaylia, Brokk stepped forward. "*No.*"

The ferocity of the word caused the emperor's eyebrows to rise. "No to *you*… or to *her*?"

Brokk had revealed too much with that single move, but he wouldn't let Kaylia suffer because of him. He loved her too much for that.

"I'll take *all* of it," he said. "It's *my* brothers who are leading the search. They'd give up if you gave them my remains."

It was a lie. They'd continue to hunt for Kaylia, but if he could buy her some time, maybe she'd gain her freedom. The ophidians would kill her one day, but the longer she lived, the better her chances were of breaking out or being found.

CHAPTER FIVE

KAYLIA COULDN'T BREATHE as the emperor and Brokk stared at each other. She wasn't afraid for herself in this situation… or at least not *only* herself.

After all her time in this hellhole, she hadn't been defeated or broken. She wouldn't welcome death and wasn't ready for it, but she couldn't lose Brokk.

If she remained in this place without him, her will to live would deteriorate. She couldn't imagine not having him next door, not being able to touch him, and having to live with the knowledge his bright soul was gone because of *her*.

Her heart felt as if someone was gripping it in their hand and squeezing as it labored to pump blood through her. Panic made her ears ring.

She couldn't lose him; she cared too much for him to lose him. She couldn't take another blow like that; she wouldn't survive it.

No. She wouldn't let anything happen to him.

Unfortunately, she couldn't think of a way to stop it. Her powers were useless in this cell, and she couldn't touch the bars without excruciating pain.

But she might be able to stop them from taking him out of his cell today. Swallowing the lump in her throat, she stepped forward, but before she could speak, the emperor did so.

"You must be hungry, my dark fae, vampire friend. Our food will only satisfy one of your three hungers, correct?"

When Brokk didn't respond, the emperor's attention shifted to her. "Show me your wrists, witch."

Kaylia almost hid her wrists behind her back but managed to keep herself from doing so. Instead, she refused to look away from the snakelike creature before her. She wouldn't let him see that he unnerved her.

She didn't want to do anything he commanded of her, but defying him might only make things worse for Brokk. When she stepped closer to the bars, Brokk edged toward her, but he was as helpless to stop this as her.

Holding the emperor's gaze, Kaylia kept her wrists turned toward her as she lifted her arms. The tattered ends of her filthy tunic fell to her elbows.

She didn't know why she bothered with the shirt anymore. It was nothing but a rag at this point, but she'd feel far more vulnerable around these things if she were nude, and she couldn't stand the idea of pressing her bare skin to the dirt floor.

"Kaylia," Brokk growled.

She had no choice but to show the emperor her marks, and they knew it. If she didn't give the man what he sought, he'd have the doors opened, and the ophidians would hit her with one of those sticks that had the same effect as the bars.

Once she hit the ground, they'd examine her wrists anyway, but they'd be more annoyed by then. Kaylia took a deep breath before turning her wrists so the emperor could see them.

His mouth twitched toward a smile, and his forked tongue slid out before retracting again. "At least she's satisfying your vampire thirst, Brokk of the house of the dark fae. Do you get enough blood from her?"

Brokk didn't reply.

"I'm guessing not, considering how thin you've become," the emperor continued. "Are you the witch his brothers are looking for?"

When the emperor's gaze shifted toward the two other witches, Kaylia blurted, "I am."

His smile grew before he nodded. His gaze swung between her and Brokk as his tongue flicked out again.

Finally, he shifted his attention to the other cells and slithered away. Kaylia's tension didn't ease; instead, it escalated as he studied the occupants of the other cells.

CHAPTER SIX

SOME CRINGED AWAY FROM HIM, and the amsirah sobbed at the end, but most prisoners stood with their shoulders back while glaring at the emperor. They'd lost many of their friends down here, but only a few went out pleading for their lives.

The emperor made it to the end of the cells and paused to rub his chin before turning toward them again. He still looked pensive, but Kaylia suspected he already had a target and was just tormenting them with this show.

Kaylia couldn't resist looking at Brokk. They were most likely the ones to be led from here today, and if this was her last day, then she would absorb everything she could about him.

Fury simmered in his red eyes when they met hers, but she also saw his concern and… something more. She couldn't quite put her finger on what that something more was, but the answering emotion rising inside her created a lump in her throat.

I can't lose him.

The emperor paused outside Ryker's cell, his head tilting from side to side as he studied the amsirah general. "You're also a wealthy, popular man, General Ryker. Your king very much wants you alive."

"Where is he?" Ryker grated out.

"Somewhere safe."

The emperor moved on to Kaylia's cell. "Why would they search for you too, witch? Why are you so special to them? What makes you so important?"

"Nothing. I'm just a witch," she replied.

"She's more than that," Brokk stated. "She's the oldest witch in existence."

Kaylia knew Brokk was trying to give this asshole reasons to keep her alive, but she didn't think it mattered to this man. If he wanted them dead, they would be.

"She's also good friends with *the* Queen of Dragonia," Brokk continued.

"Are you now?" the emperor inquired. "Is that why they're searching for you too?"

Kaylia didn't know what to say to this man that might stop this, but she was pretty sure nothing would.

"So, she would miss you both?" the emperor asked.

"Yes," Brokk answered.

"Maybe she'd be happy with only having one of you back." The emperor's head swiveled toward Brokk. "The new queen is engaged to your brother, isn't she?"

A muscle twitched at the corner of Brokk's eye as they burned impossibly brighter. "She is."

"Interesting. I've heard this new queen is very powerful."

Kaylia bit back the question on the tip of her tongue... *Is she okay?*

If the dragons were here and searching for them, that most likely meant Lexi was awake. Kaylia wasn't about to let this monster know anything had ever happened to her; it was far better if he believed Lexi was near omnipotent.

"She is," Brokk said.

The emperor rubbed his clean-shaven chin again. "Hmm.

Since she doesn't rule here, that doesn't matter to me." He thrust a finger at Kaylia. "Take her out."

CHAPTER SEVEN

KAYLIA'S HEART plunged into her stomach, her throat went dry, and everything inside her screamed against what was to come. Her back had just finished healing from the last beating she received. The last time they put her on the rack, they broke her arm and dislocated her other shoulder.

She somehow managed to clamp her teeth against screaming at them to fuck off. She'd endured their torture before; she would survive it again, and they wouldn't see her break.

She told herself this would be no different than the other times, but the emperor rarely came here, and his presence almost always spelled death when he did. And if not death, then it would be so bad she'd probably yearn for death by the time they finished with her.

Two ophidians donned thick, metal gloves and broke out a set of keys as they slithered toward her. They clasped their long, silver poles before them. They'd jab her with those poles before, rendering her useless.

"*No!*" Brokk exploded. "Take me instead!"

Kaylia shook her head but couldn't speak past the lump in

her throat. She'd gladly go with them rather than watch Brokk suffer in her place.

"Wait." The emperor held up his hand, and the ophidians stopped slithering toward her. The man's head tilted as he studied Brokk with a furrowed brow; then, his expression cleared. "Is she your consort, vampire?"

Despite her resolve to remain motionless, Kaylia's jaw dropped before she could stop it. *No, that can't be.*

But then a prickle of unease ran up her spine, causing the hair on her nape to rise. *It can't be, can it?*

Slowly, her head turned toward Brokk. Her lungs burned for oxygen, but she couldn't breathe. It was impossible as shock held her body in its vice.

Am I his consort?

The possibility had never occurred to her before; vampires rarely found their consorts, and while they were supposed to recognize it instantly when they did, Brokk was only half vampire. His dark fae nature would probably rebel against being tied to another in such a way.

Has the possibility occurred to him?

She finally sucked in a breath of air as she searched Brokk's face for some reaction to the emperor's question, but his face remained far more impassive than hers. Then, it hit her... his lack of a response was more of an answer than if he'd spoken.

He wasn't astounded by the man's question, which meant he *had* considered the possibility. This possibility made her unbelievably sad, and her shoulders slumped as her fingers itched for him.

She fisted them to keep them at her sides. Her nails dug into her palms as she tried to sort through her tumultuous emotions.

During their time together in the Valley, she'd grown to respect and admire him, and yes, though she didn't understand how it was possible, she'd grown to love this brave, selfless man with a heart of gold. He'd become her friend, lover, and salvation in a place where little good existed.

But she could never give her heart to him as completely as he deserved. Part of her heart still belonged, and always would, to Fabian.

She could never change that, and she didn't want to. Fabian deserved to still be loved; his memory continued to live on, and she would never deny him that.

But if she was Brokk's consort, he could never let her go. He had a deep, instinctive need to keep her with him... always. It also meant he would love her with everything he was and never get the same kind of love in return.

No. She inwardly wept for him as she outwardly tried not to fall apart in front of these assholes.

"I don't know," Brokk replied.

The emperor tapped his chin as he studied Brokk. "But I think you do."

"Take me instead," Brokk grated through his teeth.

"Do you *really* wish to take her place, Brokk of the house of the dark fae? Think about it before responding because you will go on the spikes."

Brokk glanced toward the rack with the spikes before focusing on the emperor again. "I have no doubt. Take me instead."

The emperor shrugged. "As you wish."

"*No!*" Kaylia finally managed to find words again. "No! I won't let him sacrifice himself for me. It's *my* turn!"

No one paid attention to her as they opened the door to Brokk's cell. Before the ophidians entered his prison, they jabbed him with the end of one of those poles.

Brokk went rigid; his arms slammed down against his sides, and his teeth clamped together before he fell over. One of them slithered into the cell, grasped his foot, and dragged him out.

"No!" Kaylia screamed.

Without thinking, she threw herself forward, and her fingers stretched toward him. As soon as she touched the bars, she shot backward across the small space and into the far wall.

Her legs shot out, something in her back cracked, and stars danced across her eyes before gravity took over, and she fell to the ground. Cool dirt filled her mouth and nose; the smell wasn't crisp and refreshing like the earth she loved to plunge her fingers into when gardening. It was stagnant and stale, and instead of flooding her with vitality, it filled her with sorrow.

Her fingers jerked as she planted them on the ground and turned her head toward the front of her cell. The figures there jumped and swayed as her vision blurred, but she saw enough to watch as they strapped Brokk onto the table of spikes.

CHAPTER EIGHT

KAYLIA HAD VOWED these monsters would never break her, but she wasn't the one on the table. She wasn't the one with her back against the spikes as the ophidians turned the chains, locking Brokk's hands and legs to the table.

Every twist of those chains pulled Brokk's arms and legs a little further apart. They also pulled him further down onto the spikes.

As the metal pierced deeper into his flesh, blood seeped out to flow down the metal, turning it a darker shade of red. The muscles in his throat and arms stood out as he fought against being stretched and impaled further, but the machine was stronger than him, and when the emperor waved his finger, his minions twisted the chains again.

Kaylia crawled toward the front of her cell as the lingering effects of touching the bars and Brokk's suffering pummeled her system. Her breaking heart made it difficult to breathe through the sobs choking her throat.

She stopped a foot away from the bars and sat as tears slid free. They ran so fast and freely that they dripped off her chin, fell onto her hands, and wet the floor.

Despite the countless times she'd almost cried since coming here, this was the first time she shed tears. She'd seen them torture Brokk before, watched as they beat him, but this was different.

This should have been *her*, and he'd taken her place because he loved her. She had no doubt about it, consort or not, this man loved her.

Would Fabian have taken my place here?

She didn't know where the thought came from and tried to shove it away, as Fabian's memory had no place here, but it refused to go away. The answer to the question should be simple, but it wasn't.

Brokk had taken her place without complaint, and though Fabian still had a piece of her heart, and her love for Brokk could never be absolute, she would have done the same for him. But Fabian… Fabian… and with a strange sort of twisting realization, she realized Fabian wouldn't have done this.

He would have let them take her from the cell and watched on while they tortured her. He was gone and couldn't say that for himself, but deep in her soul, she *knew* it was true.

She didn't know what to make of her realization; she couldn't judge a dead man because he would have chosen to look out for himself. But did it indicate that maybe he hadn't loved her as much as she did him?

But he asked you to marry him. Immortals don't do that unless they're deeply in love with another.

That was true, but Kaylia felt confused as she tried assimilating this new information into everything she'd been *so* sure about. Her head spun as her tears continued to fall and the ophidians turned the chains again.

While she'd hated to watch him suffer all those other times, this one shredded her heart and sliced deep through her soul. It didn't help that she was certain they'd kill him. The emperor was here; he was annoyed that Brokk's family was searching for him, and he had the source of his irritation at his mercy.

Please, Hecate. Please let him survive this.

Her head bowed, and she rested her useless hands on her knees. Whatever magic the ophidians used on the bars kept her magic suppressed, but she'd give anything to unleash her power on these monsters.

"Stand up," Ryker hissed under his breath.

Kaylia glanced over at him, unsure if she'd heard him. The amsirah general stared straight ahead, but when he whispered words again, she knew he was talking to her.

"Get up. Don't let them see you like this."

He was right; they enjoyed this as the emperor smiled at her before shifting his attention to Brokk and waving his hideous finger again. She was giving these monsters what they sought and hated herself for it, but she felt so defeated and battered by everything here that she wasn't sure she could stand.

Yes, you can. Get up!

Kaylia closed her eyes, wiped away her tears, and took a deep breath before gathering the strength to make herself rise. With her hands fisted at her sides, Kaylia straightened her wobbly legs and lifted her chin as the emperor looked at her again.

She longed to close her eyes and shut it all out, but Brokk deserved better, and it would only amuse the ophidians. Ryker was right; she couldn't let them see her fall apart.

With trembling hands, she wiped away her tears. They stopped falling from her chin, but everything inside her continued to weep as more of Brokk's blood flowed down the spikes.

When they twisted the chains again, Brokk's back bowed as he tried to pull himself off the spikes, but they were embedded too deeply now. Sweat slid down his temples and dripped onto the floor as his face became florid; still, no scream issued from him.

Oh, Hecate, please make it stop.

It didn't stop, and they twisted the chains three more times, sinking the spikes halfway into Brokk before the emperor finally called a halt to the torture. The man slithered down to stop at Brokk's head.

The emperor's head tilted back and forth as he studied Brokk before resting his hand on Brokk's forehead. "This is going to get *far* more interesting."

Kaylia's blood ran cold, and her nails bit into her palms as those words sent a shiver down her spine. She didn't see how anything could get any worse than *this*, but she felt she would learn how.

"Release him," the emperor commanded, "and return him to his cell."

With that, the emperor looked at Kaylia and gave her a chilling smile before slithering out of the room.

CHAPTER NINE

"Brokk. Brokk, can you hear me?"

Kaylia's whispered words barely pierced through the haze of agony that kept him locked within its brutal depths. Fire licked over his skin as he tried to slip back into the oblivion of unconsciousness.

"Brokk."

The distress in her voice finally penetrated his pain, and he turned his head toward the sound of it. His lashes felt like something was coating them as he tried to open his eyes.

He knew his eyes finally opened because light filtered through the darkness, but he couldn't make out anything more than that brief flare. Every part of him hurt. His back was wet, what remained of his clothes cleaved to him, and every beat of his heart shot pain through him.

"Brokk." The relief that came from Kaylia with that one word tugged at his heart.

He lay on his stomach with the earth against his cheek. He'd hated sleeping on dirt, but now its coolness was a welcome reprieve from the burning of his back.

What happened?

"Brokk, are you okay?"

He was as far from okay as it got. He was so weak he was pretty sure a newborn could take him out right now.

"You need blood," Kaylia whispered.

The mention of blood caused his fangs to lengthen so fast that they sliced into his bottom lip. For the first time, something replaced his pain as starvation consumed him.

"Come closer to the bars… if you can," Kaylia whispered.

Brokk's fingers twitched against the dirt floor. He shifted a little toward the sound of her voice. The second he moved, a fiery blaze raced across his back.

It screamed through his temples as his head exploded into fragments that scattered across the ground. Blackness rose to engulf him before releasing him again.

He didn't know how long he was out, but he didn't think it was too much time as Kaylia breathed, "Oh, Brokk. I'm so sorry. I'm so, so sorry."

Dim memories of what happened filtered across his mind. She hadn't done this; he was sure of it. They hadn't been able to do more than hold hands for weeks… months… *years*?

How long have we been here?

His mind spun from one detail to another as he tried to focus on what happened and why she'd apologized. And then, he saw the emperor standing before Kaylia's cell, telling his brainless followers to *"Take her out."*

This could have been her. He could have been in his cell watching while they tortured Kaylia. That would have been far worse than what he'd gone through and continued to endure.

He'd rather go through it all a thousand more times before ever witnessing her experience it. He couldn't do much for her here, but he could and would do this.

"Brokk, if you can get to me, you can have my blood. It will help you heal, but you *have to* come closer."

It took some doing, but he finally dragged his battered and

burning body closer to her voice. His vision remained little more than pinpricks of light as she urged him on.

"Stop," she whispered.

He collapsed on the ground, his breath coming in small wheezes as his heart raced faster than it ever had before. The light left his vision, his head spun, and everything faded.

CHAPTER TEN

WHEN HE CAME TO AGAIN, it was to the gentle brush of Kaylia's fingers against his cheek. And he knew it was her as her tender touch eased the worst of his agony.

Even in this place of melancholy, dirt, blood, and excrement, her inherent scent of earth and newly forming leaves pierced through. A rush of emotion flooded him as she brushed back his hair while whispering soothing words.

"Brokk."

He heard her tears and wanted to tell her not to cry for him. He didn't regret anything, but the words wouldn't come. He was too weak to speak.

Her hand trembled as it caressed his thick beard before her wrist pressed against his lips. "Drink. It will make you stronger."

She didn't have to tell him twice as the sweet lure of her blood and the beat of her pulse called to him. His fangs sank into her wrist.

Her potent blood hit his tongue, and he drank it down. Coppery and honeyed all at once, it flooded him with strength as it seeped into his drained cells and pulsed through his arid veins.

He ached to grasp her hand and hold it closer, but he didn't have the energy to make the small move; dragging himself over here had left him depleted. Dimly, he heard her talking while another, deeper voice spoke in the background.

He couldn't make out the other's words or who it was, but he understood her.

"He's burning up," Kaylia said.

There was a pause and the rumble of more words before she spoke again. "I think his wounds are infected, but I can't get a good look at them, and if I could, there's nothing I can do to clean them."

The low voice spoke again before Kaylia responded. "They'll come back soon. They never leave us for long."

Those words and the possibility of the ophidians' return roused him a little. They couldn't come back while he was this weak; he couldn't stop them from taking her if they did.

He managed to lift his hand to clasp hers while he continued to drink. He stroked her fingers as he tried to comfort her.

Finally, he reluctantly retracted his fangs as his body clamored for more. He hadn't taken nearly enough to sate him, but he couldn't take more; if he did, he risked weakening her too much.

"Drink more," Kaylia commanded.

"Taking... too... much," he managed to get out.

"*I'll* decide when it's too much. *Drink more.*"

"When they come back... you... need your... strength."

"*Drink. More.*"

Brokk wanted to argue further as her blood spread out to repair his body, but it couldn't heal all of it. His cells and veins screamed for more. They were broken, empty, on fire...seeking sustenance, and she was offering it to him.

A *little* more wouldn't hurt, but he would be the one to decide when to stop. She felt too guilty about him taking her place on the rack and would give far too much because of it. He wouldn't let that happen.

Clasping her wrist, he bit into her again and held back a

groan as he drank. A little more of the fire dimmed, but she could never provide enough to put it out fully. He was too far gone for that.

"Take as much as you need," she said.

He drank a few more gulps before releasing her and licking away the blood on her skin. "Enough."

"Brokk—"

"*No*. Enough."

He edged away from the bars before her lure became too strong to resist. He didn't know how far he made it before he collapsed and allowed the darkness to take him over again.

CHAPTER ELEVEN

KAYLIA SAT against the solid back wall with her knees drawn up to her chest and her arms around them. Her muscles ached from sitting in the same position for hours, but she remained where she was as she kept her gaze pinned on Brokk.

She had no way of knowing how long he'd been unconscious since feeding from her, but it felt like endless days of worry. The ophidians had returned a few times to give them food and water.

They always opened the cells with their metal gloves and poles at the ready while one of them shoved food and drink inside. Occasionally, someone would still charge them, but those futile escape attempts lessened as time passed.

Anyone who tried to flee always paid the price, but though Kaylia hated seeing her friends suffering after these attempts, it gave her some hope to see that the others hadn't given up yet. There was still hope here, even if it was dwindling.

She'd also tried charging the ophidians a few times, as had Brokk. They'd failed, but she wouldn't give up.

However, she didn't bother trying to run now as the ophidians opened her door, removed the bucket she used for her waste, put down a tray of food, a cup of water, and two new buckets. Kaylia glowered at them as they shut the door and retreated.

It wasn't until after they left that she crept forward to see what they'd left behind. The food was the usual unappealing slop they always delivered, but she would eat it. She had to keep up her strength, especially since she needed to feed Brokk once he woke again, and beggars couldn't be choosers.

One of the buckets was empty and ready for her to fill. She wrinkled her nose at the idea, but by now, she'd done it so many times it didn't make her want to cry. This was simply another necessity for their survival.

The other bucket was full of cold water and soap. From past experiences, she knew a cloth would be at the bottom of the suds floating on top. The ophidians didn't often give them a chance to clean themselves, but this cold, soapy water was glorious when it came.

Her mouth watering over the possibility of scrubbing some of this filth off, Kaylia looked at Brokk and relaxed when she saw his back's slow rise and fall as he lay on his stomach. It was far too slow for her liking.

He hadn't moved since feeding on her, and though she couldn't get closer to examine him, she knew an infection was still ravaging his system. Immortals didn't get infections unless they were *extremely* weakened.

Or maybe the ophidians put something on those spikes, and *that* was battering his system now. They possessed venom, but Kaylia suspected they would have stuck around to watch some of the show if they'd done that, even if it wasn't anywhere near as entertaining as torturing someone directly.

Brokk muttered something incoherent and started to lift his head before flopping onto the ground again. Tears burned her eyes as she watched him suffer; she could help him if they'd let her, but these monsters would never offer such an option.

So, she sat helplessly by while he suffered because of her.

Healing would be difficult without proper nutrition, but he *had* to pull through this.

Kaylia sighed before shifting her attention to the bucket; she shed her clothes and dunked her hand into the chilly water. She didn't flinch as she removed the cloth and scrubbed herself with the coarse material.

Her nipples puckered, and goose bumps broke out on her flesh as she worked, but it was still wonderful. She cleaned herself until all the water from the bucket was gone and the dirt beneath her turned to mud.

She twisted her hair to wring out the water. When she finished, she gathered her clothes before retreating to the back of her cell again. She set her dirty shirt on the ground and sat on it to eat her slop while watching Brokk.

CHAPTER TWELVE

BROKK REMAINED unconscious for too long. During that time, he missed the death of another amsirah and a beating with a cat o' nine tails that tore off Ryker's old scars.

Tattered scraps of Ryker's skin still dangled from what remained of his wounds as he sat in the cell beside her, bare-chested and glowering at the doorway across from him. Blood still trickled from his injuries, but he didn't pay any attention to it.

After the beating, Ryker had cleaned himself the best he could and was now sitting on the tattered remains of his shirt. He'd also stripped out of the ruins of his pants; they lay at the front of his cell by the door.

Most of them had given up on clothes, the last remnants of their former lives. They were nothing but prisoners of the ophidians now, stripped down to flesh and bone... in some cases, literally, as before he started to heal, some of Ryker's shoulder blade was visible from his beating.

When Brokk groaned, excitement flared through Kaylia, and she lurched toward her cell, catching herself before she hit the bars. "Brokk?"

His head turned toward her. His eyes cracked open, and when they met hers, they weren't as unseeing as the last time she saw them.

"Brokk?"

"I'm okay."

His voice came out raspy but stronger than when she last heard him speak. A lump lodged in her throat as she wiped away the tears sliding down her cheeks.

She moved closer to the bars. "Take some more of my blood."

"Too soon."

"No, it's not. You've been unconscious for a few days at least."

"I have?"

"Yes. Take some more of my blood."

Brokk seemed to debate this, but eventually, he used his fingers to drag himself closer to the bars. The torches the ophidians lit while last here had nearly burnt out, but she thanked Hecate for their glow as Brokk moved closer.

He collapsed a few inches from the bars and let out a low, rattling breath that spiked her anxiety. She caressed his cheek and was relieved to discover the blistering heat she'd felt there before was gone.

His skin was cool and clammy; the fire had gone out of it. Red burned from his eyes as they met hers.

Lowering her arm, she rested her wrist against his lips. His lips skimmed back, and she felt his fangs before they pierced her flesh.

While he fed, she tried to lean closer to examine his back, but the blood adhering the remains of his shirt to his skin made it impossible for her to get a good look at the damage inflicted on him.

When his fangs retracted, she stroked his face again. "You can take more. I can handle it."

"Later."

"Brokk…."

But her protests died as he pushed himself up. With careful movements, he started to peel his shirt away. He winced when it clung to his skin.

"I can help," she offered.

He scooted closer, and together, they finally removed the dried, bloody remnants from his back. Kaylia gulped at the puckered holes on his back that still hadn't completely healed.

But the sight of those red holes that should have already healed wasn't what made her stomach plummet. It was the dullness of his ciphers.

It was difficult to get a good look at them through the dried blood still clinging to him, but she saw enough to know their vibrant black color had faded to a dull gray. She'd never seen such a thing happen before and hadn't known it was possible, but she couldn't deny what her eyes were telling her.

He shuddered, and her fingers quivered as she traced those faded marks symbolizing a dark fae's power. And Brokk's power was fading.

CHAPTER THIRTEEN

KAYLIA TRIED to keep her distress over this realization hidden, but he must have sensed something as he edged away from the bars and dropped the remnants of his shirt on the ground. "I'm fine," he stated.

But they both knew that wasn't true. She wasn't going to argue with him. "They brought us some water to clean ourselves."

His head twisted toward the front of his cell. "Good."

When he rose, his legs wobbled until he braced his feet apart and rested a hand against the back wall to keep himself upright. When he was steadier, Brokk removed his boots and ruined pants before tottering to the bucket; he knelt before it.

Kaylia examined each of his movements while he carefully scrubbed himself with soap and water. She'd relished touching, exploring, and bringing pleasure to his body before they were trapped here.

She'd learned what made him happy, what he enjoyed, and what it was like to make him lose all control. During that time, she memorized the dips and ridges of his muscles, the swirl of his ciphers, and the scar over his heart; she'd learned every inch of a body that fascinated her.

But now, she barely recognized it as his ribs and collarbones stood out starkly against his flesh. The once dark, black ciphers running from his wrists, across his shoulders, and back to his waist became more visible as he washed away the blood; they were grayer than she'd suspected.

She believed many of the dark fae kept some of their ciphers, and therefore the depth of their power, hidden. Brokk's power was dwindling fast.

He could deny that starvation was weakening him, but his ciphers couldn't, and she had no way of giving him the other nourishment he required. He could have her blood, but with these bars between them, she couldn't feed the dark fae part of him.

She would give anything to help him, but all she could do was sit here and watch him waste further away until the ophidians killed them. She hated this place and this helplessness.

When he finished washing, Brokk gathered the cold, gross food the ophidians left behind and retreated to the back of his cell. Like her and the others, he settled onto his dirty clothes while leaving his ruined shirt by the door.

"I'm glad you're awake again," she told him. "I missed you."

A smile tugged at his lips before vanishing. "I'm glad to be awake again."

"What you did for me... you... you didn't have to do that."

He stopped eating, and his red eyes narrowed on her. "Yes, I did, and I'll do it again. If I can stop them from going after you, I will. Every. Single. Time."

The emotion constricting her chest and throat made it difficult to breathe, let alone talk. She'd never believed it possible for her to love another after Fabian, but she did.

Finding love twice was already such an impossibility for immortals, but a bigger one was starting to take place inside her

—she might love Brokk *more* than she'd loved Fabian. While the realization caused the familiar guilt to rear its ugly head, that emotion wasn't anywhere near as brutal as it once was.

How could she feel guilty about loving this man when he'd sacrificed himself for her and would continue to do so? He would do it until it killed him, and she couldn't allow that to happen.

"Brokk—"

"Please don't argue with me, Kaylia. I just want to sit here and enjoy seeing you again."

"I'm not going to argue with you, but there's something you should know."

"What's that?"

She held his red eyes as she placed her hand against her heart. "I love you."

Brokk froze as he stared at her with his spoon halfway to his mouth. At first, he was too shocked to respond, and then, for the first time in *far* too long, the lopsided smile she loved so much lit his face.

In the dim illumination of the dwindling fires, the red faded from his eyes, and their beautiful aqua-blue color returned, as did their twinkle. Her heart felt near to bursting, and she knew it was true; she loved him more than Fabian.

It wasn't right, and it wasn't wrong. It was simply the way of things.

"Good," Brokk stated. "Because I love you too."

CHAPTER FOURTEEN

KAYLIA WASN'T sure how much more time had passed before the ophidians made their presence known again. Brokk was still too weak, and even Ryker, who wasn't as starved as Brokk, wasn't healing as fast from his last lashing as he should.

The torches they lit last time had burned out, plunging them into darkness again. She lay with her hand in Brokk's, but she couldn't see him; she was just glad to be able to feel him again.

He'd fed on her a few more times, but her blood wasn't enough to keep him going. His dark fae side also had to be nourished, and he'd lost so much blood on the spikes that the meager amount he took from her wasn't enough to replenish it.

Kaylia was helping sustain him, but he weakened further every day. She was fast becoming not enough for him.

When the approaching torches cast shadows over the window in the locked door, Kaylia contemplated releasing Brokk. However, the ophidians already knew about them, and she wasn't ready to let him go.

They could fuck right off.

Remaining on her side, she held Brokk's hand as the ophidians opened the door and slithered into the room. They spread out as they removed the spent torches and replaced them with the new ones they brought.

A dim glow illuminated the dungeon. Shadows danced from the torches as the ophidians lined up outside their cells while the emperor slid in last.

The sick feeling in the pit of her stomach turned into a strangling knot. Reluctantly, Kaylia released Brokk and pushed herself into a seated position.

The last time the emperor came, Brokk nearly died, and he was still far too weak to go up against these things now. She wouldn't let him suffer again because of her.

The emperor didn't pretend to examine the rest of the prisoners; his gaze fell on Brokk, and a smile curved his mouth. "Well, look who's finally awake. I cannot say how happy that makes me."

Kaylia glanced at Brokk as he leaned against the back wall with one knee drawn up to his chest and an arm draped over it. He was unfazed by the emperor's words, but blood pounded in her ears as her heart battered her ribs.

What does this vicious asshole intend for him?

The emperor slithered over and stopped in front of Brokk's cell. "They continue to look for you, dark fae, but Doomed Valley and my followers have ensured they don't survive. We can't do anything about the dragons, but they won't find you here."

"They'll find your pyramid," Brokk stated. "It's not easy to see from above, but they'll find it."

Kaylia gulped as her gaze darted between the two men. The jewels in the emperor's nemes headdress sparkled in the flickering torches, as did the gleam in his eyes.

She didn't like Brokk antagonizing this monster but understood his unwillingness to back down. Ryker shifted slightly in the cell to her right before settling into stillness again.

"Do you think the dragons will destroy it?" the emperor asked.

"I have no idea what the dragons will do. I'm not the one controlling them."

"If they destroy my pyramid, they'll destroy you too."

Brokk shrugged. "You already plan to do so, so let them destroy it."

Kaylia stopped breathing when the emperor's gaze shifted to her. "Are you so flippant with her life?"

Brokk's jaw clenched as his eyes clashed with the emperor's. He didn't say a word.

"You're looking a little worse for the wear, Brokk of the house of the *dark fae*. You must be *starving*."

Kaylia's skin crawled as the tension in the dungeon amped up, and Ryker shifted again. Still, Brokk didn't speak, but his gaze flicked to her.

The hunger blazing in them as his eyes roamed her nude body turned them a deeper shade of red. Kaylia's eyes fell to his lengthening shaft.

They were trapped in this dirty, gross, *awful* place, but he was starving, and she was naked. Truth be told, even if this place made her sick, she'd give anything to feed him and make him stronger. These cells didn't matter. *He* did.

"What if I told you I could ease your hunger?" the emperor inquired.

A muscle in Brokk's jaw twitched as he tore his gaze away from her and back to the monster before him. Their eyes clashed before the emperor grinned.

"Oh, what fun we shall have, dark fae. I'll accept your thanks when you're done."

When the emperor lifted a hand above his shoulder and gave a little wave, two of his followers slithered from the room. They returned with a beautiful, dark-haired woman who sauntered into the room.

She wasn't upset to be with these monsters as she strolled over to stand next to the emperor, stuck out a hip, and rested her hand on it. The torchlight played over her naked form, revealing her plump breasts and the triangle of dark hair between her legs.

The woman was a nymph, an immortal creature who relished sex, and the seductive smile she sent Brokk made Kaylia's stomach turn. She had no idea why a nymph was with these assholes, but the woman's skin glowed, her hair shone, and her figure was filled out in all the right places. There was no way she was a prisoner, too.

"I brought you a present, dark fae. You should be *very* happy about that," the emperor said.

His attention shifted to Kaylia, and he smiled before focusing on Brokk again. "I *never* reward my prisoners, but I've decided to try something new. I can personally attest that Jobee here is an *outstanding* fuck, dark fae. She'll keep you happy and fed for *days*. Open his cell."

CHAPTER FIFTEEN

No, no, no, no! The word ran on a loop in Kaylia's head as four ophidians came forward. Two wore the thick metal gloves required to open the cells, and the others carried the silver poles.

Brokk remained unmoving as the muscles in his neck stood out against his flesh. His punctures had finally healed, but his ciphers remained faded, and he was nothing more than skin and bones.

He was starving, possibly *dying*, and the only way to keep him from dying in this place rose on her toes to kiss the emperor's cheek. Brokk remained unmoving as the nymph strolled into his cell.

Kaylia winced when the door clanged shut behind her. No one in the dungeon moved. She didn't dare breathe as time slowed, her heart shriveled, and anguish tore at her insides.

Unable to look into Brokk's cell, she kept her gaze straight ahead. She could feel the emperor staring at her but kept her attention on the torch across from her as she tried to calm the riotous emotions pummeling her.

Brokk was fading fast, and they'd locked a banquet into his

cell. Unable to resist anymore, Kaylia glanced into his cell as the nymph strolled closer.

Brokk's eyes rolled, and his nostrils flared as he scented the nymph's desire… even Kaylia could smell it. He was a starving, feral animal on the brink of losing control.

The nymph licked her lips in anticipation of the brutal, frenzied fucking about to unfold. "Oh, what fun we're going to have," Jobee whispered.

When she skimmed a finger down Brokk's chest, he shuddered as he bit out, "*Don't.*"

His voice came out stronger than Kaylia anticipated as he seized the woman's hand and held it in the air between them.

"*Don't* touch me."

Brokk's eyes were a fiery red, and his body trembled as he fought his hunger, but then his gaze shifted to her. Kaylia's breath sucked in when those savage eyes met hers.

Suffering emanated from him. He needed this, and she couldn't give it to him.

He'd sacrificed himself and gone on to those spikes for *her*. Having this occur in the cell next to her would slice nearly as deep as losing Fabian, but it would strengthen Brokk, which was necessary in this place.

If he didn't feed, he would fade further away in this place, and his ciphers proved he was fading. Afterward, he would hate himself for this… but she wouldn't.

He might never forgive himself, but she would. And hopefully, her forgiveness would help him heal from what happened here.

He'd sacrificed himself, and now, she'd give him permission to choose strength and life… even if it shattered her heart. But she would survive this blow, and so would he.

And once they were free of this place, they would build a life together and move on from this. She was confident they could do it; they could do *anything* together, but he had to be strong enough for them to get free.

Tension continued to vibrate through the air, and Brokk caught the nymph's other hand when she tried to touch him again. She gave a playful little pout and whimper as she edged her body closer until her breasts brushed his chest.

Brokk jerked her back, but before he could speak, Kaylia did. "It's okay, Brokk."

CHAPTER SIXTEEN

UTTERING those words took more strength than Kaylia had ever known she possessed. It took more strength than surviving Doomed Valley, the Lord's war, and Fabian's death, but they were the right words to say.

"You *have* to feed. You need to regain your strength." She shot a pointed glance at his faded ciphers. "You have to do what's necessary to survive. This... is... it's... okay."

She'd meant for her words to come out stronger and to hide how much this anguished her, but she couldn't stop her voice from breaking at the end. She refused to shed the tears burning her eyes as Brokk's eyes held hers.

If he saw how much this devastated her, he'd keep fighting the nymph, but they both knew it was a losing battle. Ultimately, his need to feed would win over his love for her.

He'd been pushed too far and was wasting away. No starving man could turn away from a feast.

They both knew it was only a matter of time before he caved, and it would be better if he did so with her permission. She hoped it would make him loathe himself a little less if he saw she understood and wouldn't hate him.

"No matter what happens in here, no matter what they do to us, *we'll* be okay," she vowed, and she meant it.

Her words probably challenged the emperor, but she didn't care. Fuck him and all his scaled minions. All that mattered right now was Brokk.

If they hadn't starved him for so long, she didn't doubt he would *never* stray from her. The dark fae loved to bounce from partner to partner, but he loved her, and immortals didn't stray from those they loved.

Plus, she might be his consort. They hadn't discussed the possibility since the emperor first mentioned it, but she suspected he believed it was true, and a vampire was like a lycan with their mate when it came to their consorts.

She'd spent centuries hating vampires, but that was one good thing she could say about them: they were loyal to their consorts. Even though this would happen, Brokk's heart belonged to *her*.

The ophidians were to blame for this, not him.

"It's okay," she whispered.

She yearned to retreat to the back of her cell, close her eyes, and clap her hands over her ears, but the ophidians would bask in her misery, and she couldn't let that happen. So, she would have to stand here, stare straight ahead, and pretend none of this bothered her while listening to him have sex with another woman.

And she could never cry over this in front of him; it would only make Brokk hate himself more. But when she got the chance, she would tear *every one* of these monsters to shreds. She'd pull out their hair, descale them, lock them away, prod them with sticks, tie them to racks, starve them, and skin them alive before feeding them to the dragons.

Brokk held her gaze before shifting his attention back to the nymph. The fire in his eyes burned hotter when she wiggled closer again.

Then he jerked the nymph against him and sank his fangs into her throat. Kaylia knew all about the bloodlust that could take over a vampire and make them go wild for sex while they fed. It was one more thing he'd be unable to deny.

When the woman's hands wrapped around him and her fingers dug into his back, Kaylia shifted her gaze ahead while inwardly weeping. The sounds of Brokk's feeding were the only ones in the dungeon as the ophidians raptly watched what was happening in his cell.

The emperor smirked as Brokk continued to feed. He was taking too much; he'd weaken the nymph, but Kaylia didn't care.

She hoped he drained the bitch dry. If that woman was working with these assholes, she deserved to suffer.

Then the sounds of his feeding stopped, and while it surprised her that they hadn't already started, she knew the ones of a sexual frenzy were soon to follow. Instead of grunting and moans, a loud crack filled the air.

A slurpy, grinding, rending sound turned Kaylia's stomach. Unable to resist looking, she turned toward him as Brokk tore the nymph's head from her shoulders.

His blood-coated lips twisted into a sneer as Brokk heaved the head at the cell door. A second later, it hit the gate with a bang, and the nymph's body crumpled to the ground.

The emperor's eyebrows rose as he studied the parted mouth of the nymph. "Well, now, that was an interesting twist. Until next time, then. Come along."

With a wave of his fingers, the emperor turned and left the dungeon. His followers trailed after him.

CHAPTER SEVENTEEN

BROKK STARED at the body of the woman he killed. Every part of him had hungered for what she offered, but she wasn't who he *craved*, and he couldn't do that to Kaylia.

No matter what she said, he couldn't hurt her like that. She may forgive him for it, but he'd hate himself forever.

Despite the woman losing her head, almost no blood littered the floor as he'd drained her nearly dry before killing her. Thanks to the nymph's and Kaylia's blood, the vampire part was full for the first time in a while.

The dark fae part of him though... oh, the dark fae was *ravenous*, but even the dark fae knew this wasn't the feast it sought. *Every* part of him craved the woman in the next cell, but while the vampire part of him was stronger, the dark fae had grown weaker.

He looked down at his hands; when he flexed them, the bones stuck out against his flesh as they moved. But then, all the bones in his body stood starkly out against his skin.

And he was very aware of his ciphers fading. He'd never heard of such a thing happening before, but he couldn't deny their jet-black color had been replaced by an ashy gray.

If he wasn't in this cell, he wasn't sure he could draw the shadows to him anymore or control the elements. Those were the fundamental powers of a dark fae, yet he questioned his ability to wield them.

Brokk lifted the body and carried it over to the front of his cell, where he dropped it next to her head. He hoped the ophidians removed the woman before she started to smell; this place reeked bad enough without the bonus of rotting flesh.

When he finished, he retreated to the back of his cell and slid down the wall to sit. He drew one knee to his chest and draped his arm over it while extending his other leg.

His heart raced as he stared at the wall directly across from him while trying to calm the riotous beat of his heart and the lingering lust still battering his system. He couldn't look at Kaylia.

He'd managed to stop himself from fucking that woman, but he'd been far closer than he would ever admit. The sight of Kaylia, naked and in her cell, already had him ravenous, even in this forsaken shithole where sex should be the last thing anyone desired, but he did.

Despite her not being the woman he wanted, Jobee's naked body brushing against his had aroused him further. He still had the erection to prove it.

A rustle from Kaylia's cell drew his attention as she settled near the bars. "It would have been okay. I would have understood."

Shadows rimmed her translucent, pewter eyes filled with sadness. It would have been okay, and she *would* have understood if he'd slept with that woman, and not because she didn't love him, but because she *did* and couldn't stand to see him like this.

"I know," he said.

"And it's not because—"

He cut her off before she could say anything more. "I understand, Kaylia. I do."

He'd willingly put himself on those spikes for her, and she'd put herself on a different torture device for him. She would have forgiven him, but he was sure she believed he wouldn't require forgiveness.

He never could have looked at himself in the same way. Right now, he was physically weak but still mentally strong and could withstand the torments these monsters had planned for them.

And he was sure he'd have to prove that once more. The emperor had discovered a new way to torture them; it was only a matter of time before he twisted the screws again.

Brokk prayed the emperor didn't turn someone loose in Kaylia's cell next time. His hands flexed as he contemplated the possibility; such a thing would send him into a spiral of rage and madness.

When Kaylia slid her hand through the bars, he grasped it and bent to kiss her palm. He couldn't let them harm her in such a way.

"Do you think I'm your consort?" she asked.

He didn't hesitate before replying. "Yes."

"Next time, take care of you," she said.

So, he wasn't the only one convinced there would be a next time. He didn't tell her that he'd fight it next time, too; it would only upset her.

And he couldn't stand the idea of possibly lying to her.

CHAPTER EIGHTEEN

MORE DAYS AND WEEKS PASSED, though Kaylia doubted it was more than a month, but she couldn't be sure. They lost more of those who entered the dungeon with them. Only her, Brokk, Ryker, a witch named Leland, and two amsirah, Kenneth and Tucker, remained.

Part of the ophidians' torture was watching their friends being picked off one by one and speculating who would be next. And those numbers were dwindling toward a near certainty on who they'd claim as their next victim.

During that time, Brokk killed two more of the nymphs the emperor placed in his cell. She didn't know how many more of the beings the ophidians had in their pyramid, but they didn't care about watching them die.

Probably because the ophidians knew that one day, Brokk would break and give them the show they craved. His ciphers had faded further as he weakened more; it was only a matter of time before the dark fae fed.

Until then, at least his vampire half was sated as he'd drained the nymphs dry before killing them, and he continued to take

Kaylia's blood. She believed that was more for the connection it created between them than an actual need to feed, and she welcomed it.

The ophidians had flogged Ryker's chest and back again recently. The whip had stripped nearly all the flesh from him.

Like Brokk, his torture was wearing on him, and he didn't heal as fast or as completely as he did before. The ophidians might not have to outright kill those who remained; they might all waste away and die in these awful cells deep in the bowels of the pyramid.

The amsirah general sat in the center of his cell, his legs crossed and his shoulders back, though the position had to be pulling at his recently torn flesh. His hands rested on his knees while he stared at the door.

For some reason, Brokk and Ryker had become the ophidians' two favorite targets, probably because they remained the most defiant. A part of her wished they would break at least a little and maybe get a reprieve, but the bigger part hoped they never caved to these monsters.

When they came for her again, Brokk screamed at them to take him instead, but they didn't listen this time. Instead, they placed her on a rack and twisted until the bones in her shoulders popped out of joint, one of her wrists broke, and both her ankles dislocated.

It still bothered her that she'd screamed when it happened. It hadn't been a full-blown scream; she'd managed to hold most of it back, but too much sound had left her lips.

Those bastards had smiled as they unstrapped her from the table. Unable to walk, she hung limply between them as they dragged her across the floor; the movement made the pain in her ankles worse, and she gritted her teeth against screaming again.

She also should have healed by now but still walked with a limp. The fact they hadn't killed her didn't mean her death wasn't coming soon. They were running out of immortals to play with, and Kaylia had no idea what was coming next; they could only watch and wait for the next blow to fall.

CHAPTER NINETEEN

BROKK KILLED ANOTHER NYMPH. Ryker's wounds healed before they flayed him open again, and the ophidians removed Kenneth from his cell. He never returned after they tore him apart.

Kaylia's injuries healed, as did Ryker's back, but it took more time than it had before, and now dozens of new scars criss-crossed his chest and back. All of them were weakening daily, and while she retained hope they'd escape this place, it had become a small bubble inside her.

When the ophidians returned with the emperor, Kaylia closed her eyes against the wave of sorrow swelling in her chest. Most likely, another nymph was about to be brought in, or one of them would leave their cell to meet their end.

Thankfully, they didn't leave the nymph's bodies behind and usually removed them after what she guessed was a day or two. She couldn't handle that stench on top of all the others.

Brokk's bones were more noticeable; the dark shadows under his eyes had grown as his ciphers faded further. He was wasting away, and no matter what she said, he refused to nourish the dark fae half of himself.

It was only a matter of time before he couldn't hold out

anymore and his survival instinct finally overrode his determination. She'd prepared herself the best she could for this, but it was still going to hurt worse than anything these fuckers had done to her.

Brokk's fingers squeezed hers. He kissed her knuckles before they released each other.

Kaylia's whole body ached as she pushed herself into a seated position. She still used the tattered remnants of her shirt to provide some protection against the dirt ground, but it didn't offer any warmth or comfort.

The remnants of her pants sat next to the bucket of soap and water the ophidians brought them yesterday. At least they still had that tiny piece of luxury in this place.

Standing with her arms at her sides, she lifted her chin as she waited to see who would suffer today. It had been a while for her, and she mentally braced herself for the agony that would probably come soon.

When two ophidians donned their gloves and slithered toward her cell, her shoulders went back as they produced a set of keys. Whatever they did to her, she wouldn't scream again.

Brokk growled as he prowled toward his cell door. "Take me instead."

"No," Kaylia said. "It's my turn."

Brokk's head swiveled toward her, and his eyes flashed a violent shade of red. His lips skimmed back to reveal his extended fangs.

"Kaylia…." His words trailed off as the key turned in her lock and a click sounded. "*Take me!*" he shouted at the emperor.

The man didn't look at Brokk; he focused on Kaylia as she strode from the cell with her chin raised. She wouldn't give them the satisfaction of jabbing her with one of those poles.

When the emperor's gaze raked over her naked body, there was nothing lustful in his eyes but something more analytical and colder. She was aware she'd lost weight since arriving here, not as much as Brokk, but her curves had flattened out, and her bones stuck out.

Her hair had grown since she cut it off in the mirror realm and hung in a tangled mess beneath her shoulders. It wasn't enough for her to shield her breasts, but even if she could, she wouldn't hide from him.

"Take me," Brokk said again.

For the first time, the emperor's eyes went to him. "The dragons have returned."

"There's a simple solution for that," Brokk stated. "You can let the rest of us go, and the dragons and searchers will leave your realm."

"And your brother will unleash war upon us."

"My brother will pay you well for all of us."

"I have no doubt, but we don't seek riches."

"Then what do you seek?"

"Pleasure, fun, little distractions such as yourselves. They keep us entertained. We haven't been able to capture more of you, but we hope to fill our cells again. Until then, you'll be our distractions."

"If you let us go—"

"If I let you go," the emperor interrupted Brokk, "your brother will rain down hell on this valley. Do you think I haven't heard whispers about the Shadow Reaver? I bet the shadows hunt for you, too, but they haven't found you yet."

No one had any idea how big Doomed Valley was. The emperor might know they were here because she was sure the man had eyes and ears all over this valley, but Cole and the dragons could be searching an area thousands of miles away.

They could also be opening portals into the same area over and over again and not knowing it because of how similar the jungle looked. Or they could be five miles away, but because the vegetation was so thick, they couldn't see the pyramid.

"If you let us go, I'll make sure my brother stays out of the

Valley, as well as Lexi and the dragons," Brokk vowed. "No one from Dragonia will ever enter here again."

The emperor chuckled. "There's no way you'll walk away from this... *any* of you. I let you go, and you'll return. I don't doubt it. You'll die here, dark fae; you all will."

CHAPTER TWENTY

KAYLIA'S HEART RACED, and she gulped down the lump in her throat as she gazed wildly around. It was one thing to suspect this; it was something entirely different to have it confirmed. These monsters would torture them until they murdered them.

She searched for some way to escape, but ophidians surrounded her, and she couldn't go anywhere. If she lifted her hands to cast a spell or open a portal, they'd stab her with one of those poles before she could wiggle her fingers, and then she'd be useless.

There had to be *some* way out of this, but she'd been here this long and never seen an opportunity to flee. Time was slipping away, and today, they'd taken her from the cell.

"Of course, I intend to reward you before I kill you, dark fae," the emperor continued.

Kaylia's fingers twitched as she contemplated her best course of action. Depleted from the oppressive air of this place, her powers weren't what they should be.

The only source of real energy here was Brokk. And this place had so drained him that she didn't allow herself to brush against the little strength he still possessed.

"And why would you do that?" Brokk inquired.

"Because it's been such a joy to watch you resist me. But you're so depleted now, you'd probably drain the next woman you fucked until you killed her. You won't be able to stop yourself from doing so."

Kaylia's fingers twitched again as the ophidians grabbed her arms. She lifted her hands to draw air to her, possibly using it as a weapon against them. If she could push them away and free herself, she *might* have enough energy left to open a portal.

Unlike the rest of Doomed Valley, the pyramid was an easily recognizable place she could return to… with an army. If she broke free, she could save the others.

The emperor would know that the second she entered a portal, he'd have to flee this place. He wouldn't have time to kill the others before then.

She loathed the idea of leaving Brokk behind, but she would if it gave her the chance to save his life. It was the only small hope they had.

Heart hammering, Kaylia felt the pressure of air building against her palms as she worked to gather the element. Before she could do much more than feel it against her, the ophidians seized her hands, grasped her fingers to cease their movement, and yanked them above her head.

"*Stop it!*" Brokk exploded.

"Open his door," the emperor commanded.

Kaylia's eyes widened as the emperor's words came back to her. When he first uttered them, she'd been more focused on trying to devise a plan to get free, but now they sank into her panicked mind…

"But you're so depleted now, you'd probably drain the next woman you fucked until you killed her. You won't be able to stop yourself from doing so."

And what better show would it be than to watch him kill *her*?

Kaylia started to struggle in their grasp before going limp.

She didn't want to die; every part of her rebelled against it, but they were going to put her in with *Brokk*.

She'd finally hold him and have his arms around her again. And while the emperor was probably right that he was so weak he would drain and destroy the next woman he had sex with, but not *her*.

If she was certain of anything in this forsaken place, it was *that*. The vampire part of him would protect its consort, and the man would not lose the woman he loved.

More ophidians donned the thick metal gloves before slithering with the key to Brokk's cell. They held the poles before them like jousting rods, keeping them at the ready as they approached Brokk's cell.

Brokk's eyes burned a fiery red as they opened the cell door and jabbed the poles into the small space until he retreated from the gate. The ones holding her slithered toward the opening.

When Brokk's eyes met hers, dread emanated from them as he realized what was happening. The ophidians jabbed the poles at Brokk again, pushing him back as the others carried her to the doorway, lifted her off the ground, and threw her inside.

Unable to keep her feet under her, she tripped and staggered forward before her still-not-quite right ankle gave way, and she fell to the ground. Behind her, the door clanged shut with an air of finality.

CHAPTER TWENTY-ONE

FEAR CREPT like a spider up Brokk's spine. Its numerous legs scratched his skin as the hair on his arms rose, his mouth went dry, and the dark fae screamed to *finally* be sated.

She's here!

The one he'd craved so badly since being dragged in here—the one who could ease and infuse him with power like no other.

The one he loved... and could very well kill if he went anywhere near her.

Slowly, Kaylia lifted her head, and her striking gray eyes met his as her hair fell across her face. Goose bumps broke out on his flesh, and blood flooded his cock.

Ever since entering this place, he'd dreamed of holding her again, but not like this, and not in this *pit* with the ophidians looking on in amusement. Plus, the emperor was right; he might kill her if he took her now.

Brokk hadn't given much thought to what would happen and how he would replenish the dark fae when they escaped this place. He'd been too focused on surviving the torments unleashed on them and trying to figure out how to get free—something he'd failed to do.

And now, the problem of how he'd strengthen himself again was being taken from him by the creatures he loathed most in this world. He was too drained, depleted, and out of his mind to go anywhere near Kaylia.

Then her scent hit him; that sweet aroma caused saliva to fill his mouth as his dick grew harder. Her scent wasn't as strong as before they entered this place, but it was still there, and he recalled what it was like to have it envelop him as she pressed her body to his.

He had to stop this, but he couldn't tear his eyes from her as the ophidians moved away but didn't leave the room. *None* of them would miss this show.

They'd trapped a deer with a starved lion and were eager to watch the bloodbath sure to unfold. They anticipated a good time.

He already loathed that she was so bared to them and they could see every part of her. He'd give anything to cover her up, shield her from them, and protect her from these assholes.

To have them watching them was something he couldn't stand. He wouldn't allow it.

Not to mention, what he'd do to her should never be done to anyone... especially Kaylia.

Brokk didn't realize he was edging away from her until his back connected with the wall. Slowly, Kaylia rose, and her shoulders went back as she stood proudly before him.

Her body wasn't as lush as before they entered this place, and they'd left scars on her belly and back, but she was still so unbelievably beautiful and *his*. Every part of him screamed to possess her again, to ease his hunger, but he didn't go any closer.

"Brokk," she whispered as she stepped toward him.

"Don't," he growled. "I can't control myself around you."

And he wasn't about to rip off her head, although that might be better than what he would do to her.

"Then it's a good thing you don't have to."

Her voice was far stronger and more confident than it should be for someone approaching the man who could kill them. "Kaylia—"

"You won't hurt me, and you certainly won't kill me. I *know* it."

She may know it, but he was far less certain as he drank in the miracle of her while she glided closer. She was offering herself to him, but he didn't think she fully grasped the possibility that it could be as a sacrifice.

The ophidians had continued to taunt him with nymphs while watching him grow weaker; he suspected the emperor was planning this all along. It would be far more fun to watch him destroy Kaylia.

"Not in here," he said. "Not like *this*."

"Then where? This could be our last chance, and I want it. I don't care about them; this is about *us*."

"No." If he touched her now, it would be ugly. "No."

Before she could get any closer, Brokk finally found the strength to move. He threw himself to the side and into the bars there. The second he connected with them, they launched him backward.

CHAPTER TWENTY-TWO

WHEN BROKK HIT the ground and crumpled into a heap, Kaylia's heart sank, but she wasn't astonished by what he'd done. He was trying to protect her, but she didn't require it from him.

Without hesitation, she strode closer and knelt before him as anticipation sizzled throughout her. He wasn't the only one who was hungry.

She wasn't starved in the same way as him, but she craved feeling his touch again... one last time. He wouldn't be the one to kill her—she was convinced of that—but she could feel their time here coming to an end.

The emperor would soon call for their demise, and she *had* to know the joy of him again before that time came. Their joining would be rougher than before, desperate, and he'd probably take more than he normally did from her, but she'd walk away from it.

He didn't have faith he'd stop himself before it went too far; she did.

She tenderly caressed his cheek as his head rolled to the side; his red eyes briefly met hers before his lids closed again. Her fingers rested against the white starburst scar over his heart from where a dark fae ran him through with a sword.

Most dark fae would have succumbed to such a blow, but not him. Other scars crisscrossed his chest from the beatings he'd sustained while here. They weren't as numerous as Ryker's, as the ophidians had shifted their attention to tormenting Brokk with women.

She couldn't see them, but on his back, he also bore the marks of the spikes. His ciphers remained a dull gray as they swirled over his flesh; after this, she hoped some of their vibrant color returned to them.

"Don't do that again," she told him.

He didn't respond; he was probably still too dazed by the bars to form words. She was playing with fire and hoping to get burned as she rested her hand against his cheek and kissed him.

The kiss was familiar and strange all at once. She easily recalled the warmth of his lips, the way it sent tingles through her, and his fresh-rain-and-man aroma, but the last time they kissed, he didn't have a beard that tickled her cheeks and chin.

The way his kiss made her body come alive was a welcome reprieve from this abysmal place. She broke the kiss to plant more on his forehead, cheeks, and neck as her fingers found his chest and roved over the changed contours of his body.

He was far thinner but still so powerful as her fingers explored the etched muscle of his physique. Every part of her became focused on him as excitement raced through her.

She was *finally* able to feel so much of him again. She'd dreamt about what it would be like for them outside of here, but she'd always awoken to the nightmare and her inability to do anything more than hold his hand.

But this wasn't a dream; it was a reality she'd plunged herself into. She forgot all about those watching them while she continued to explore him.

She loved him so much that nothing else mattered, and no

one else existed outside them. When she stroked his erection, he found the strength to grasp her wrist, halting her movements.

Leaning back, she met the vibrant red of his eyes as he gazed at her with longing and distress. "Kaylia—"

"I want this as much as you," she assured him.

She didn't give a shit about anybody else. She didn't care they would watch everything they did together, but she hated them for their intrusion into this private world of her and Brokk's making.

This would most likely be their last time together, and she would seize the opportunity without hesitation. Let them watch; she wouldn't let that stop her from having this man.

She was sure being watched wouldn't be a first for Brokk. The dark fae weren't known for their modesty or discretion; it would be a first for her.

Witches embraced their sexuality, but she'd never ventured into voyeurism before. And she never would have with him either, simply because he was *hers*, and she'd never share him with anyone in such a way.

They didn't have a choice here. They either grasped this moment or let it slip away from them.

"No. I won't let them see you—"

"They already see me, and it doesn't matter. Nothing else exists but you," she whispered.

"But it does."

"Not to me. Not anymore."

As their gazes remained locked, she saw a softening in his. "I'll hurt you."

"No, you won't. I'm sure of it."

When she bent to kiss him again, he didn't respond, but when she nipped his bottom lip, he stiffened, and his shaft jumped in her hand. She didn't take joy in knowing she would win this battle; she simply took pleasure in *him*.

His mouth moved against hers, and his fingers slid into her

hair as he pulled her closer. Kaylia's heart raced, and her entire body screamed with anticipation.

Her skin erupted in tingles that raced over her. She hadn't forgotten how alive and powerful he made her feel, but the memory had faded beneath the horror.

Now, her body recalled all the power that flooded her when they were together—the awakening that had pierced through her grief and self-imposed isolation from her loss of Fabian.

Brokk broke through *every* horrible thing that ever happened to her, including this place. He buried the bad memories under a wave of pleasure and love. He awakened parts of her she'd never known existed and made her feel alive in a way she never had before him.

She was his, and he was hers, and no matter the circumstances, everything was *right* when they were together.

"Turn away," Ryker commanded.

Somehow, his words broke through the bubble protecting her from the outside world, but they were the last sounds she heard from anyone other than *them*. All that existed was their love.

CHAPTER TWENTY-THREE

THE LAST REMAINING shreds of reason slid away from Brokk. It was useless to fight Kaylia on this, especially when he desired her so badly.

He hated those things out there, watching them, waiting for a show. He wouldn't give it to them.

Oh, he'd take her. He'd been denied too long to resist anymore, but he'd keep her protected. If he had to, he'd grasp hold of those bars and never let go if it kept him from harming her.

His fingers tightened in her hair as he deepened the kiss, and his other hand settled on her waist. *Oh fuck, she feels so good.*

Every part of him screamed to be sated by the woman lying against him. Her breasts skimmed his chest as she moved further on top of him.

The other women the ophidians threw into his cell would have nourished and helped strengthen him, but Kaylia would *complete* him. They could never do for him what she could, and his ravenous body thrummed in anticipation of what was to come.

When she settled fully on top of him and guided his cock toward her entrance, his temples pounded with the blood rushing to them. His body tensed in anticipation of being inside her again while his brain screamed against this.

And on this, his brain was right.

Shaking off the lingering effects of the bars, he wrapped his arm around her waist and pulled her to the side. She could shut out the rest of the world and pretend these monsters didn't exist, but he'd be damned if they saw more of her than they already did.

He didn't care what it took; he would keep her shielded from them. As he adjusted his grip on her, she moaned her disappointment and wiggled against his shaft. She was already wet for him as she teased the head of his dick.

Stifling a groan, he turned, put his hand down, and rose. He also wouldn't take her in the dirt. He couldn't give her the luxury she deserved in this place, but he could give her that much.

He carried her to the back of the cell, as far from those assholes as he could get. Once there, he pressed her back against the wall and held her as he pulled away a little to look at her again.

She's here. She's really here.

It seemed too good to be true, but it was her beautiful eyes on his and her warm body in his arms. His heart swelled with love as a smile curved the corners of her full, swollen mouth.

Passion darkened her eyes, and her breath came faster as he ran his fingers down her side. Her nipples puckered against his chest.

She'd always been so beautiful to him, but she was more so now as love shone from her gaze. It hadn't been there when they were together before.

That love enraptured him more than the woman who slid her legs around his waist and dug her heels into his back to draw him closer. She loved him; there was no denying that.

And she's mine.

His gaze fell to her neck and the rapid beat of her pulse as his fangs lengthened, the dark fae screamed, and something primeval tore free. She was already wet for him, but he should prepare her further for what was to come.

His control was spiraling away as hunger twisted his insides into knots and battered his restraint. His lips skimmed back as saliva filled his mouth, and his cock became impossibly hard.

"Fuck me, Brokk."

Those three words completely undid him, and unable to stop himself, he thrust into her as he sank his fangs into her vein. He groaned against her throat as her hot, wet sheath enveloped him while her blood rushed into his mouth.

She fit perfectly around him as she cried out from his invasion and her fingers dug into his neck. He placed his hands on the small of her back when it bowed, and she ground against him.

He managed to retract his fangs but couldn't stop himself from moving within her. "I'm sorry."

"I'm not."

He sank his fangs into her shoulder and feasted as the pleasure she gave sent him spiraling out of control. He plunged beyond hearing as the remaining shreds of his reason disappeared.

Hard. Too hard.

But he couldn't stop as he feasted on the sexual energy rising between them while he consumed her blood. He was taking too much.

The ophidians had starved him, and she offered the most exquisite banquet Brokk had ever encountered. He had to stop.

He couldn't.

She was so sure he wouldn't hurt her, but that trust had been misplaced as he couldn't get enough of her. When she cried out and her sheath tightened around his cock, his body stiffened as he came with her, but it still didn't stop him.

He finally managed to retract his fangs while his hips continued to move. He could kill her; that knowledge hammered at him, but he couldn't stop.

Now that he had her again, he would gorge himself on her.

CHAPTER TWENTY-FOUR

BROKK DIDN'T KNOW how much time passed before he finally pulled out of Kaylia and brought her to the ground to hold her. With his back to the ophidians, he locked himself protectively around her while cradling her against him.

The most they could see of her was the foot she slipped between his legs. She was still alive but weakened as she yawned.

And every part of him nearly vibrated with renewed vitality. His ciphers still weren't the deep black they should be. However, their color had deepened until they were almost black again instead of that sick gray color.

"I'm sorry," he whispered. "I'm so sorry."

"I'm not." She placed her hand over his heart and lifted her eyes to his. "I'm tired but fine. I swear, Brokk, I'm fine."

"You must be sore."

"It's a good sore."

"I was too rough."

"And it was *fantastic*."

He searched her face for some sign she was lying to protect him, but a sweet smile curved her mouth, and her eyes shone with love. He could have destroyed that love, but somehow, he'd maintained enough control to ensure he didn't.

"I love you," she murmured.

Brokk closed his eyes as anguish and joy radiated through him. She was everything he ever could have dreamed of in this life and more. Together, they could have an *amazing* life with children, a home, and so much laughter and love... if they ever got free of this place.

And that was proving to be impossible as their time swiftly ran out. The emperor was growing bored with them; soon, he would destroy them.

He was sure he'd disappointed the man by keeping Kaylia alive. *She* would be the one to pay for that.

He kissed the tip of her nose and then her forehead. "I love you too."

She'd sated the sharpest edges of his hunger, but it remained. While the dark fae part of him still hungered, it was also content in a way it hadn't been before.

He shouldn't feel that way, considering they were still locked in these cells and surrounded by monsters, but he had her in his arms again, and she loved him. It couldn't get any better than this.

That was more than he'd ever dared to hope for after learning about her ex and their engagement. Then, he wasn't sure she could ever love another, but he'd been blessed that she could... and it was *him*.

"Get her out of there."

A cold bolt of terror lanced down Brokk's spine, and he lifted his head at the emperor's command; the man had sounded disgusted. His arms constricted around Kaylia as he turned his head to watch the ophidians slithering closer; they'd already donned their metal gloves and held their poles at the ready.

Kaylia shuddered against him, and her fingers dug into his

chest as she rested her head against him. He rubbed his hand along her spine to ease her sorrow.

He'd *just* gotten her back; he wouldn't let them take her again. He didn't know how he'd stop it, but he would.

His eyes found the emperor's, and the man's lips curled as he gave Brokk a scathing look. They'd expected him to kill her when they set her free in here, and he'd disappointed them... *again*.

They'd also planned on having him one day cave and fuck a nymph, and he'd managed to stop himself. The ophidians enjoyed watching the nymphs die, but it wasn't the show they wanted, and neither was this one.

Now they would make him suffer because of it, and the best way to do that was with Kaylia.

CHAPTER TWENTY-FIVE

"I'M NOT GOING to let them take you," Brokk vowed.

She turned her face into his throat and kissed him. "We don't have a choice. I regret nothing that's passed between us. Not. One. Thing. You showed me how to love and live again, and I'm so grateful."

With those words, he understood she knew this would be the end for her. If they took her from this cell, he would never see her again.

He clasped the back of her head and held her close. They'd have to kill him to get to her; he'd far prefer death to life without her.

Brokk kissed her cheek before reluctantly unraveling himself from her. If he had his way, he'd never let her go again, but he couldn't lie on the ground when they came for her.

Rising, he felt the difference in his body as his bones didn't crack, and he didn't sway as he braced his feet apart to stand protectively in front of her. She'd flooded him with strength, and he would use it against these bastards.

Behind him, Kaylia shifted as she rose. He glanced back at where she stood proudly with her shoulders back.

He searched her for any sign of weakness, but while he'd taken too much and she was a little paler, she'd handled what he'd done to her well. A weakness might soon reveal itself in her movements and speed. However, he'd probably helped replenish and strengthen her, too.

When the key turned in the lock and the cell door opened, Brokk remained firmly in front of Kaylia. "You're not taking her."

The ophidians snickered. They were all here because the ophidians wielded a magic stick that prevented them from using their abilities.

They remained here because these bars possessed the same magic and were impossible to touch. Despite numerous attempts, none of them had broken free before, but he wasn't about to let that deter them from trying now.

He'd fight to the death for her.

Ryker moved to the front of his cell as the ophidians at the end of one of those poles used them to open the door further. When they did, Brokk moved.

He couldn't transport, the bars kept him from using that vampire ability, but with the influx of power Kaylia had given him, he moved faster than he had in months… something the ophidians didn't anticipate.

Grasping the end of one of the metal sticks, Brokk yanked it forward and smashed the ophidian holding it into the bars. The creature's scream abruptly cut off when the bars flung it backward.

Brokk ripped the weapon free of the ophidian, spun it around, and dodged to the side in time to avoid another pole coming at him. Thrusting his own forward, he pulled the trigger and grinned while the other ophidian screamed before falling to the ground.

Brokk darted out of the cell and turned to use the stick to hold the door open so Kaylia could escape. Before she could, another one of those monsters slithered forward and threw themselves into the door, slamming it shut. They screamed as the current threw them backward.

"Capture him!" the emperor shouted as the other ophidians closed in on him.

CHAPTER TWENTY-SIX

BROKK SPUN to the side to avoid the wave of ophidians approaching him. Jabbing out with the stick, he jammed it into another asshole and fired.

The creature jerked and spasmed as he pummeled her with the brutal energy of the thing they wielded against others. Brokk grinned as he released his hold on the trigger. He didn't know if these things packed an infinite punch or would eventually dry up, so he had to be careful.

The next ophidian lashed out with its tail, and Brokk jumped over it. These serpents had removed all the weapons from the dungeon they'd stripped from them upon capture, but some had swords strapped to their backs.

His fingers itched to get a hold of one of those blades as he leapt over another tail, threw himself to the ground to avoid a pole, and rolled. He came up onto one knee and stabbed the end of his pole into another ophidian.

This one had a sword. As the male crumpled, Brokk pulled the blade free from the sheath, and, with the one-handed training his father had given all his sons, he swung the weapon into the ophidian's neck.

He released the pole, gripped the sword in both hands, and ripped it free of the tendons, trying to keep it trapped. With another swing, Brokk cleaved the man's head from his shoulders.

Smiling grimly, Brokk reclaimed his pole and leapt to his feet. Undeterred by the death of their friend, the ophidians closed in on him. He didn't have help—they outnumbered him at least thirty to one—but he couldn't let them take him.

The possibility of losing Kaylia propelled him onward. He didn't have time to open a portal; if he stopped, they'd destroy him, but if he could somehow get away from them long enough to do so…

Another pole jabbed at him; Brokk dropped the sword to catch the end of the pole. Gritting his teeth, he bent the pole upward as a sword emerged from the mix of snakes closing in on him.

Twisting to the side, he avoided a more solid blow from the sword, but it skimmed his stomach to spill his blood. Kaylia gasped, but it was the only noise his fellow survivors made.

Having expected to plunge the sword into him, the ophidian wielding the blade put too much weight behind it and fell toward him. Brokk caught the monster in the back of his head with a solid punch that sent him flying to the ground.

He lifted his foot and stomped on the man's back; an audible crack pierced the air despite the fact he wasn't wearing boots. If he could, he'd stomp every one of these things into the ground.

Sensing more closing in on him, he twisted and flung out his elbow to catch one in the face while another stabbed at him with a metal pole. Brokk brought his arm down on top of the pole, knocking it down.

They were all around him now, a mixture of human faces and snake bodies blocking the rest of the dungeon. Tongues flicked at him, and firelight gleamed off their lethal fangs as they hissed at him.

There were too many as they surrounded him in a wall of

bodies. Kaylia's scent still lingered in his nostrils, fueling him. He'd gotten further than anyone else and couldn't let her down now.

When another tail swung at him, he jumped it but missed the next coming at him. That one swept his feet out from under him, and he hit the ground with enough force to drive the breath from his lungs.

Knowing that he couldn't stop moving, Brokk leapt to his feet again and, drawing on his dark fae powers, drew the shadows toward him. Despite feeling stronger thanks to Kaylia, his weakness showed as the shadows were sluggish in coming.

Jumping another tail, he plunged the end of his pole into another one and rejoiced in the creature's gurgled screech. The shadows started sliding around him, but they were too late as one of the ophidians struck him.

Brokk managed to avoid the fangs dripping venom, but a tail crashed into the back of his head. Staggering forward, he lost his hold on the shadows, and they slipped away.

His vision blurred, and white stars exploded before his eyes, but he managed to keep enough of a grasp on consciousness to teleport. He didn't make it nearly as far as he would have liked.

He managed to get outside the circle of ophidians, but the movement drained him in a way it never had before. *Kaylia. Keep going for her.*

Thoughts of her sent adrenaline crashing through his system and flooded him with strength, but it wouldn't last. He was fading fast.

He tried teleporting again but found himself unable to do so. Drawing the shadows to him once more, he'd nearly slid into oblivion while the ophidians closed in on him with a speed that rivaled a vampire's.

He was almost concealed in darkness as he sprinted toward the doorway. The emperor shouted something but remained unmoving as he watched with an amused smile.

He could draw them away and possibly open a portal if he could get through the doorway. If he could get the key, he'd come back here; if not, he'd get help.

Every cell in his body screamed against leaving Kaylia, but he'd do whatever it took to free her from her cage. He was almost to the doorway when more ophidians entered.

Brokk skidded to a halt as his hope of escape exploded like a balloon filled with too much air. He should have known they'd have more guards in the hall, but he'd been too focused on breaking free to contemplate the possibility.

His heart hammered his ribs while he strove to formulate a new plan. They were all around him now; not even the shadows could keep him safe. They knew where he was because he couldn't break completely free of the ophidians.

He dodged the swing of a blade and drove the tip of his pole into the stomach of another. When they fell back, it created a brief opening, and the ophidians quickly filled it with more bodies.

Fangs glistened, scales shimmered, and a sea of hostile faces surrounded him. He jumped another tail but missed the one that crashed into his back, whipping him forward a few feet.

Brokk stopped himself from crashing into the ground by bouncing off another ophidian and staggering back. Leaping forward, he encircled his arms and legs around another.

The man reeled back as Brokk seized his face and twisted his head to the side. When his neck snapped, the ophidian hit the ground, and Brokk had the opportunity to break free of the circle.

It vanished when something jabbed him in the side. Electricity, magic, or whatever they used in those poles slammed into his system.

His hand clenched around his pole, and he willed himself not to give in, but as he did so, another tail hit his back, and he faceplanted onto the ground. More ophidians jabbed him with their sticks until he lost his hold on the shadows, and his body spasmed beyond his control.

No! Kaylia!

The wordless scream in his head never got uttered as his body was far beyond his control.

"Stop it!" Kaylia screamed, but they didn't stop.

CHAPTER TWENTY-SEVEN

KAYLIA'S HANDS went to her chest. Brokk remained on the ground, his face in the dirt as more ophidians jabbed him with their sticks.

His feet and hands twitched and jerked as he convulsed while they tortured him. The monsters smiled as they jabbed at him.

"Stop it!" she screamed, her voice surprisingly strong, considering everything in her felt twisted and broken. "*Stop it!*"

"You're only making it worse," Ryker growled. "Your reaction is fueling them."

She knew he was right; her anguish only encouraged their brutality, but she couldn't stand here and do *nothing*. Unfortunately, she didn't have a choice.

She was as close to the bars as she could get and had to resist the impulse to grasp them while screaming at the monsters torturing Brokk. If she did such a thing, she'd only succeed in launching herself into the back wall, but at least she'd be doing *something*.

This nothing was more than she could bear, especially since Brokk was suffering because of her… again. He'd tried to break free to save her, and now he was suffering the consequences of it.

And he'd been so close. So. Fucking. Close. He would have made it, too, if there hadn't been more of those assholes in the corridor. It was almost like they'd planned this but were too arrogant to anticipate it.

"Flog him," the emperor commanded. "Don't leave a fleck of skin on his back."

"No!" Kaylia screamed before she could stop herself. "I'll take his place!"

None of them acknowledged her as they grabbed Brokk's arms and lifted him from the ground. His head hung down as they dragged him toward the chains hanging from the ceiling and bolted into the floor. Ryker's blood still stained the dirt beneath them.

"I'll take his place!" she shouted.

"It's no longer your turn, my dear," the emperor practically purred. "But it will come again."

The foul man smirked at her in his horrific way; his yellow eyes gleamed with amusement. Knowing she couldn't do anything, Kaylia lifted her chin and made her expression blank as she shifted her attention to Brokk.

The ophidians strapped his wrists into the thick manacles hanging from the ceiling while they locked his ankles into the ones on the floor. She knew from her past experiences with the whip how strong, thick, and impossible to break those chains were.

When they finished locking him into place, the ophidians slithered back, and one of them produced a cat o' nine tails. The emperor grinned as the first blow landed against Brokk's back with a crack that made Kaylia inwardly wince while she remained outwardly immobile.

With each new crack of the whip, a part of her died a little more, but she never looked away as Brokk's blood ran free and the last of her hope died.

They were never going to leave this place alive.

CHAPTER TWENTY-EIGHT

BROKK BARELY HELD on to consciousness by the time they finished with him. His head lolled forward; he couldn't see what they'd done, but he felt it as every beat of his heart shot flames throughout the ravaged nerve endings on his back.

Blood ran in rivulets down his back and ass to drip on the floor. He didn't have to see what they'd done to know they'd taken all the flesh from him.

"Throw him in her old cell," the emperor commanded before slithering out of the room with a number of followers.

He didn't know how many remained, but the emperor was gone, which meant Kaylia would be safe for the rest of today. It was a small reprieve given everything else that happened, but he'd give all the skin on his body if it meant keeping her safe.

The only problem was, he couldn't keep her safe forever. They would go after her again, and once he was back in one of those cells, there was nothing he could do about it.

The chains clinked and rattled as they freed his ankles and wrists. Unable to remain standing, he went to his knees when his arms fell to his sides.

Determined not to let them see him like this, he started to rise as two ophidians each clasped an arm. A third started pulling on the metal gloves to open the cell while the other two dragged him toward his cell.

Brokk struggled to get his feet under him rather than have them drag him. With effort, he lifted his head to take in the dungeon through blurred vision. At first, he thought he was seeing things or *not* seeing things, but as Brokk blinked rapidly and his vision cleared, he realized the rest of the ophidians were gone.

It *was* just him and these three.

Brokk stopped trying to get to his feet and went limp in their hold. His toes scraped the dirt as they dragged him toward the cell Kaylia used to occupy.

Most of the strength he'd regained from his time with Kaylia now seeped down his back and decorated the floor, but he still maintained some of it. They believed him too weak to do anything, and normally, they'd be right, but she'd reinvigorated him far more than they could have anticipated.

As did the knowledge that it would be their last chance if he failed now. Once those bars closed on him again, their deaths would become a guarantee. Weakened and mangled or not, he'd never have another opportunity like this.

His eyes briefly met Kaylia's as she turned to follow their movement. The grief, hopelessness, and unhappiness emanating from her only fueled his urge to get her away from this awful place. She was a being of nature, light, and beauty wasting away in this pit of despair.

The only problem was he didn't know if he was strong enough to do anything. Yes, some of the power she'd returned to him remained, but was it enough?

It has to be.

Brokk lowered his head again but kept it high enough to watch them surreptitiously as he remained limp in their grip. His toes scratched the dirt. The one with gloves shifted his hold on his pole to produce a set of keys from the pouch secured to his waist.

The ophidians holding him had left their metal poles against the wall near the manacles once binding him. They didn't think they were necessary, and judging by the lax way the other held his pole, he didn't consider Brokk a threat.

You have to move. You have to go now*! This is the first mistake they've ever made, and if you don't take advantage of it, you're all dead.* Kaylia *is dead!*

With those words hammering in his brain, he eyed the distance to his cell and the way the ophidian with his gloves continued to hold his pole loosely. Adrenaline flowed through him as his drive to survive and to ensure Kaylia did, too, gave him strength.

He watched and waited as they dragged him closer to his new cell. Five feet... Four... Three... Two... One.

CHAPTER TWENTY-NINE

THEY WERE ABOUT to toss Brokk inside the cell when he jerked his feet forward and planted his heels in the ground. At the same time, he threw all his weight to the side.

His flayed back screamed in protest. Fire lanced across his tattered nerve endings as what remained of his muscles and tendons protested the movement.

The ophidian he'd shoved himself into hadn't expected any movement from him and was thrown off balance by it. As it skidded away, its tail curled toward him as the man fell into the bars.

Whatever scream the ophidian had been about to issue died away as gurgled sounds emanated from him while he spasmed against the bars. Jerking and heaving, the ophidian's tail lashed across the floor while the man convulsed.

Brokk staggered away from the sweeping tail as the ophidian on his left tightened his grip. Spinning, Brokk launched a punch at him.

The man swung his head to the side, but not in time to avoid the blow that caved his cheekbone and shattered his eye socket.

When his hands flew to his ruined face, he released Brokk, who went for the one with the keys and the pole.

That one was recovering from his shock but not fast enough. A savage sound issued from Brokk when the man stabbed at him; he grasped the pole and knocked it aside. Before the serpent could recover, he leapt on the ophidian.

With wild swings, the ophidian pummeled his back with his metal gloves. To keep from screaming, Brokk clamped his teeth down and bit into his tongue. Blood filled his mouth, but he kept his teeth shut against the agony racing along his spine.

He was too focused on survival to let the pain stop him, but it was a constant reminder of what they'd done and what they'd continue to do if he failed. Brokk's fingers enveloped the ophidian's throat, and his thumbs found the sensitive spot under his chin.

Red filled his vision as he shoved up to expose the man's vein. He sank his fangs into the serpent's throat and tore it out.

He wanted to finish what he'd started by ruining the man's speaking ability, but the one still clinging to his face was slithering toward the exit. That would keep this ophidian quiet while buying him time to return to the other.

Leaping off the creature, he snagged the pole the ophidian released. He ignored the growing weakness trying to drag him down as his racing heart pumped more of his dwindling blood from him.

Before the ophidian could flee the dungeon, Brokk caught up to him and jammed the pole into his back. He bared his teeth in a mockery of a smile as the ophidian started going down.

Brokk released the pole and leapt onto his back as the creature hit the ground. He wrapped his arm around the ophidian's throat and cinched it.

Needing to replenish the blood he was losing, he bit into the ophidian's jugular and sucked his blood in greedy gulps. He depleted the man so fast the ophidian never had a chance to recover from the effects of the stick before he was too weak to attempt to fight Brokk.

The ophidian wasn't dead when he finished, but Brokk released him and let him hit the ground. The blood wasn't enough to start the healing process on his back, but it would keep him going.

Turning, he ran toward the other two as the one with the gloves started rising high onto his tail while the other had fallen limply by the cell. Kaylia was wide-eyed and wordless as he ran up the tail of the monster with the gloves and launched himself onto his back.

He grasped the ophidian's head and jerked it to the side. The reverberating crack caused him to smile as the ophidian went limp beneath him.

As he rode the creature to the ground, he twisted until he tore the head free and threw it into the open cell. The ophidian hit the ground, and Brokk knelt to tug off the metal gloves before setting them near the keys.

The last one was starting to wake when Brokk pounced on him, and with a flurry of uncontrollable punches, he beat the man's face into a bloody mess. By the time he finished, no bones had remained intact, and it was impossible to tell a head once existed.

Sitting back, his shoulders heaved as his breaths came fast and deep. A red haze still clouded his vision, but with the last one dead, his strength was fading. When he tried to rise, he staggered and nearly went down.

"Brokk."

Kaylia's whisper infused him with another rush of adrenaline. He'd come this far and couldn't fail now; he had to free the others.

With a deep breath, he placed his bloody and broken knuckles on the ground. He hadn't realized he'd split the skin on his hands open and broken his bones during the fight, but now they ground together when he moved them.

Donning the gloves, Brokk gathered the keys and strode toward Kaylia's cell. She glanced nervously behind him as she shifted from foot to foot while wringing her hands before her.

He understood her anxiety; they'd been trapped for so long that this seemed too good to be true. They were seconds away from freedom, and he kept waiting for the ophidians to return. He didn't know if he could open a portal if they did return.

But somehow, the ax he felt hanging over their heads didn't fall as, with trembling fingers, he managed to unlock her door and pull it open. Kaylia's mouth parted, and her eyes found his.

For a second, she didn't move, and then she rushed forward. She was about to throw her arms around him, but her momentum jerked to a stop as she recalled his back and skidded to a halt in front of him.

The joy on her face made all his agony vanish as she rested her hands on his chest and rose onto her toes to kiss him. He wanted to pull her closer, but now that the adrenaline was wearing off, the ruins of his back were making movement difficult.

Instead, he settled for resting his hands on her hips as he returned the kiss. He'd love to lose himself to her and celebrate this small bit of freedom, but they had to move fast.

CHAPTER THIRTY

HE BROKE THE KISS, gave her the keys, and shook off the gloves to hand them to her. "Free the others."

"I will."

With unsteady steps, Brokk returned to the last living ophidian, who had dragged himself halfway out the door before collapsing onto the ground. With glee, Brokk straddled the man with one foot on each side of his chest and bent over him.

He stuck his fingers into the hole he created in the man's jugular and gritted his teeth against his growing weakness. His broken fingers ground together as they protested the movement, but he managed to tear off the man's head.

He tossed the head aside and turned back as Kaylia freed their three remaining friends from their cages. Kaylia dropped the key and the gloves. Her fingers moved as she tried to open a portal, but nothing happened.

Brokk's heart sank. Somehow, the ophidians' magic kept them from opening a portal; they would have to find their way out of the pyramids and back into Doomed Valley before escaping.

He barely had the energy to stand, let alone make it out of

this pyramid. He had no idea how many enemies they'd encounter along the way, and they were too depleted to put up much of a fight, but at least they had the poles and gloves.

Still, he didn't know how he would walk out of here. He'd used all his fight to get this far, and weakness was fast closing in on him.

They'll have to go on without me.

The idea of Kaylia being out there without him created a new adrenaline rush, but it dwindled as soon as it came. She'd have to go on without him; he'd only slow her down.

She had a chance to get free, and he would make sure she took it. Before he could give voice to his decision, Kaylia spoke.

"I'm too weakened. Someone else has to open a portal into the human realm so we can get to Dragonia from there."

He *had* taken too much from her earlier, but while he hated himself for this, he was also relieved they might not be as trapped here as he'd believed.

"I can do it," Leland said.

With the last dregs of his strength, Brokk rose and limped back toward Kaylia as Leland waved her fingers and a portal opened before her. That portal was one of the most amazing things he'd ever seen, and judging by the faces of the others, he wasn't alone in thinking so.

But his joy at their impending freedom couldn't stop his legs from quaking so badly that his knees gave out. Ryker caught him before he hit the ground; he carefully put his arms around Brokk's waist to hold him up.

"Thank you," Ryker said.

"I'd like to say anytime, but let's never do this again," Brokk replied.

"I have to agree with that," Tucker said.

Kaylia hovered at Brokk's side as Ryker walked with him into the portal and toward freedom.

CHAPTER THIRTY-ONE

THE LARGE SHADOW passing overhead drew Lexi's attention to the sky. She smiled as Alina, the speaker of the dragons, soared above them before she shifted her attention back to Skog and the other dwarves.

After the Lord destroyed the dwarves' realm of Drumbledon, they decided to stay in Dragonia and make a new home in the mountains. Lexi tried to visit at least once a month to see how things were going and check in with her friends.

Unfortunately, this wasn't a fun visit. They'd come here to recruit more help for another exploration into Doomed Valley, a realm that had already taken more than a few dwarves.

"We plan to leave tomorrow," Orin stated.

Lexi didn't like it but kept her uneasiness hidden. She'd prefer if he and Sahira would stay and recuperate for at least another week before diving into Doomed Valley, but they insisted they were ready to search for Brokk and Kaylia.

This time, her dad was determined to go with them. She didn't try to talk him out of it; he wouldn't change his mind about going with his sister into the place that had claimed too many lives... or at least she assumed most of those they'd sent were dead.

They never found most of the bodies or any sign of those who had vanished. She hoped she was wrong about that.

She wasn't ready to give up on Brokk and Kaylia and was determined to find an answer about what became of them. And she knew Brokk's brothers wouldn't give up until they knew what happened to him.

So tomorrow, Orin, Sahira, her dad, and others would return to Doomed Valley. She tried to keep her distress over that hidden. *No one* had returned yet, but the three of them were adamant they would, and she couldn't stop them.

She would send more dragons this time; they were the only immortals who regularly returned. Cole wasn't thrilled with the idea, especially since the ghouls were making more aggressive moves toward other realms, and there were rumors they planned on coming at Dragonia, but they had to find out what happened to Kaylia and Brokk.

As much as she loved and missed them, they couldn't keep sending immortals to die in Doomed Valley. She would prefer to *only* send the dragons, but Alina said that because the jungle was so thick, it was difficult for the dragons to see anything on the ground. They were mostly there for backup and air support.

Alina also said the dragons had no idea if they'd repeatedly search the same areas of the jungle or different parts, as from land or sky, everything looked nearly identical. She'd reported that sometimes there were breaks, clearings, rivers, and abnormalities in the landscape, but it was mostly dense, green trees.

It was all so disheartening, but Lexi refused to give up hope. Even if all they brought home was Brokk and Kaylia's bodies, at least they would bring them home.

"We have two volunteers to go with you," Skog said with the slightly English accent of the dwarves. "I'd like to tell you we had more, but we've lost too many to that place. Those are the only ones willing to go."

Skog rubbed the grayish-brown beard hanging to his chest while he spoke. His intelligent, hazel eyes focused on her, and while she'd come to learn his grumpy demeanor was more of an act, it wasn't this time. He'd prefer not to have any more dwarves enter that place, but, like her, he wouldn't stop them.

"It's more than we could have hoped for," Lexi admitted.

There weren't many other immortals who were willing to go either. They'd all heard about those who vanished in the jungle and weren't eager to add their names to the list.

Some were still adventurous and arrogant enough to believe they'd survive, but most weren't willing to find out. They'd found enough for this trip, though; she didn't know what would happen if it also failed because she refused to think about losing any more of her loved ones, especially when they'd *just* gotten Sahira and Orin back.

Another dragon soared into view. Unlike Alina, who circled lazily above, this one's bellow quaked the ground and rattled some pebbles from the mountain. Skog stepped out of the way of the stones bouncing toward him as they all shifted their attention to the sky.

Lexi frowned as Alina stopped circling to turn herself upright. She flapped her wings as she kept herself suspended above.

When the other dragon roared again, Alina turned and dove straight toward them. Lexi's heart raced as the dragon's sense of urgency gripped her.

Shielding her eyes, she stepped forward as shadows raced across the ground toward Cole. They gathered around him and her as the powerful, red dragon with flecks of yellow decorating the underneath of her wings and belly landed.

Dust and air kicked up around them as Alina settled on the

ground and closed her wings. Lexi stepped toward her, but before she could speak, Alina did.

"Brokk and Kaylia have returned."

At first, everyone was too astonished to respond, but Cole finally found the ability to do so. "What?"

"Your brother and Kaylia have returned to Dragonia. I will take you to them."

Cole's Persian blue eyes were troubled but joyful when they met hers. She sensed his fear that this was somehow a mistake and they'd discover that someone else had entered Dragonia.

"Brokk is in rough shape," Alina said.

Cole's nostrils flared, and his jaw clenched. Lexi took his hand and clasped it in both of hers. "Let's go."

He nodded, and some of his tension eased as he squeezed her hand. "You'll take all of us?" Cole inquired as they strode toward Alina.

"Yes."

Lexi was the first to scramble up Alina's leg and settle on the thick scales behind her head. Cole settled himself behind her and slipped his arm around her waist.

Despite the apprehension battering her, Lexi relaxed in his grasp as warmth spread through her. One small touch from him could make the worst of her apprehension a little better, but her heart continued to hammer, and her pulse raced with her need to reassure herself they were *really* here.

When she looked over at where Sahira and Orin had stood near Skog, she saw Sahira had started toward them while Orin remained planted in place.

"Come on," Cole called over to his younger brother.

"Fuck no. I'm not getting back on a dragon."

Sahira's eyebrows rose, and Lexi suppressed a chuckle as she recalled how much Orin hated flying on the dragons. She was glad the exasperating man made her aunt so happy, but she still enjoyed watching him squirm.

"It will take at least an hour to ride back to the palace," Sahira said.

"Someone should take the horses back."

"We'll get them back for you," Skog assured him.

When Orin scowled at him, Skog grinned as he leaned back on his heels and rubbed his beard.

"You're an asshole," Orin muttered.

"But you're still a bigger one."

Lexi suppressed a laugh as Sahira rolled her eyes and scrambled up Alina to settle behind Cole. Finally, Orin trudged toward Alina. He hesitated before using his one hand to climb up to sit behind Sahira.

When Alina rose and started flapping her wings, Orin muttered, "Oh shit, oh shit, oh shit."

Despite Alina's revelation that Brokk was in rough shape, Lexi chuckled at Orin's discomfort as Alina lifted into the air and soared back toward the castle. No matter what, they would save him.

CHAPTER THIRTY-TWO

UNABLE TO WALK on his own anymore, Ryker held Brokk under his shoulders, and Tucker carried his feet as they walked Brokk up the hill toward the palace with its golden turrets.

Soon after entering Dragonia, Brokk lost consciousness, and his chin rested against his chest. A trail of blood followed them up the pathway to the palace.

Kaylia hovered nervously at his side. She couldn't see the extent of the damage done to his back, but his ciphers had faded to that awful gray color again.

Some of Dragonia's citizens trailed them up the hill. The second they'd come through the portal from the human realm, a commotion had spread through the town.

When the realization of who the bloody, naked, filthy, and barely functioning new arrivals were sank in, chaos spread. Shouts filled the air, and the guards rushed forward to help them, but Kaylia waved them away.

She didn't expect the ophidians to follow them here. If the ophidians had discovered their escape, then the snakes probably planned to leave the pyramid behind.

Those serpents wouldn't dare enter this realm. The guards

here would slaughter them, but she still told the guards, "We'll be fine. You have to stay here and remain *extra* vigilant with the portals."

One of the lycan guards nodded as they retreated to the portals and held their weapons at the ready. That didn't stop some of the merchants and buyers in the town from following them as a dozen dragons circled above.

When the dragons' bellows vibrated the air, Leland glanced nervously up at them. Her light brown skin was darker from the grime covering it, but patches of her natural tone poked through.

Tangles matted her long, black hair, and her honey-brown eyes were troubled as she searched the sky. Like the rest, she'd lost weight and had fresh scars, but those factors couldn't obscure her natural beauty.

Brokk's low groan drew Kaylia's attention back to him. She rested her hand on his forehead and was relieved to find that he didn't have another fever.

He'd been brutalized and weakened again but was still infection-free... for now. She hoped he remained that way, and once they got him to the infirmary, she would do everything she could to ensure he did.

"The dragons don't seem happy," Leland murmured.

"They won't attack us," Kaylia assured her. "They're just letting others know we've arrived."

"Are you sure? They're not exactly known as friendly."

"The Lord compelled the dragons to do his bidding, but Lexi wouldn't use them in such a way. The dragons love her, and she loves them, and she would never command them to kill without their consent, and she especially wouldn't use them to attack those she loves. The throne won't rot her mind like it did the Lord's."

"I hope you're right."

A large shadow fell over them as a gust of wind blew back Kaylia's hair and caused Leland to stumble as she threw up her arms. Ryker and Tucker came to an abrupt halt as a large red dragon settled onto the ground ten feet in front of them.

"Oh shit," Ryker muttered.

"Alina," Kaylia breathed.

The dragon took up so much space she didn't see her riders until Orin slid off the Speaker's back and staggered a few steps before righting himself. He was paler than normal, but his black eyes instantly found hers.

Orin was the last person she'd been looking forward to seeing again, but for some reason, a sob lodged in her throat, and she nearly fell to her knees as reality hit her. They were in Dragonia, but she hadn't felt safe or fully accepted her new reality until now.

They were *free*. Those monsters wouldn't follow them here. They had protection, food, medicine, and *family*.

Sahira, Cole, and Lexi followed Orin off the dragon. The tears she'd been holding back spilled free, and she wiped them away as Cole's attention shifted to Brokk. Concern and rage etched his features as his gaze traveled over the weakened group with his brother.

"What happened?" Cole demanded as he stormed toward them.

Shadows shifted across his eyes and followed him across the ground. "He looks less friendly than the dragons," Tucker muttered.

Orin, who had regained some of his color, caught up with his brother as a thunderous expression descended over his face. Lexi and Sahira ran after the murderous-looking brothers as the air crackled with electricity.

CHAPTER THIRTY-THREE

"DON'T," Kaylia warned Ryker. "It will only make things worse. They're Brokk's brothers."

Some of the crackling eased from the air, but Kaylia still felt the prickle of electricity against her skin. She wiped away her tears, and her shoulders went back as she met Cole's shadow-filled eyes.

"We have to get him inside. I can tend to him there," she told him.

Lexi pushed ahead of Cole, but his eyes went to Ryker as he seized her wrist to halt her. She didn't notice as she arrived at Kaylia's side and used her free hand to grip her wrist.

Her hunter-green eyes, with their flecks of emerald, were full of concern. The flight here had pulled some of her auburn hair from its braid to wave around her face.

Cole's eyes remained focused on his brother. Lexi's gaze shot nervously to Brokk before her attention shifted back to Kaylia.

"You look like you're about to pass out," Lexi said.

Kaylia yearned to hug her friend and sob into her shoulder, but she couldn't break down. She had to tend to Brokk.

"*I'll* be the one to tend to his wounds," Kaylia stated.

"Are you okay?" Sahira asked.

Sahira stepped close to Lexi's side as Cole and Orin moved closer to Brokk. "We'll take him," Cole stated.

"Be careful of his back," Ryker said. "It's bad."

"Did you do this?" Orin demanded.

"Yeah, that's why we're here. We beat him and then decided to carry him to the immortals who would destroy us over it," Ryker retorted.

When Orin glared at him, the air started to crackle with electricity again. Cole's eyes narrowed on Ryker, and his gaze ran curiously over him before he moved to stand at Brokk's head.

"They're friends," Kaylia interjected before things could get ugly. "They're good friends, and you can trust them."

Cole relaxed and rested his hand against Brokk's cheek before moving toward Ryker again. "Give him to me."

With care, Ryker handed Brokk over to him. Orin remained unmoving as he scowled at Ryker.

"Orin, let's go," Cole commanded.

Orin didn't tear his gaze away from Ryker as he moved to take Brokk's feet from Tucker. As he wrapped his arm around Brokk's feet, Kaylia noticed his missing hand but didn't ask; she had more pressing matters right now.

"Who are you?" Cole inquired.

Ryker's shoulders went back. "I'm Ryker Locke, amsirah general; who are you?"

"King Colburn of the dark fae."

"Your brother has spoken highly of you."

"And you're an amsirah. Interesting."

"We can do introductions later!" Kaylia snapped. "We need the infirmary... *now!*"

Lexi squeezed her wrist. "Then let's go."

Lexi turned toward the drawbridge and moat only fifty feet away as Alina shifted out of their way. Before they could move,

Alina's three children, Astarot, Belindo, and Nithe, burst out from under the open portico.

The three baby dragons were much larger than Kaylia remembered. They were all now the size of a small car as they tumbled, leapt, and fell over top of one another in their excitement to get to their mother.

Little puffs of smoke coiled from their nostrils, and their squeals echoed down the hillside as they pounced on their mom. The bundles of joy would have flattened anyone else, but Alina sighed as they climbed over her.

"Easy, children," she murmured when they settled close to her head to nuzzle her.

"Holy shit, it talks," Ryker breathed.

"She's not an it," Lexi said kindly. "She is Alina, speaker of dragons."

"Amazing," Leland breathed.

Yes, it was all so wonderful, but they were wasting time. The longer they stood there, the more blood Brokk lost and the more suffering he endured.

"We have to go," Kaylia said brusquely.

She rested her hand on Brokk's thigh as they carried him toward the palace. They were safe here, but she wouldn't leave his side.

"I'm so happy you're home," Lexi whispered.

A single tear rolled down Kaylia's face as love broke through the panic gripping her. Releasing Brokk, she threw her arms around her friend and pulled her close.

Lexi clung to her as Kaylia fought not to fall apart. They were safe; she could let it all go, but she had no time for such luxuries as she had to care for Brokk.

When Sahira rested her hand on Kaylia's back, she half turned to embrace her other friend as they continued toward the palace.

CHAPTER THIRTY-FOUR

RYKER DID MOST of the talking while Kaylia, Sahira, Leland, and a witch Sahira introduced as Elsa worked to clean Brokk's back while he lay face down on one of the beds. After the final battle against the Lord, this room was full of injured immortals, but Brokk was the only occupant now.

Once they finished cleaning his exposed muscles and nerves, Kaylia applied a poultice while the others created a healing and pain potion. It would help speed up his recovery process while easing his suffering.

She had just finished applying the poultice when Varo rushed into the room. His nearly white-blue eyes filled with concern, and his black hair stood at angles around his face as he rushed to Brokk's side.

"What happened?" he demanded as Del and Maverick entered behind him.

"A lot," Cole replied, filling him in on everything Ryker had revealed.

Adrenaline and her desperation to ensure she did everything she could for Brokk kept her going even as her eyelids drooped and her legs trembled. When she slumped against the side of the mattress, Sahira wrapped her arm around Kaylia's waist.

"Why don't you let Lexi take you to your room so you can shower and dress," Sahira suggested.

Kaylia shook her head; it was all she could manage, as words wouldn't come.

"Then at least sit down." Sahira led her over to one of the chairs next to the bed. "You're about to drop, Kaylia, and you won't do anyone any good if we have to tend to you too."

Kaylia reluctantly slumped into one of the chairs. Brokk's hand was up by his head; she clasped it in hers as she leaned closer to listen to his shallow breaths.

She would prefer it if his breathing was stronger, but he wasn't wheezing and still didn't have a fever, which were both good signs. She wished he'd wake up, but that wouldn't happen until his body had more time and blood to heal.

After Ryker told their tale, Maverick and Del showed him and Tucker to some guest rooms. Though she could also use some rest, Leland stayed behind to help them.

"We have to help them find their king." Kaylia felt like she was pulling words from the sticky white substance that had sucked her into the mirror realm, but she had to tell them this. "We promised we would, and the ophidians have to *burn*."

"We'll do both those things." Cole rested his hand on her shoulder and squeezed. "Right now, all you have to worry about is ensuring you both stay healthy. Rest, Kaylia."

She knew Cole was right but couldn't stop herself from adjusting the padding covering Brokk's poultice.

"His ciphers," Orin muttered from where he stood on the other side of the bed. "I've *never* seen them fade like that before."

"They starved him," she whispered.

"From the looks of all of you, they starved you too," Lexi said.

Sitting in the chair across from Kaylia, Lexi's hands glowed white as she kept them against Brokk's side. Her arach ability to heal would also help speed up the process, but none of it was fast enough for Kaylia. She wanted to see and talk to him *now*.

"They did," Kaylia agreed, "but not as bad as him. If he hadn't been able to drink my blood through the bars and that of the nymphs they stuck in there with him, then he'd be far worse off than he is now. And it wasn't until yesterday or today, or whenever it was, that he finally fed the dark fae part of himself."

"Was that when they put nymphs in with him?" Varo asked.

"No. He killed all of them."

"Why would he do that?" Orin demanded.

All their eyes bore into her, but she was too tired to go into details. Besides, they'd figure it out soon enough.

She rested her head on the bed beside Brokk's and yawned as her eyes drifted closed. "How long have we been gone?"

"A little over three months," Lexi replied.

It was such a short time, but it felt like an eternity. "Did anyone from our group of searchers ever return?"

"You're the first to return out of the *many* who entered the Valley."

"I hate that place."

And those were the last words she uttered before passing out.

CHAPTER THIRTY-FIVE

WHEN KAYLIA WOKE AGAIN, it was to discover that someone had draped a blanket over her. She pulled it closer and nestled into its warmth before memories returned, and her head shot up.

Instantly, she focused on Brokk. He remained unmoving, his breathing sluggish, and his hand in hers. She squeezed his fingers before carefully releasing them.

Since he hadn't been able to feed, his ciphers remained faded. That would only slow his healing, but she couldn't do anything about it while he remained unconscious.

With tender fingers, she peeled back a section of the cloth on his poultice to inspect his back. The thick paste protected his brutalized body, but she could see enough to know he was healing.

It wasn't as swiftly as it should have been. She settled the cloth back into place and rested a hand over his as she stroked his cheek and beard. At least he still didn't have a fever.

Clasping his hand again, she lifted her gaze to Sahira and Orin, who sat across from her. Sahira held Orin's hand in both of hers.

Kaylia's eyebrows drew together as she stared at those hands. *Orin and Sahira?*

She couldn't think of a more unlikely pairing; not even she and Brokk were that odd, but she was too concerned about Brokk to question it.

"Has he shown any signs of waking?" she asked.

"Not yet," Sahira answered.

Kaylia closed her eyes as anguish twisted inside her, and with her free hand, she pulled the blanket tighter around her shoulders. Now that everything had settled down and she wasn't rushing around to ensure Brokk's treatment, the stench of her filled her nostrils.

While in the dungeon, surrounded by filth, waste, death, and blood, she'd grown accustomed to the reek of that place and her. Free of the dungeon, with the fresh scent of herbs, fresh linens, and clean immortals, the unbearable stench made her stomach turn.

Wrinkling her nose, she tried to shut out the smell, but it was an ever-present thing that wouldn't let her go. She'd give anything for a shower.

"I should change his dressing," she murmured.

"I did it half an hour ago," Sahira said when Kaylia started to rise. "Sit and rest. He's not the only one who endured a lot."

Kaylia hovered nervously over her chair as her gaze went from Brokk to Orin and Sahira, and back again. Finally, she settled onto her seat again.

"What happened to your hand?" she asked Orin.

The corners of his mouth twitched toward a smile. "You aren't the only one who was gone for three months. We only returned a few days ago and were preparing to go into Doomed Valley to search for the two of you. Thankfully, you found your way home instead."

"Thanks to Brokk," she whispered as she caressed his cheek. She'd bathed him the best she could when he first came to the infirmary. She'd taken away layers of dirt and blood, but she still smelled the dungeon all over him too, and his shaggy beard, a product of their time in that shithole, remained.

Her fingers itched to shave that reminder away, but she wouldn't take it from him while he slept. It was his decision to make.

"Is there something between you two?" Orin asked.

"Yes," Kaylia said.

"*That's* why he didn't feed on the nymphs."

"Yes." Kaylia lifted her head and looked pointedly at their joined hands. "And I'm guessing three months away changed the two of you too."

"In so many ways," Sahira said.

"Are you going to tell me about it?" Kaylia waved toward Orin's missing appendage. "And the hand?"

"We were trapped in the Cursed Realm."

Kaylia didn't speak while listening to their story, which was as brutal and awful as hers. By the time they finished, she didn't know what to say.

She never would have believed Orin could be selfless in any way or he would *ever* care for another the way he did for Sahira. However, love filled his eyes whenever he looked at her.

"I'm sorry for all you endured," Kaylia murmured when they finished.

"I'm sorry for all you endured, too," Sahira said.

"And no one is sorrier about it than me."

Kaylia turned as Lexi entered the room; she pushed a silver cart laden with food.

Lexi stopped the cart beside the bed and lifted her sorrow-filled eyes to look at them. "All of you were in those awful places because of me."

"That's not true," Kaylia said. "We were there because Amaris betrayed and nearly killed you. We were there because we *chose* to be; we knew there were risks when we left here."

"You didn't know about the ophidians, and they didn't know the Cursed Realm existed."

"I would do it all over again," Sahira said. "It was awful and terrifying, but something fantastic came out of it, and I would *never* change that."

Orin lifted their joined hands and kissed Sahira's knuckles. "Neither would I."

"And neither would I," Kaylia assured her.

Because, despite every *awful* thing that happened over the past three months, some good had come from it. She had Brokk now, and she was never going to let him go.

And, like everyone else in this room and so many outside it, she would do whatever it took to keep Lexi on the throne. She was the true queen of the realms and the only one who could handle the power of the arach throne without being driven mad by it.

Kaylia had also come to love the young woman and would protect her. Without her, someone else would assume the throne, go mad, and turn the realms into a living hell. They could *never* let that happen again.

CHAPTER THIRTY-SIX

LEXI RESTED her hands on Kaylia's shoulders before bending to hug her. "I missed you."

"I missed you too." Kaylia leaned into her friend before pulling away. "You shouldn't touch me; I smell so bad."

Lexi laughed as she returned to the cart. "That you do, but I'll take it if it means you're here."

She pulled the lid off a platter of bread, fruit, cheeses, and assorted pastries. Kaylia's stomach rumbled, and saliva flooded her mouth as the tantalizing scent of those delicacies drifted to her.

"You must be hungry," Lexi said. "You fell asleep before you could eat anything."

When she started to rise, Lexi waved her back and removed another lid to reveal a meat platter. "I'll make you a plate. I know you don't eat meat, but I thought Orin might want to eat too."

Orin sat back in his chair and stretched his legs before him as he smirked at Lexi. "That's Uncle Orin to you."

Lexi stopped using the tongs to place some cheese on a plate and lifted her head to frown at him. Sahira rolled her eyes, and Kaylia suppressed a smile as warmth filled her.

Brokk was still out of it, but they were home, surrounded by family, friends, and love, and they were *safe*. It was everything they'd dreamed about for the past three months.

"You two aren't married," Lexi retorted.

"*Yet*," Orin said.

Lexi's eyebrows shot up, and Kaylia's mouth fell open at this revelation. Things had *really* changed while she was gone.

"Well, if you do get married, you'll always be just Orin to me," Lexi retorted.

"Oh, we're getting married," Orin replied. "There's no doubt about that."

Kaylia didn't know how to respond, and Lexi didn't seem to either, as her mouth opened and closed. Neither of them was used to *this* Orin; he was much the same but also *very* different.

Orin was the *last* immortal she'd ever imagined hearing talk about *his* marriage. She was going to have to check, but she was pretty sure Hell had frozen over.

Brokk had to wake up to see and hear this. He'd never believe her when she told him later.

"I hope that does happen," Lexi said, "but you'll still *never* be Uncle Orin."

Lexi handed Kaylia a plate heaped with goodies. Her gaze fastened on the bread, cheeses, fruits, veggies, and sweets. It was a little bit of heaven in her hands, but she had to make sure Brokk was set before she ate.

"Has he had any blood lately?" Kaylia asked as she shifted her hold on the plate to wave at Brokk.

Orin's amusement vanished as his attention shifted back to his brother. "I gave him some blood about half an hour ago; he had some more healing and pain potion afterward."

"Good."

Kaylia set her plate on the edge of the bed to focus on her

food. She munched on some cheese and grapes, but while her mouth watered and she yearned to shovel all the delicious goodies in, she ate slowly.

After the gruel she'd survived on these past three months, she'd make herself sick if she ate too fast. Her stomach was so shrunken that by the time Lexi finished making plates for everyone, Kaylia couldn't put another bite into it.

She set her plate aside and brushed the hair back from Brokk's forehead. "Have you seen Ryker and the others?"

"Some of the kitchen staff took some food to their rooms while I brought up this cart," Lexi said. "But no one has seen them. Like you, I assume they've also been asleep for the past day."

"We've already been back for a day?"

"You have."

"Time keeps slipping away," Kaylia murmured. "He should be awake."

"He has a lot of healing to do," Sahira said, "but he'll wake soon."

Lexi came to stand beside her and rested her hand on Kaylia's shoulder. "Why don't we get you cleaned up? You'll feel better after showering, and maybe you can eat more afterward. You could also use some rest."

"I just slept for a day."

"I meant a rest from keeping vigil."

"I haven't watched over him for a whole day."

"Kaylia, you may have slept, but you haven't left his side, and you didn't sleep well. You were constantly twitching, muttering, and sometimes crying. You have to take care of yourself too."

"Would you leave Cole's side?"

Before Lexi could respond, Sahira spoke up. "I think a shower and a break is a great idea. We won't be gone long, and Orin will watch over him."

"I'm not going anywhere," Orin said.

"Cole and Varo will be here again soon, too," Lexi said. "They had to go to the Gloaming to meet with Elvin."

"How is the rebuild going there?" Kaylia asked in the hopes of distracting them from their current plan.

"Good! They've rebuilt all the homes and sown the crops. Most of the dark fae have returned to reestablish their lives there. Those who haven't are probably wandering the realms for a bit, have decided to go rogue, or are dead."

"That's good news about the rebuild," Kaylia said.

"Come on," Lexi said and squeezed Kaylia's shoulder. "Let's get you taken care of now."

Kaylia debated arguing, but when Sahira rose and walked around to join them, the fight left her. She'd love to scrub all the dungeon off her skin; that place would forever haunt her memories, but at least she wouldn't have to wear its filth anymore.

CHAPTER THIRTY-SEVEN

KAYLIA HAD every intention of taking the quickest shower of her life, but once she entered her bathroom, still filled with all her favorite soaps and shampoos, she couldn't tear herself away from the shower. She sobbed as the hot water pounded against her back while washing away the blood and dirt covering her.

She scrubbed herself clean, and when she finished, she did it three more times. Her skin was raw and red when she emerged from the shower and into the steam-filled bathroom, but she contemplated doing it all over again.

She'd already been away from Brokk for too long, and while she could still smell the dungeon, it wasn't possible that its stench still clung to her. The scent was a memory that had etched itself into the very fiber of her being.

Oh, Hecate, don't let that be true.

Kaylia tried not to think about the possibility she might never completely rid herself of the awful aroma as she removed one of the soft towels from where she'd stored them in the closet. She buried her face in it and inhaled its fresh, lavender scent.

While in Doomed Valley, she hadn't allowed herself to dwell on the luxuries she was missing. She'd had a mission and was determined to fulfill it, but she reveled in all the things she'd missed out on while gone.

When she finished drying off, she shrugged into the white robe she'd left hanging on the back of her door many months ago. A cloud of steam followed when she opened the door and entered her beautiful room.

The floor-to-ceiling windows making up the entire wall across from her allowed enough sun to enter that the cream-colored walls turned a pale yellow. At night, during a full moon, they were a silvery color.

Five different lamps with glass shades of multiple hues also sent beams of color around the room, even though they weren't lit. She'd positioned them to catch and reflect as much of the sun as possible.

In the corner was her favorite yellow chair, and her desk was a deep blue hue. A multihued quilt covered her bed; her mother had made it for her when she was a girl, and it was one of her favorite possessions.

She walked over to run her fingers across the familiar, bumpy surface. Her mother had interwoven hundreds of strands of color throughout the separate patterns. There were so many different shades that she occasionally found a new one.

Tears pricked her eyes as she recalled the woman who had so lovingly crafted this for her. Every night she slept beneath it, she felt her mother's love.

She heard the door click closed from the adjoining room that she'd turned into a storage place for a treasure trove of potions, crystals, gems, and myriad other ingredients. A second later, Sahira and Lexi entered the room.

"Was someone here?" Kaylia asked anxiously.

Did Brokk wake up while I was in the shower? She'd never forgive herself if he did.

"It was a guard," Lexi said. "He came to report there's been no change in Brokk, so you don't have to rush back."

That news filled her with both relief and dread. It didn't matter what they said; she had to get dressed and get back to him soon. She'd been gone too long.

Striding over to her closet, she opened the doors to reveal her eclectic mix of pants and tunics next to the much-loved dresses she hadn't worn in months. She'd spent so much time fighting recently that she'd put aside her once daily wear of dresses in favor of more snug clothing that wouldn't catch on things.

She didn't regret that her peaceful life in the crone realm had come to a screeching halt the day Sahira and Brokk entered her life. She *loathed* the fighting and death that followed, but they'd all done *so* much good for the realms, and she'd do it again if necessary.

However, she was so tired of fighting, and the fight wasn't over yet... it may *never* end. Countless, greedy immortals would do anything to remove Lexi from her throne and claim it for themselves.

They'd also promised Ryker they would find his king, which meant a return to the place that nearly destroyed her and Brokk. Every part of her rebelled against entering Doomed Valley again, but she'd uphold their promise *and* see an end to the ophidians.

Brokk and his brothers would also be determined to make the ophidians pay for what they'd done. She would be there to help them, but she was ready to feel at least somewhat normal again.

Removing a cheerful yellow dress with dark blue and red flowers, she removed her robe to tug on the lightweight material. She smiled when it settled into place around her.

The supple fabric soothed her raw flesh. Before the war against the Lord, the dress had hugged her frame, but now it hung off her shoulders and flowed freely around her waist.

She shoved aside the sadness creeping into her; she'd regain the weight, and one day, it would fit as well as before. She and Brokk were alive, and that was what mattered. Lamenting things she couldn't change wouldn't do anyone any good.

"Do you feel better?" Lexi asked when she emerged from the closet.

"Yes," she said, but mostly to put Lexi's mind at ease.

She wouldn't feel better until Brokk was awake again. Pulling her skirt forward, she settled at her dressing table and picked up her brush. She ran her fingers over the bristles while smiling at the simple design that made life easier.

When she went to brush her hair, her hand froze as, for the first time, she saw Doomed Valley's effect on her. Her cheeks and eyes were sunken, and the once shiny hair that flowed to her knees was dull and tangled around her shoulders.

The rosy color once blooming on her cheeks had taken on a dull pallor that made her look sickly, and perhaps she was. She hadn't eaten well in months and was denied access to the vibrant nature that nourished her soul.

Like her weight, they were changes she could correct over time. She'd never considered herself vain, but Kaylia couldn't look in the mirror when she lifted the brush to her hair. That woman in the glass was one more reminder of the dungeon.

CHAPTER THIRTY-EIGHT

SAHIRA RESTED her fingers against Kaylia's brush when her hand trembled. "Let me help."

Unable to deal with the mess of her hair and feeling drained from all the effort it had taken to shower and dress, Kaylia handed the brush to her. With tender care, Sahira started working the knots out.

"What happened to your hair?" Lexi asked as she settled onto the seat beside her.

"I cut it off. It was getting in the way," Kaylia replied.

"It looks beautiful."

"It's lopsided."

"I can fix that when I finish brushing it," Sahira assured her.

"Thank you, but I have to get back to Brokk; my hair can wait."

"You and Brokk...?" Lexi's voice trailed off into a question.

"I love him." Kaylia pressed her hand to her chest when it flipped strangely. "And he loves me."

Lexi leaned against her side. "That's wonderful."

"Yes. Something amazing, and what I believed to be *impossible*, came from all that horror."

"Why would loving him be impossible?" Sahira asked. "Because he's part vampire?"

"No." Kaylia had forgotten that Sahira didn't know about Fabian. "I was engaged once to a man who was murdered by a vampire."

Sahira's hand was still, and Kaylia glanced in the mirror to discover Sahira's mouth agape. "I didn't know… I'm so sorry. How *awful*."

"Thank you." Kaylia's gaze lowered to the hands she'd clasped in her lap. "It happened centuries ago, but I still love him."

"*That's* why you created the crone realm. You went there to grieve."

"Yes."

Lexi placed her hand on Kaylia's knee; she knew this story. Adjusting her hold on the hairbrush, Sahira bent to hug Kaylia.

When tears burned in her eyes, Kaylia closed them before she started crying again. She was afraid she'd never stop if she started.

She squeezed Sahira's arm and held on to her before releasing her friend. Sahira rose and squeezed Kaylia's shoulder before returning her attention to the knots in her hair.

"I never thought I'd fall in love again; I didn't think it was possible," Kaylia whispered. "Immortals *don't* love twice."

"You have one of the biggest hearts I've ever encountered," Lexi said. "It only makes sense that it would have room to love more than once."

"I guess." Kaylia closed her eyes and tried not to fall asleep while Sahira brushed her hair. "It's just so unusual and believed to be impossible, but I *do* love Brokk. He can't replace Fabian, and I don't want him to, but he's claimed a huge piece of my heart."

"That's a good thing."

"But you feel guilty," Sahira said.

"It's impossible not to. It got better while we were in the dungeon, but before then, my love for him and the guilt felt like they were tearing me in two. It doesn't help...."

"What doesn't help?" Sahira asked when Kaylia's words trailed off.

"It doesn't help that I've come to love Brokk more than I loved Fabian," she admitted in an ashamed whisper.

"Kaylia—"

Kaylia couldn't stand to hear what Lexi was going to say. It would be something forgiving, and she shouldn't be forgiven.

"I didn't think that was possible," she interrupted. "Fabian was *everything* to me. Yes, it took a while for our relationship to grow into what it became, but before it did, he was my best friend. Over time, he became something more.

"And then, the same thing happened with Brokk; it took time for my love for him to develop, and a whole lot of shitty things happened before it did, but that's not why I fell in love with him. I couldn't help that. He's such a good man with a kind heart, and he would do *anything* for me. He deserves to be loved completely, and while I love him more than Fabian, I can never give him everything he deserves."

And she *hated* herself for that. No one spoke as they digested her words.

"I feel like I'm betraying Fabian with Brokk," she finally said, "and that I'm failing Brokk."

"You're not," Lexi assured her. "Fabian has been dead for hundreds of years, and you've loved him all that time, and now you're getting the chance to move on and love again. That's an amazing thing."

"Every immortal I've ever known has gone to their grave still loving the one they lost... if it happens to them. As long as they live, they grieve the loss of their love."

"But you're different than them. We're *all* different, and we all love in numerous ways."

"I just... I never believed I'd love at all... until Fabian. It wasn't something I was looking for. I enjoyed being single; I had fun with my friends and different men and wasn't looking for that to change.

"Then Fabian came along, and everything changed. Initially, I didn't find him attractive, and he certainly wasn't my type. Brokk is far more my type than Fabian, but he captured my heart."

Sahira continued to work the tangles from her hair while she told them how she'd met Fabian at a Samhain party. At first, she rebuked his advances, but they became friends. Over time, that friendship developed into something deeper.

As she retold the story, her guilt over Fabian increased, and so did her shame of talking about him while Brokk lay in the infirmary, waiting for her return. She admitted all of this to them as she closed her eyes and battled the conflicting waves of love, sadness, and wrongdoing battering her.

"I know things take time, but I'm sick of feeling this way," she admitted.

Sahira's brow furrowed, and her lips pursed as she set the brush down.

Kaylia frowned at her friend's troubled expression. "What is it?"

Sahira's eyes darted up to meet hers in the mirror. "Hmm?"

"What's bothering you?"

"Oh, nothing... nothing. Are you sure you don't want me to cut your hair?"

"No, it can wait. I've been away for too long already. If Brokk wakes, and I'm not there, I'll never forgive myself."

Kaylia rose and turned to face her friends. Opening her arms, she smiled as they embraced, and their love enveloped her. She needed to get back to Brokk, but she also needed *this*.

"I missed you so much," she whispered.

Lexi hugged her closer. "We missed you too."

CHAPTER THIRTY-NINE

SAHIRA WATCHED as Kaylia slipped her feet into a pair of moccasins. The most powerful witch in existence and a woman who once shone with vitality had withered away, but despite her weakened exterior, the courage and strength of her soul remained intact.

Kaylia and Brokk would survive this, regain all the vitality they'd lost, and continue their lives. They'd love each other, and Kaylia might one day come to terms with her love for two men... or maybe she wouldn't.

Sahira nibbled her bottom lip as she pondered Kaylia's revelations and the terrible, niggling doubt they'd evoked. She should say something, but Kaylia had just returned.

Sahira didn't know if she was right. If she was, it could be worse than if she were wrong.

Plus, while they'd united to help Lexi reclaim her throne and become good friends during that time, Sahira easily recalled what it was like to have the oldest witch hate her. Right or wrong, she could evoke Kaylia's anger again, and she'd just gotten her friend back.

And now you know why she hated vampires more than most

witches; her fiancé was killed by one. She might evoke that hatred again if she expressed her concerns and understood why.

Now that she had Orin, she knew what it was like to love another so deeply she would bind her life to them. If someone killed Orin, she would go on a rampage against all those involved.

She understood Kaylia's hatred and didn't want to do or say something to make it return. But could she keep her mouth shut and not mention it? Was that fair to Kaylia?

And if she decided to do so, how long should she remain silent? Until Brokk woke, a month, a year, or forever?

She couldn't live with these doubts for days or months. She'd have a difficult time looking Kaylia and Brokk in the face, and it would ruin her friendship with them. And how much would they both hate her if they found out she hadn't said anything?

She would have to tell Orin; she could never keep it from him, and then what? He'd *never* remain quiet about it.

Maybe she could wait until Brokk was awake and he and Kaylia were more settled, healthier, and happier, but she would still have the issue of Orin. And out of the two of them, these doubts would be a lot less upsetting coming from her than Orin, as he didn't do gentle when it came to words.

"Kaylia...." Her voice trailed off when her friend turned toward her.

"What is it?" Kaylia asked.

Sahira glanced at her niece, but Lexi didn't know the doubts running through her mind. Lexi tilted her head to the side and frowned as she studied Sahira.

"How... ah... how old was Fabian when you met?" Sahira finally asked.

A small smile tugged at Kaylia's mouth as she recalled her lost love. "He was around seventeen hundred years old when we first met, five hundred years older than me."

Sahira gulped and looked at Lexi again as she tried to decide what to do, but her niece's attention was on Kaylia.

"Are you ready?" Kaylia asked as she strode out of her bedroom and into the one full of witches' supplies.

Sahira's throat felt like something was creeping up inside it as she followed Lexi and Kaylia. Whatever that something was, it sought to spread its fingers around her voice box.

She should listen to it and keep her mouth shut. She shouldn't say a thing, but as her conscience warred with anxiety over losing her friend, she blurted, "Do you think he could have used a love potion or spell on you?"

Kaylia's hand froze on the doorknob. The room went deathly silent; she didn't even hear the birds singing anymore. It was as if the whole realm was holding its breath in expectation of her response.

CHAPTER FORTY

KAYLIA'S HEAD turned toward Sahira, and her brow furrowed. Lexi didn't move as her gaze shifted from Sahira to Kaylia and back again.

Kaylia finally broke the hush. "*What?*"

Sahira wished she could suck her words back in; she should've waited for a better time to express her concern, but when would be a better time?

When Brokk's not in a coma, maybe.

Sahira resisted the impulse to slap herself in the forehead, but the words were out there now, and she couldn't take them back. She'd uttered them because she couldn't pretend everything was fine, but they would only cause Kaylia more unhappiness if she was wrong.

"What do you mean?" Kaylia asked. "Brokk doesn't have that kind of power."

Sahira blinked in response to Kaylia's odd reply. She had no idea why her friend's brain had shifted from Fabian to Brokk when they'd been discussing the warlock she was engaged to or why she'd assumed Sahira meant Brokk when the dark fae didn't possess such magical abilities.

Judging by Lexi's expression, she wasn't the only one confused by this, but it also made Sahira question if maybe she was right. If Fabian did do something to Kaylia, he'd also made it so she never suspected a thing.

There were witches and warlocks capable of doing such a thing—Kaylia was one of them. But Fabian was older than her and, therefore, stronger.

"I'm not talking about Brokk," Sahira said kindly. "Brokk doesn't have that ability, but Fabian was a warlock."

Sahira hadn't thought it possible, considering how pale Kaylia already was, but the color drained further from her face. "*No*. I would know if somebody used a love potion or spell on me. I'm a witch."

"I know, but he was older and more powerful than you."

Kaylia's eyebrows drew sharply together over the bridge of her nose. The cleft in her chin became more noticeable when her lips pursed.

"I'm not trying to upset you," Sahira rushed to get out. "You have a *huge* heart, and I believe you could love two men so deeply, but… but the way you are about Fabian and something you said while talking about him bothered me."

"And what was that?" Kaylia's voice had taken on a defensive tone.

"Sahira…." Lexi warned in a low whisper.

But she'd come this far, and it was too late to turn back. "That you weren't attracted to him at first and he wasn't your type. Believe me, I get it when it comes to men *not* being your type. Orin certainly isn't mine.

"I've always hated arrogant assholes who consider themselves a gift to women and the world, and Orin is *the* king of them, but I was always attracted to him, even when I didn't want to be. And yes, deep, lasting love does come from friendship; those are some of the best relationships out there—"

"Then why are you questioning what happened between me and Fabian?" Kaylia interrupted.

Sahira clasped her hands before her as she resisted wringing them. *What did I start here?*

But no matter her regrets, she *had* started it and would see it through. She didn't have a choice.

"It's your eyes." Sahira had noticed it while brushing Kaylia's hair. "They're not the same when you talk about Fabian and Brokk. They sparkle when you talk about Brokk, even though you're drained, battered, and exhausted. That same twinkle doesn't come into your eyes when you speak about Fabian."

Kaylia frowned while pondering this. "It's been *centuries* since Fabian passed."

"I know, but you still claim to love him; shouldn't that spark be there?"

Kaylia looked to Lexi, who remained unmoving while absorbing Sahira's words. When Kaylia's attention shifted back to her, Sahira didn't look away as Kaylia's eyes burned into hers. She could practically see her friend's mind racing while she tried to process everything.

"I don't want to upset you; that's the last thing I'm trying to do after everything you've been through," Sahira said, "but I... I... I *had* to say something."

"And now you have," Kaylia muttered.

With that, she opened the door and strode into the hallway. Sahira remained standing beside Lexi.

"I had to say something," Sahira whispered.

Lexi gave her a tremulous smile as she squeezed Sahira's arm. "Yes, you did. It will be fine."

Sahira hoped she was right.

.

CHAPTER FORTY-ONE

AT FIRST, Kaylia strode down the hall with irritated strides that left Sahira and Lexi trailing her. But as she walked, Sahira's words dug deeper into her brain.

What Sahira suggested was *impossible*. She was the strongest witch in existence. She had a *lot* of power and would know if someone was casting a love spell over her or using a potion against her.

She was infuriated with Sahira for suggesting she could be so weak or that Fabian, the man she'd loved for *centuries*, would ever be capable of doing such a thing. He was far different than Brokk, but he was a good man who had *loved* her.

An immortal didn't ask someone they didn't love to marry them. *But would that love drive him to use a potion or spell against me?*

She hated herself for thinking it as guilt surged back to fierce life. *He was a good man! How dare you doubt him!*

Kaylia's step slowed as it became difficult for her to keep walking. She should close the door on all her doubts; they weren't fair to a man whose life was unfairly cut short, but now that it had been cracked open, her mind churned.

I have a lot of power now, and I did then too, but not as much as Fabian. He was older and more experienced. He knew things I didn't and still don't.

Warlocks were more likely than witches to dabble in darker magic and more likely to use those arts against another than witches. Fabian hadn't been one of those warlocks.

At least as far as you know. It's not like they make their practices well known.

Most warlocks were secretive about their abilities, but so were the witches. They couldn't risk exposing any vulnerabilities to an enemy.

She'd believed she'd known everything about him, but looking back, they never discussed their practices with each other. They each had their separate time with their covens, which was a private thing.

I have no idea what kind of magic he practiced.

The realization was like a kick to the gut—one that left her laboring to breathe as her steps slowed enough that she could hear Lexi and Sahira behind her again.

I would have known if he cast a spell or used a potion on me!

But there were plenty of times he'd given her a drink before they got together. They'd been friends. She'd gone to his home, and he to hers.

They'd swapped tales, recipes, and concoctions. All of them had been innocent things, like a better way to help a tree grow or to cast bones. They'd shared their knowledge but never delved deeper into their practices.

Fabian had been arrogant, boastful, and not much for the work that went into some spells, but he was also fascinated with her, and they'd worked well together. There hadn't been an instant spark, and as much as she hated acknowledging it, he hadn't made her become completely unhinged during sex like Brokk did.

The sex between them had been great, but with Brokk, it was

fantastic. She never had that level of chemistry with Fabian... or any other man until Brokk.

When she first met Fabian at the party, she found him too smooth and perfect. When he extended his hand to take hers, not one speck of dirt marred his skin.

His was the hand of someone who *never* got dirty, and she'd always preferred her men willing to plunge their hands into the earth. She'd liked them rougher, less composed, and without their hair so perfectly styled.

Fabian had made advances on her that night, but when she politely rebuked them, he'd taken it all in stride. It wasn't until later in the night, when she told another witch she would be hunting for shantoo mushroom tomorrow, that he overheard her, and they started a conversation again.

He knew of a place where the fungus grew in abundance and would be happy to take her there. Kaylia had planned to spend most of the day trying to find the shantoo, but Fabian's help would give her more time to create the potion she required to chase the imps from her garden. The small creatures disliked the smell of them and would flee from it.

Eager to get the annoying creatures away from her herbs, she'd agreed to go with him. The following morning, they gathered the mushrooms and learned more about each other.

She told him about the loss of her sister, Mina, and he revealed he was the oldest of three siblings. A lycan had killed his youngest brother over a hundred years ago, and they bonded over their shared grief.

By the time she had enough mushrooms to create her potion, she already liked him more than she had the day before. Plus, he didn't mind getting his hands dirty as much as she'd first assumed, even if he had worn gloves the whole time.

When they returned to her home, she brewed the potion and sprinkled it around her garden while he made lunch. It had been such a fun day, and by the end of it, while she wasn't attracted to him, she'd grown to like him.

After he left, she didn't see him again for a couple of weeks. When she did, she'd run into him at the marketplace run by witches and warlocks. They had dinner that night, caught up, and shared some laughs.

When they parted, they agreed to meet again the next week. After that, they saw each other about once a week for the next couple of months until things started changing, and they started seeing each other daily.

She found herself not caring about his too-perfect demeanor and was excited to be in his company. Yes, he was a little too charming, perfect, and refined, but she started to like that more.

And then, before she knew it, she woke up one day and realized she'd fallen in love. It wasn't the wild tumble she experienced with Brokk but a gradual descent into something she'd always seen as beautiful.

There was no way that love was because of a potion or spell. It couldn't have been fake. *It was real!*

But now that doubt had hooked its claws into her, she couldn't shake it. Her head spun as guilt and self-hatred battered her. These doubts were one more betrayal to Fabian, but he *was* stronger than her, and she had refused him at first.

He was arrogant. He never liked hearing the word no and always had an air of superiority around him that irked me even after we fell in love. He also made me plenty of drinks, many of which were when I wasn't watching.

She couldn't deny those things because they were all the truth.

CHAPTER FORTY-TWO

Resting her hand against the wall, Kaylia stopped walking as her head bowed, and she inhaled a tremulous breath. "If it was a love spell, his death would have broken it."

She sensed Sahira and Lexi behind her, but neither spoke.

"The same would be true if it were a potion," Kaylia continued.

"That's true," Sahira finally said.

"And he's dead."

Again, neither of them said anything.

"His brother came to my door. He told me about Fabian's death, and I never saw him again. And if he was alive, there would have been sightings of him in the realms. They're vast and numerous, but *someone* would have seen him."

Even as she insisted on this, she knew it was foolish to be so certain. The realms were numerous, and it would be easy for someone to become lost in them.

Plus, it wasn't as if everyone in *all* the realms knew about their relationship. There were even plenty of witches and warlocks who they didn't associate with and who wouldn't have cared who was fucking or marrying who.

If Fabian was alive, he could be anywhere, and no one would know or care about the relationship he once shared with her.

"But why would he hide?" she muttered. "Why would he fake his death?"

Again, Lexi and Sahira said nothing as they let Kaylia sort through her thoughts and emotions. She shouldn't question her love for Fabian; she was wrong to do so, and that knowledge squeezed her chest until she could barely breathe.

A gentle hand on her arm turned her attention to Lexi. Her friend's face swam as Kaylia's vision blurred. She realized it was because she had tears in her eyes.

"It's okay. We'll figure it all out together, but you have to breathe," Lexi soothed.

Until Lexi said this, Kaylia hadn't realized she'd stopped breathing. She inhaled a tremulous breath while struggling to keep her emotions under control.

When she felt a little better, she lifted her gaze to Sahira, who stood beside Lexi. Concern etched Sahira's features as she bit nervously on her lip.

"I shouldn't have said anything," Sahira whispered. "I was wrong to do so."

"No. You were right to voice your concerns."

Kaylia shifted her attention back to the infirmary door, only fifty feet away. She had to see Brokk again, to hold his hand and reassure herself that he was okay while she tried to calm her tumultuous emotions.

Once that happened, she could think more clearly and figure out what was happening. Lexi's hand fell away as Kaylia threw her shoulders back and started down the corridor again.

While she walked, she reminded herself that any love spell or potion Fabian created would have broken when he died. *But what if he's not dead?*

She recalled the devastated look on his brother's face as he stood outside her teepee. Tears had shone in his eyes while he broke the news to her.

Someone couldn't fake that level of grief... or could they? *Of course they can.*

She knew well the cruelty of immortals and mortals; she was still suffering the effects of the ophidians. There were so many wonderful living creatures in the realms, but there were also a lot of monsters.

Kaylia hesitated outside the infirmary door. As she twisted the knob, she told Sahira, "Make an antidote. I'll drink it."

She didn't look back at her friends as she entered the room.

CHAPTER FORTY-THREE

KAYLIA HELD Brokk's hand while stroking his forehead. She'd reclaimed the position next to the bed she'd left behind. Cole, Varo, and Orin sat across from her. The three brothers were stone-faced while holding vigil over Brokk.

"Did he show any signs of starting to wake?" she asked.

"He was talking a little bit," Orin said, "and I thought he was going to wake, but he slipped back into unconsciousness."

Kaylia buried her disappointment as she checked his poultice and removed the cover. She gathered a bowl and some towels before returning to carefully wash away the pasty, magical concoction she'd placed over his brutalized back.

When she exposed his raw flesh, she set the bowl aside to examine the wounds more closely. A thin layer of red skin covered the muscles and veins so cruelly exposed by the ophidian's whip.

She was going to cover it again but decided against it. Some air would help it heal and dry out before she covered it for the night.

Kaylia rested her hand against his forehead and smiled when

she discovered his cool skin. His mouth and fingers twitched, and he issued a small sound before settling again.

She suspected he'd wake up soon and prayed to Hecate she was right. She *needed* to hear his voice again.

While she worked on Brokk, Sahira glided around the infirmary. Kaylia tried not to notice her stirring a cauldron while adding handfuls of herbs to her potion.

The scents of lavender, mint, milk thistle, dandelion, and eucalyptus filled the room as Sahira worked. Kaylia knew a lot more was going into the antidote Sahira created, but those aromas were the most prevalent.

Standing by the window, Lexi rubbed the snout of a dragon who'd stuck their head in to say hello and check on her. When the creature decided to leave, it created a small breeze as it propelled itself back into the sky.

Kaylia didn't know how to feel about anything right now. Her love for Brokk was the only thing she was certain of anymore.

But even with that love held fast in her chest, her emotions had taken too much of a beating lately, and she'd settled into a state of numbness. Her brain stopped running through all the doubts Sahira had aroused, and she focused on Brokk.

He was the truth. He was hers, and she could rely on everything she felt for him. She knew their love was true but wasn't so certain about what occurred between her and Fabian.

And whenever she doubted it, guilt and self-hatred came to the forefront again. She couldn't handle the never-ending cycle anymore, so she shut it down.

She brushed Brokk's dark blond hair off his forehead before giving him more blood mixed with the healing and pain potion. It was difficult to get him to drink while he was lying on his stomach, but she got a fair amount in him before wiping his mouth and removing the towel she'd placed under his face.

When she kissed his cheek, his eyes fluttered beneath his

lids, but he still didn't wake. Kaylia sat down and reclaimed his hand as she recalled their first time together in Doomed Valley.

She'd felt her body awakening before they came together in the small shelter Ryker had given them. But being with him had *really* reawakened her.

Life had flooded her, and power exploded out of her when she came apart. She'd never experienced such a thing before. It felt like she was coming alive all over again, breaking free of something… had it been a love potion or spell or something?

Was it part of her trying to break free? Had her experience with Brokk somehow pierced through a part of whatever hold the spell or potion had on her?

If anyone could break through and save her from something beyond her control, it was Brokk. She did not doubt that.

But had she really been under the control of a spell or potion? It had been over three hundred years since Fabian died; could she have been held captive by some outside force that whole time?

The possibility made her skin crawl and the hair on her nape rise. That would mean that for three *centuries,* she wasn't herself. She'd been under the control of someone else, and *everything* she'd done since then had revolved around something that didn't exist.

The possibility was terrifying.

CHAPTER FORTY-FOUR

ANOTHER COUPLE of hours passed where no one spoke, and the crackle of the fire beneath Sahira's antidote was the only sound filling the room. Brokk stirred and murmured her name a few times before settling into sleep again.

Kaylia sprinkled a powder on his back to help him heal faster but decided to wait on the poultice. His back looked a little less red, and his skin had completely closed over his muscles and veins.

After another hour, Sahira tapped her wooden spoon against the side of the cauldron hanging over the fire. "It's done."

"What is it?" Orin asked.

Kaylia, Sahira, and Lexi didn't respond. Their silence drew curious glances from the brothers.

"What is it?" Orin asked again.

"It's something for me," Kaylia replied stiffly.

Lexi rose and smoothed down the front of her green tunic before looking at Cole. "It's best if the three of you leave."

Varo and Cole were slightly perplexed by her words, but Orin's face darkened. He crossed his arms over his chest and leaned back in his chair. "I'm not going anywhere."

"Yes, you are," Sahira said. "This should be done in private. I promise you, Brokk will be safe with us, and we're not giving him anything."

"If it has to be done privately, then you should all take it there."

"Orin—"

"He's my *brother*. You wouldn't leave Lexi."

"I would leave Lexi in Cole's hands if he asked me to. Obviously, Brokk wants her here; he keeps muttering her name, and Kaylia loves him. You have to respect that."

When Orin's eyes narrowed on her, Sahira glared back at him. The rest of them watched with amusement and curiosity as to who would win this battle of wills. Kaylia was anxious for them to go, but this wasn't her battle.

When Brokk murmured Kaylia's name again, Orin's arms fell. "Fine." He planted his hand on the side of Brokk's bed while rising. "You'd better take good care of him."

"I will," Kaylia vowed.

As long as she lived, she would protect Brokk with everything she had. Cole and Varo also stood. Cole kissed Lexi while Varo rested his hand on her shoulder and squeezed before leaving the room.

The hush following their exit felt too heavy yet somehow loud. She couldn't hear the crackle of the fire until Sahira set a mug of steaming liquid in front of her.

The combination of smells from it caused Kaylia's nose to wrinkle as sounds rushed back in. The birds sang outside, a dragon roared in the distance, and the fire crackled.

Kaylia stared at the mug like it was a scorpion about to sting her, but she didn't move to pick it up. Her stomach churned as her entire being protested drinking it.

Putting that stuff in her body was a betrayal to Fabian. It was a decision she could never take back and one that would forever haunt her love for him.

But is that love real?

The question caused a clammy sweat to break out on her body. She wiped away the beads forming on her upper lip.

Lexi came to stand beside her as another dragon soared by the window. "We'll leave, too."

Kaylia watched the rising steam in her mug until it dissipated in the air. "No. Stay."

If they left, she'd dump the potion out the window; she was certain of it. That certainty frightened her as much as the idea of being trapped in the ophidians' dungeon again.

She felt out of control of her body, as if something else possessed it. She shouldn't dread drinking this potion... but she did.

Kaylia wrapped one hand around the warm mug and slid her free fingers between Brokk's. When she squeezed his hand, he twitched in response, and fresh tears burned her eyes.

She hated how emotional she'd become and despised the uncertainty, terror, and guilt twisting like a tornado within her. This was wrong; she shouldn't do it, but if she was so certain in her love for Fabian, she shouldn't hesitate to drink it.

She should be more than happy to show Sahira, herself, and the realms that her love for him was true. *Then why won't my hand move?*

For too long, she sat there watching as the steam faded while the mug's contents cooled. The temperature of the potion didn't matter; it was as effective cold as it was hot.

Still, she couldn't bring herself to drink it as the clock in the corner ticked away the seconds and minutes. Sahira and Lexi didn't say anything while they waited for her.

She gulped and finally managed to lift her trembling hand off the table. It took more strength than she'd ever admit to steady her hand enough to bring the mug to her lips.

There, it rested for another minute before she parted her lips and drank it.

CHAPTER FORTY-FIVE

THE SECOND SAHIRA'S concoction hit her tongue, a screaming started in her body. She'd never experienced such a sensation before, but she could hear all her cells shrieking against the antidote, filling her mouth to the point where she couldn't swallow.

While her body screeched to the level of banshees, her mind berated her for being a traitorous bitch who'd tossed aside her lost love for another man. The hair on her arms rose, bile surged up her throat, and she almost spewed the foul-tasting antidote all over Brokk.

Except, it shouldn't taste so bad. She knew what went into a potion meant to break a love spell. Its ingredients should give it a crisp, refreshing taste. It shouldn't make her feel like she'd poured liquid garbage into her mouth.

Sahira poisoned me.

As soon as the ludicrous idea crossed her mind, she knew it was wrong. Sahira would never do that, but her brain continued to shout it at her while her ears vibrated from the shrieking of her cells.

The antidote burned into her tongue in a way it never should have. In her mind's eye, she had a vivid image of her tongue turning black and shriveling before rotting off.

Though a lump had lodged in her throat, Kaylia gulped the liquid down. Lexi patted her on the back when she choked and coughed.

She contemplated heaving the mug across the room but lifted it to her mouth to force the rest down. The antidote burned as it seeped through her bloodstream, turned her insides black, and withered them.

I'm dying.

Her cells proved this as they stopped screaming and shriveled inside her. She was dying, breaking apart, rotting from the inside out, and it was all because she hadn't trusted her love for Fabian.

It wasn't the potion doing this to her... it was her betrayal of *him*. She was a rotten bitch who deserved everything she was getting.

The empty mug fell from Kaylia's grasp. It bounced off the bed and shattered when it hit the floor.

"Oh," Lexi cried.

Kaylia dimly realized Lexi bent to pick up the pieces, but she couldn't focus on anything other than the shattering inside her. She was breaking apart like a sandcastle beneath the relentless waves of the sea.

At first, only little pieces of herself were washing out to the ocean. Then, a massive wave crashed over her; it swept away everything, leaving nothing of her behind.

After that final wave, silence descended. Her brain stopped telling her how terrible she was, and the screeching finally ended.

Unable to move, Kaylia sat there, cold, numb, and unfeeling. She couldn't hear or see anything. She couldn't feel anymore; it was impossible when nothing of her remained.

Then, the ocean rolled forth once more. As it crashed against the beach, it brought a rush of outside noise back in as her body revolted.

CHAPTER FORTY-SIX

RISING, Kaylia staggered toward the trash can tucked neatly beneath the counter. She would have gone for the sink, but it was too far away.

She was going to throw up; everything dead and broken inside her was going to come out, and it was going to happen soon. With a hand against her mouth, she tried to hold back the tidal wave of broken things, but they burned their way up her throat and erupted before she made it halfway to the can.

Sahira and Lexi gasped as black bile coated the floor. Unable to remain standing, Kaylia dropped to her knees as she threw up again.

The black toxin erupting from her not only coated her lips but became a part of them as it tattooed its foul, bitter taste onto her. It was so vile it only made her gag and vomit more.

"Kaylia!" Sahira cried.

When arms embraced her, she quaked within her friend's hold as more vile stuff spewed from her. Her vision blurred, her head spun, and for a second, she feared she'd pass out, but she didn't get the chance before vomiting more.

"What's going on in here?"

"Get out!" Lexi commanded.

Kaylia had no idea who had opened the door, but when Lexi yelled at them to leave, the door clicked shut again. A dragon roared outside, and the fire crackled while her heaving breaths came out as strange wheezes.

With the next purge of black goo, the truth hit her. It wasn't her insides coming out; it was *poison*.

It was the poison Fabian had given to her with the food they shared and the drinks he made. It was the poison that had rotted her insides for centuries and turned her into someone who loved him deeply... except that love was never *real*.

He'd poisoned her slowly to make her growing love for him more believable. When, after a few months of growing closer to him, she'd decided she was in love with him, her change of heart was plausible to her and the friends who'd watched it happen.

They'd all known how she felt about him at first—he was nice but not her type, and despite being very handsome, she wasn't attracted to him. When she started telling them how she and Fabian spent more time together and enjoyed laughing, talking, and sharing stories, they believed things were naturally changing between them... just like her.

Some of the best relationships were those built on friendship first, where the unexpected bloomed into something vibrant. It was all so miraculous to her at the time; she'd discovered a love that would last for eternity.

And it was all based on poison and *lies*.

So many lies were coming out of her as she threw up again and again. There was so much wrong that could never be fixed.

Those friends who had stood by her side throughout everything with Fabian were gone. She pushed them all away when she retreated to the crone realm, and none of them still lived.

It had taken many years of coming to terms with her grief over a lost *love* before she started to regret the loss of those friendships. By then, it was too late.

Not only had Fabian used, twisted, and made her into someone she wasn't meant to be, but he'd also stolen years of her life from her. She'd wasted *centuries* grieving him in the crone realm.

Anger, hatred, and sorrow became her constant companions. She'd literally thrown Brokk and Sahira out of her home on their first encounter.

Like all witches back then, she'd hated vampires, but she hadn't *loathed* them with the same intensity she did after Fabian's death. After he died, she'd considered burning the realms to kill *every last one* of them. She'd yearned to destroy everything... including herself.

Kaylia had believed a part of herself died with Fabian, but that wasn't true. A part of her died *because* of him.

None of what she'd believed to be the truth was. It was all a sick game by a manipulative piece of shit who'd reveled in his control over her.

All the time she'd spent fighting her attraction to Brokk in Doomed Valley was more lies. Guilt had eaten at her and made her hate herself... and all of it was also based on a lie.

All. Of. It.

He'd used her.

An awful wailing sob tore from her; she clawed at her chest as sorrow and betrayal battered her heart. Unable to make it stop, she grasped at her throat to cut off the noise, but it wouldn't cease once it started.

Even back then, she'd been one of the most powerful witches to walk the realms... and a *fool*. Fabian was stronger, and he'd used that to his advantage.

She should have seen it coming and sensed something wrong, but she'd been too blinded by her growing love for Fabian to question any of it. She'd been lost to the joy that became a part of her life after he entered it.

Lexi and Sahira hugged her as they whispered words of

solace. Their presence didn't eradicate her misery, but they warmed the chill encasing her heart as their love helped ease her grief.

"What the *fuck* is going on?"

Kaylia barely heard the words over the awful noise escaping her. Lexi eased away from her, and a new warmth encompassed her as bigger, stronger arms enveloped her.

Some of her wailing eased as she relaxed into Brokk. Her joy over his waking broke through some of her melancholy, and she turned into him. Her fingers dug into the wall of his chest as her tears wet his skin.

"What happened?" Brokk demanded, his voice ragged and raw.

He ran his hand over her hair, looking to soothe her. She couldn't see him through her tears, but feeling and hearing him again was a magic she hadn't expected to experience again.

"Shh," he murmured in her ear when shivers wracked her. "Shh, I'm here, love. I'm here."

She'd vomited all the poison inside her, but it would take years for her to purge the emotions battling her.

"What happened?" Brokk demanded again.

"That's her story to tell," Sahira said softly. "Be gentle, Brokk, it's not a happy one."

Kaylia listened as they retreated from the room and closed the door behind them.

CHAPTER FORTY-SEVEN

BROKK BARELY FELT the weakness still penetrating his muscles and shaking his legs, which made moving difficult as he held Kaylia against his chest. None of it mattered as he tried to ease the sorrow breaking his heart.

They'd spent a lot of time trapped in that dungeon, and he'd never heard her cry like this. She'd been beaten, starved, thrown into a cell with him, locked in darkness, and never broken down.

He had no idea what could have possibly caused this reaction from her. It wasn't because she'd feared he would die; he was holding her, and she was still shaking like a leaf in a hurricane.

The black pool spreading across the floor shimmered in the sun. He was clueless to what the thick liquid was, but it had come from her; he felt that truth in his bones.

As she continued to weep, her despair penetrated his soul, radiated through his bones, and pushed aside the hunger he'd woken with. The flesh on his back ached when he moved, and he dimly recalled the whip tearing away his skin, but that memory faded beneath the onslaught of her distress.

Her arms slid around his neck as she pressed closer. Despite her emotional state, she was careful not to touch the healing skin on his back.

Brokk inhaled her fresh, earthy scent mixed with the lavender drifting from her hair. Though she smelled amazing, her breath had something foul on it, and he realized the same odor emanated from the black puddle.

He had no idea what to do to help her but didn't assure her it would all be okay. He didn't know what was wrong, and he'd never seen her like this before.

Instead, he ran his hands over her hair and down her back, whispering, "I'm here. I'm here for you. I'll always be here."

And he did not doubt that. Whatever transpired, he would be here to help her through it.

Brokk had no idea what had happened since they left Doomed Valley, but a pit of blackness had swallowed him and kept him clasped in its dark hold until her cries somehow pierced it.

He'd managed to pull himself out of that darkness for *her*, and he'd help pull her out of whatever this was. He would stand by her side no matter what; he just hoped she still wanted *him*.

Gradually, her shaking and tears subsided as she slumped against him. After a few more minutes, she turned her head and kissed his neck.

"You're awake," she breathed.

"I'm awake." He felt her exhaustion as she rested her head on his shoulder. "Let's get you somewhere you can lie down."

Her head turned toward the black pool, and she shuddered. "Aren't you going to ask?"

"Do you want to tell me now, or would you prefer to rest first?"

She pondered this before replying, "I'm afraid I'll go insane if I go anywhere quiet. Everything's already too loud in my head."

His arms tightened around her, and he pulled her into his lap as he sought to protect her from the world. Whatever happened here, it was worse for her than the dungeon; he couldn't imagine such a thing being true, but she'd never worried about going insane behind those bars.

"Are you ready to talk about it?" he asked.

"Sahira said something to me earlier...."

Brokk frowned as her words trailed away. He shifted his attention to the black pool and rested his cheek on her head as he tried to piece this new information into what little he knew.

He recalled Sahira's words about this not being a happy story, but she couldn't have said something that would create this, could she?

Things hadn't been great between Sahira and Kaylia when they first met, but they bonded over their mutual love for Lexi and became good friends.

Did something happen while I was unconscious to change that?

"*Sahira's* the reason you're so upset?" He tried to keep the ire from his voice; the last thing she needed was to deal with that too, but it tinged the words coming out through his gritted teeth.

"Yes... I mean, no. This isn't her fault; she... just... she saw something I... I never did."

Her voice hitched while she spoke, and another tear ran down to wet his shoulder. He hated her suffering more than his own and wished he could pull her closer to protect her further, but they were as close as they could get.

"What did she see?" he asked.

"Fabian."

CHAPTER FORTY-EIGHT

In halting words, she told him what happened. She revealed what the black pool was and the horrible thing she'd discovered today, except horrible was too kind a word for what that *monster* did to her.

Brokk's fangs extended, and fury vibrated through him while she talked, but he managed to keep it hidden from her, or at least he hoped he did. She needed compassion and love now, but if that bastard had still been alive, he would have hunted him down and torn him limb from limb.

He would lock Fabian into a dungeon and do what the ophidians did to them repeatedly, except he'd make sure the warlock never broke free. He would keep Fabian locked away and make him suffer twice as long as Fabian made Kaylia, and he'd relish every second of those centuries, as well as the screams the man released.

"I feel so stupid, so weak," she finished in a whisper. "I should have known something was wrong."

Brokk had to unlock his clamped teeth to speak. "This is *not* your fault. You couldn't have known what he was doing to you.

He was more powerful than you; how were you supposed to know he was a monster?"

His rising anger wasn't helping the situation, but her words had rattled him. She couldn't blame herself for this.

"I wasn't some young witch," she said.

"But you still weren't as old as *him*. What he did to you should *never* be done to another. He was an abomination that never should have walked the realms."

"I understand that, and I know it's all true, but I still feel like I should have known or seen something to indicate what was happening."

Brokk didn't know what to say. He knew his words weren't enough to pierce through the haze of her devastation right now.

All he could do was constantly reassure her none of this was her fault, and he would do so every chance he got. Hopefully, one day, she would believe them because she didn't deserve this on top of everything she'd been through.

"I wasted so much time in the crone realm," she murmured. "Yes, we ended up building a wonderful place for those who sought sanctuary there, and I'm glad for that, but I spent far too much time angry and grieving a man who didn't deserve one second of my tears. And there were so many tears."

He hated the bitterness in her voice. "But you're now free from the crone realm, Fabian, and the ophidians. I promise you, Kaylia, I will give you everything you deserve in this life. I will be here for you no matter what, even if you need space to figure things out—"

"No!" she interrupted.

"This is a huge shock to you and a *giant* betrayal. I know you'll need time to come to terms with it, and I'll give it to you, but I'll always be here. Always."

"I don't want time away from *you*, Brokk. Fabian's already ruined so many years of my life and kept us apart for too long. I hated you and Sahira for no reason. I won't pretend I liked vampires before I was told one killed him, but I didn't hate them with the same intensity as I did afterward. I wouldn't have been as vicious and hateful toward you if it wasn't for *him*."

He kissed the top of her head. "You made winning your heart more of a challenge, and I do enjoy a challenge."

A small smile tugged at the corner of her mouth, as he'd hoped it would. "I wouldn't have wasted so much time feeling guilty about my desire for you in Doomed Valley if it wasn't for him. I would have given in to it and been happy about everything afterward. Instead, I grew to hate myself and vowed I'd stay away from you, but I couldn't.

"Fabian got so deep inside me with his magic that I almost didn't drink Sahira's antidote. Even after Sahira led me to have doubts about him, doubts that grew bigger and bigger, I contemplated throwing the antidote out the window. It's been centuries since I saw him, but he still had that much control over me. I think that's the most terrifying part of it all."

Brokk kissed the top of her head again. "It's over... or at least *that* part of it is."

"It's over," she murmured. "You broke through his hold over me."

He leaned back a little to look down at her, and she tipped her head back to meet his gaze. "I did?"

She smiled as she rested her hand against his cheek. "Not completely, but you chipped away at it, brought me back to life, and I love you more than I loved him. I realized that in the dungeon and *hated* myself for it."

Joy and sadness warred within him as he rested his hand over hers on his face. She had one of the kindest hearts, and that useless piece of shit, who couldn't get her without using magic, had caused her such unnecessary emotional torment.

Before he spoke again, he had to regain control of his temper. "He doesn't have control over you anymore; he's dead, which is the best thing that could have happened to him. We can start building our life together… if that's what you want?"

"More than anything, but it will take me a while to get over this."

"I'm not expecting you to get over this, Kaylia. This isn't something you sweep under the rug and move on from, but I'll be here for you through it all."

She rested her head on his shoulder again. "I love you."

"I love you too."

"There's one more thing."

Brokk braced himself for whatever she was about to say next. After everything she'd revealed already, he couldn't imagine what *more* there could be.

"What is it?" he asked.

"If the potion was still working, and it must have been as I believed myself to be in love with him, then Fabian is still alive."

Brokk's fingers bit into her a little before he eased his grip. Resting his chin on her head, he hid his smile.

Good. He was going to do some hunting.

CHAPTER FORTY-NINE

OVER THE NEXT FEW DAYS, Kaylia tended to Brokk's healing wounds while also trying to nurse her own not-so-visible ones. She was still rattled by the idea that everything she'd been *so* certain of with Fabian was nothing but lies from an evil man who still roamed the realms.

The knowledge he was still alive made her inwardly quake. She was furious at Fabian and would kill him, but she was ashamed to admit she also feared him. He'd turned her into a different version of herself for *centuries*, and that knowledge terrified her.

What if he can somehow do it again? She was more powerful than when they met, but so was he.

Kaylia couldn't imagine him somehow breaking through her love for Brokk to twist her into something else again, but she couldn't have imagined it the first time, either. She'd do everything it took to keep that from happening.

She'd already wasted too much of her life on Fabian, and she wouldn't waste a second more, but he haunted her thoughts. It was difficult to stop thinking about someone who had been a constant part of her life for three hundred years.

She wished he'd go away. Maybe once he was dead, things would be better, and she had no doubt he would die. If she didn't kill him, Brokk would.

As Kaylia sat on the window seat inside the room Brokk had returned to that morning, she watched the dragons soaring across the sky, guarding Dragonia and hunting. They were beautiful, powerful, terrifying, and she loved watching them.

She shifted her attention to Brokk's bedroom. It was very much like the man himself—simple, elegant, yet earthy and warm in its tones. The dark furniture, as did the deep blue comforter, stood out against the pale gray walls.

The sitting room, through the door he'd just entered, was the same color with dark brown couches, a bar, and a built-in book-case loaded with books. The rain and man scent he emanated filled the two rooms, making them more welcoming.

"You know," Kaylia said as Brokk settled into a chair a few feet away, "I've been thinking."

He stopped in the middle of putting his boot on to look up at her. It took a few seconds, but she finally met his gaze. His aqua eyes weren't as bright as they once were, his ciphers remained faded, and he was still too thin with his gaunt cheekbones, but he'd shaved the beard, and his handsome face was exposed.

She clenched her fingers as she resisted the impulse to lean toward him and stroke his cheek. He needed to feed on something more than blood and food, but they hadn't talked about sex.

"About what?" he asked.

"Fabian was a man of luxury; he craved the finer things in life. He didn't get his hands dirty and wore gloves when he gardened."

Brokk's eyebrow shot up at this revelation. She knew what he was thinking; Fabian was the opposite of her, but she'd always known that.

"I see," Brokk murmured.

"He was always immaculate and would *never* settle for anything less than the best."

"Which is why he set his sights on you."

Despite how awful Fabian made her feel, her heart warmed a little, and she smiled at him. "Others would disagree with you."

"They're all fools. So, you're saying he's most likely not in an outer realm."

"Not likely. In the beginning, he probably glamoured himself into looking like someone else whenever he was around an immortal we might know. But few knew about our relationship, and the ones who did are gone now, or at least the ones who would have known the whole story and come to me are. The warlocks would *never* tell me if he was still alive."

"No, they wouldn't," Brokk agreed.

"They'd all find it amusing."

Red flashed through Brokk's eyes. They couldn't go out and try to destroy all warlocks, but she was certain they'd both like to try.

Unfortunately, it would start another war, and they already had too many battles ahead. She wanted peace, but the realms seemed determined not to let that happen.

She refused to give up on the hope that one day peace would rule. *One day, we'll know what it's like not to fight.*

"I also believe he was the one who came to tell me about his death and not his brother," she said.

Brokk tugged on his other boot. "You think he glamoured himself into looking like his brother?"

"I'm not sure if he has a brother. He told me he did, but that could have been a lie... everything else about him was."

"True."

"Before that day, I had never met his brother, so he could have glamoured himself into looking like his brother or lied about having one. We originally bonded over our lost siblings, but I told him about Mina before he told me he had two brothers and one of them had died."

Brokk inhaled deeply and exhaled it on an angry breath as he flexed his fingers. "I see. So, what makes you think he was the one who came to tell you about his death and not his brother?"

"Their eyes were the same. At the time, it upset me to see those warm brown eyes in the face of another as they delivered news of Fabian's death, but I wrote it off as them being siblings and having the same genetics.

"Now, I think it was done on purpose. *He* wanted to be the one to tell me. *He* wanted to see my reaction and watch me suffer. Given everything he'd done before then, I have no *doubt* it was him."

Brokk's nostrils flared as another flash of red ran through his eyes before he suppressed it. He was doing his best to keep his rage over what was done to her concealed, but she felt it whenever they discussed Fabian.

She didn't mind his rage; she would have stopped talking to him about it if he'd pitied her. She couldn't handle that from him.

Instead of pity, she'd only ever seen anger and understanding, and she could handle those. She *refused* to be pitied.

CHAPTER FIFTY

"Do you think he could still look like his supposed brother?" Brokk asked.

"He could. I've never seen him again, but I retreated to the crone realm soon after receiving the news of his death. I didn't see many immortals after that."

Brokk sat back in the chair and clasped his hands on his stomach. "We'll have someone draw a picture from your descriptions of Fabian and his brother. We can't circulate it through the realms; if he knows we're looking for him, he'll hide, but we can send some immortals out to discreetly hunt for him. We might find him if he doesn't know we're looking. But no matter what, we *will* find him."

She nodded as she rose from the window seat and smoothed down the front of her lavender dress. Brokk tried to hide his discomfort as he stood, but she didn't miss his wince as his bones cracked.

He rested a hand on the chair arm to steady himself before rolling his shoulders to try to hide that he was still weak. He couldn't hide it from her.

"We should go," he said.

Kaylia sighed; she'd prefer not to do this, but they had to. She strolled over and slid her arm through his.

As soon as she did, the familiar thrill of desire ran through her. From under her lashes, she glanced at Brokk and saw his jaw clench before he looked down and smiled at her.

She missed that connection to him and knew he required it, but she still felt emotionally defeated. Leaning against his side, she took solace in his steady presence and the love he evoked as they made their way out of his bedroom, through the sitting room, and into the hall.

They descended the sweeping staircase spiraling down to the grand entry of the palace. Once they arrived at the bottom, they walked toward the great hall.

Along the way, they passed statues of the arach who once roamed these halls. They were some of what little decorative pieces remained after the Lord's rule.

The walls remained mostly bare as Lexi and Cole didn't have much time to decorate the palace, but despite the barren walls, the place felt warmer than it did when the Lord lived here.

Once they arrived at the great hall, they descended the five steps to the stone floor. Normally, they wouldn't meet Cole, Lexi, or others here. It was too uninviting, and while the Lord died in this room, it was full of a lot of bad memories and emanated an aura of death and suffering.

Countless immortals had filed into the great hall today, and this was the place that would emphasize Lexi's powers over the realms. Plus, the throne was a sign of power that would remind everyone who their queen was.

Far over their heads was a domed ceiling with an opening in the middle. The dragons' black scorch marks marred the interior closest to the opening.

Two dozen dragons perched on the edge, their heads craned to peer into the room below. At the first sign of a problem, they would descend and feast on any who tried to harm Lexi.

Kaylia didn't foresee that happening. Everyone here was an ally, but the dragons were a welcome reminder of what a betrayal to Lexi would cost the immortals here.

Lexi already sat on the throne at the far end of the hall. Cole stood on her right and Del to her left. Orin and Varo were beside Cole, while Sahira, Skog, and Maverick stood near Del.

Del's red sun medallion glinted in the light. Cole had given him the amulet to protect him from the sun's rays.

Behind the throne, Alina sat proudly. Her head, towering over Lexi, was a constant reminder to all those within to remain on their best behavior.

Inside the hall was an eclectic mix of lycan, witches, vampires who stood in the shadows, and demons who stood closer to the dais. Sirens, merfolk, dwarves, and some warlocks also filled the room. Above, peering over the dragons, was the giant queen, Banba, and her brother, Gibborim.

Near the front of the crowd, standing by the demons, Ryker, Tucker, and Leland had gathered. Before them was a contingent of brownies.

As she got closer, Kaylia spotted a brownie perched on Orin's shoulder. The tiny creature, with her mouselike face, had a steely expression as she sat proudly with a spear in one hand.

Sahira and Orin had told her, and later Brokk, about what happened in the Cursed Realm, and she knew about the brownies, but it still astounded her to see Orin with such a tiny creature. She waited for him to pick the brownie off his shoulder, spin her around by the tail, and fling her across the room.

Instead, when the brownie leaned over to say something in his ear, he smiled before nodding. *Times have definitely changed.*

CHAPTER FIFTY-ONE

WHEN THEY REACHED the steps to the dais, Kaylia squeezed Brokk's arm before they separated. He went to stand with his brothers and Cole's uncle while she moved to stand beside Sahira.

Standing at the top of the dais, looking over the crowd of assorted immortals, a sense of pride swelled in her chest. They'd brought these many species together through hard work and dedication.

In doing so, they enabled all these immortals to be in the same room without trying to kill each other. There were species such as the amsirah and demons who far preferred to keep to themselves, even if the demons often enjoyed jumping into a good battle.

The demons and brownies had sworn their loyalty to Lexi before she and Brokk returned from Doomed Valley. This revelation shocked her a little as the demons were known more as mercenaries than loyal followers, but Orin and Sahira's friend Zeth had a lot of pull with his uncle, the demon king.

She wasn't sure the brownies had ever sworn loyalty to anyone, but they were often overlooked creatures, discounted because of their size. The brownies were respected here, and Orin made that abundantly clear by having a brownie on his shoulder.

When Kaylia's attention shifted to Brokk, love filled her as he stood proudly beside his brothers. He was still far too thin and pale but handsome and strong. He'd remained relentlessly by her, hadn't pressured her even though he'd been starved for months, and loved her as deeply as she did him.

A lump formed in her throat as she shifted her attention from Brokk to the others on stage. They'd accomplished all of this together and succeeded in stabilizing the realms when so many others failed before them.

Despite everything revealed to her about Fabian, she couldn't recall a time when she was ever this happy or content. Friends who had become family surrounded her; she was surrounded by *love*.

Kaylia had to force herself not to smile while the different factions of immortals, who had complaints and suggestions, talked. They listened and didn't argue when Lexi spoke, not because they were afraid of her like they were the Lord, but because they *respected* her.

Standing in the front row, Ryker watched Lexi and occasionally nodded. In the days since their return from Doomed Valley, he'd spoken with Lexi and Cole about his king, and they'd agreed to help him.

Soon, they'd return to Doomed Valley, but first, they had things to take care of here. Ryker couldn't promise his king would swear fealty to Lexi, but because Ryker had helped Brokk and Kaylia, Lexi vowed to help him.

Kaylia believed there was a good chance King Leo would swear allegiance to Lexi if they managed to rescue him from the ophidians. He would definitely be grateful to be free of those monsters.

When the meeting came to an end, Lexi rose from the throne.

"Before we all go to lunch or return home, there is one more thing I'd like to discuss."

The hall fell silent as they all focused on their Queen. "We will send an army into Doomed Valley to rescue the amsirah king. We're looking for volunteers to help in this fight."

The crowd shifted as they cast uneasy glances at each other, but Kaylia was certain some of those here and from their realms would volunteer. Many immortals sought glory, even if it was in a place as atrocious as Doomed Valley.

CHAPTER FIFTY-TWO

BROKK TRIED to ignore his festering hunger as he strolled the halls with Cole, Varo, and Orin. There was something so right about being with his brothers again.

They'd clashed, killed, partied, trained, and been friends and enemies throughout their lives. The brothers were all a different mix of immortals who had been torn apart by wars... and united by them. They'd lost five of their other brothers and their father, yet they remained standing, stronger and closer because of it.

For so long, he'd been angry at Orin and Varo for siding against their father, and being a part of his downfall, but not any longer. Being trapped, beaten, and nearly killed had a way of making old hurts fade.

Life was too short to retain so much anger for two men who, despite their faults and their pasts, he loved very much. They were his brothers and no matter what happened, they would all be there for each other.

The power swirling between them crackled against his skin, and he had no doubt others could feel it too. While they remained united, they could take on anything.

It was so good to be home, where he belonged, but his time

here was soon ending. With the help of many other immortals, they formed an army to lead into Doomed Valley.

He didn't know if the ophidians remained but suspected they did. The Valley was their home, where they felt safe and believed they could withstand anything that tried to come for them.

They had no idea the wrath he and his brothers would soon unleash on them. Despite his lingering weakness, he was excited to hear those fuckers scream.

The ophidians had probably moved on from the pyramid, but they *would* find them, even if they had to root them out from the earth's bowels.

Tomorrow, they would return to Doomed Valley. He wasn't in the best condition for that place, but he'd survived the dungeon and would survive this too. Once they freed King Leonidas and destroyed the ophidians, he'd never return to that forsaken jungle again and would focus his energy on finding Fabian.

Yesterday, Maverick, who possessed an artistic ability Brokk had never known about, sat down with Kaylia and drew two pictures. Together, they worked to create a portrait of Fabian and the so-called brother who arrived at her door.

While surveying the pictures, he kept his lips pursed and his face emotionless, but hate festered inside him. If given a choice, he'd go after Fabian before the ophidians; that was how much he *loathed* the man. He'd choose his death over the monsters who tortured him and Kaylia for months.

However, he would honor his promise to Ryker and return to the Valley in search of his king. He owed him that much.

He wouldn't be solely focused on Doomed Valley while they were there. Brokk had recruited a few trusted dark fae, lycans, and dwarves to search for the man while he was gone.

He hoped that by the time they returned from Doomed

Valley, he'd have some leads into Fabian's whereabouts. And then, he'd hunt, and he'd *destroy*.

This time, all his brothers would enter Doomed Valley with him. Cole didn't like the idea of leaving Lexi, but he didn't plan to be gone long, and Lexi had the dragons to watch over her. He also planned to leave some shadows behind for protection.

If something happened while they were gone, the shadows or Alina would let him know, but Lexi insisted she'd be safe. No one was going to risk the dragons' wrath, and she could set fire to anyone who tried to attack her.

The memory of Amaris's betrayal was still fresh in all their minds, but Lexi insisted Cole go with them. She needed to show the rest of the realms she didn't require his constant presence in Dragonia to ensure her safety and control of the realm.

Cole tried to argue, but she told him that instead of him remaining behind, she'd go to Doomed Valley instead… with or without him. Brokk smiled as he recalled how swiftly that ended their disagreement.

Besides, the giant, Gibborim, would also stand watch over the land while they were gone, and he had a *big* soft spot for Lexi. She would be perfectly safe remaining behind.

Two hundred men and women had volunteered to enter Doomed Valley with them. They could have taken more as many had stepped forward to help, but two hundred should be more than enough to accomplish this mission.

CHAPTER FIFTY-THREE

When he and his brothers arrived in the garden, Brokk felt a little jolt at seeing the beautiful, blooming plants. The first time he saw this place, it was barren of anything living... or so he'd believed.

With her arach magic and touch, Lexi brought it back to life. They still didn't know everything she could do, as the arach kept their abilities mostly concealed from others, but she'd figured some of them out.

As they strode through the drooping branches, colorful flowers, and multihued leaves that created a covering over the pathway, Brokk inhaled the fragrant blooms. His step sped up a little when he caught Kaylia's scent amongst the others.

They discovered Kaylia, Sahira, Lexi, Elsa, Zeth, two other demons, and a couple dozen brownies near one of the fountains in the garden. Brokk had gotten to know Elsa and Zeth since returning from the Valley, and he liked them and the brownies, who were all playing and fighting on the edge of the fountain.

In the fountain's center was a dragon with its wings spread as it prepared to take flight. Water poured from the creature's mouth and into the pool below.

When Pip saw Orin, she sheathed her sword and scampered over to him. Without missing a step, he bent and scooped her into his hand.

She raced up his arm and settled on his shoulder, where she lifted the ruined end of her tail into the air. It was still amazing for Brokk to witness, but he couldn't deny that his brother, one of *the* biggest assholes he'd ever met, cared for the six-inch-tall creature who equally loved him.

Not only that, but Orin was handling the loss of his hand with confidence and wasn't bitter about it. He'd also fallen in *love*.

If someone had ever told him that Orin would fall in love, he would have laughed in their faces while questioning their sanity. But there was no doubt that Orin was head over heels for Sahira as he bent to kiss her, and they beamed at each other.

It was still more of a shock to Brokk than a jolt from the ophidians' poles, but it made him smile. He couldn't wait to see how this all unfolded.

Once gathered, Zeth introduced them to his son, Alrorud—or Rud, as he preferred. His wife, Vorndun, who went by Vorn, had her arm linked through his as she smiled at all of them.

Unlike Zeth, who was black in color, Vorn was a red demon with yellow eyes. Their son was a mixture of red and black coloring that swirled throughout his skin.

Zeth grinned at them as he kept his arm around his wife's waist. Brokk doubted they'd been more than fifty feet apart since Zeth returned from the Cursed Realm.

Kaylia walked over to him and clasped his hand in both of hers. His skin tingled, and he had to work to suppress an erection.

She needed time to recover from everything she'd endured, and he would give her that, but he couldn't control his body's insatiable hunger for her. He kept it hidden to ensure she didn't feel any pressure from him, or at least he hoped he did.

"How about a walk?" she asked.

Brokk smiled as he leaned over and kissed the top of her head. "Lead the way."

They said goodbye to the others before leaving to wander down the pathways twisting deeper into the vast, sprawling garden. As they walked, they passed statues, more fountains, and massive yellow trees with flowers the size of his head.

Kaylia brushed her fingers across the leaves and blooms when they moved beneath them. He could practically feel her absorbing energy from the earth as her skin glowed the radiant hue she'd lost while in the dungeon.

Her hair once again shone, and she'd regained some of the weight she lost while in captivity. She'd never stopped being beautiful to him, but he loved the vitality she radiated as nature once again nourished her soul.

"There's so much life here," she whispered. "It pulses through the ground as it strengthens me."

He squeezed her hand. "Good."

They strolled into an area full of trees whose branches stretched over them. Their sweeping limbs covered the walkway in shadows and small peach petals.

Afterward, they crossed a small bridge into an area full of bushes laden with yellow berries. They were so thick he couldn't see beyond the wall they created on both sides of the trail.

It was all so beautiful and peaceful that it helped pacify the ragged, still enraged parts of him that lingered from his time in the dungeon and the revelation of Fabian's existence. He'd never been an angry man; he far preferred partying and fucking to anger, but what happened to them should never happen to another.

After months of abuse, he couldn't shake the fury haunting him since his return. And while Fabian lived, his bloodthirst for him would never be sated.

Being near Kaylia helped soothe the raw edges of his nerves, but the bloodlust that screamed for revenge against the ophidians and Fabian wouldn't be easily satisfied.

CHAPTER FIFTY-FOUR

THEY TOOK another turn in the pathway and emerged at the edge of a small pool. Overhead, the thick limbs of the trees cast shadows over most of the pool, but the sun glinting off the center emphasized its crystalline depths and sparkling blue water.

Kaylia released his hand, kicked off her moccasins, lifted her skirt, and waded into the water. When she laughed and started to kick at the water, he smiled. It had been months since he heard laughter flow so freely from her.

Her troubles melted away as joy overtook her. He'd been so unsure if either of them would ever recover from what happened to them, but watching her now, he saw it was possible.

They had to find joy in the simple things again, take their time, and heal together. Her healing process would take longer after what Fabian did to her, but she would get there; he was certain of it.

She'd never let that asshole keep her down.

When she reached the center of the pool, she released her skirt. She let it fall into the water as she threw up her arms, tipped her head back, and basked in the sun's rays.

A beautiful smile lit her face as the sun bathed her in its

golden radiance. He gritted his teeth against his throbbing cock, but no matter how hard he tried, he couldn't will his erection away.

The hunger was a constant battle that kept him weakened while tearing at his insides, but he would ensure she didn't know how bad it was. She would have her time to heal, and there would never be another woman for him.

He was content with that knowledge. Monogamy had never been something he'd entertained much, but he had no doubt she was his; she always would be, and there would *never* be another.

He'd wait for her no matter what it took out of him. He might be weak and wasted away by then, but she was worth it.

Kaylia lowered her head and turned toward him. He ground his teeth together when the playful gleam in her eyes sent a bolt of desire through him.

If he couldn't get himself under better control, he'd have to leave, but he'd prefer not to do that to her. *You're six hundred years old; you can control yourself.*

Brokk fisted his hands as the playful look left her eyes and her smile slid away. He'd taken her carefree joy away and hated himself for it.

Tearing his attention away from her, he focused on the trees while willing his lust to subside. No matter how he struggled, it remained an incessant, ugly thing that screamed to be quenched.

The splash of water as she waded her way through it caused him to step back. She needed him, and he was afraid to be around her.

"Brokk."

She didn't say anything more, and he closed his eyes as his temples pulsed and blood rushed through him. It took everything Brokk had not to walk away; it would only upset her if he did, but if he stayed, he might lose control.

The blood thundering through his ears blocked out all other sounds as his body tensed and *every* part of him screamed for her. He didn't realize she'd left the water until she clasped his cheeks.

"Brokk."

Her touch created a firestorm of electricity across his skin as every part of him came to life. His fangs extended.

"Don't," he managed to grate out.

It was the only word he could get out past his fangs and clenched teeth. Everything inside him was falling apart and slicing open as his body screamed for sustenance.

He was *ravenous*, and she was so close.

"Don't."

CHAPTER FIFTY-FIVE

ANGUISH ETCHED Brokk's gaunt features as he kept his eyes closed and head turned away from her. She ached for his suffering as she brushed his cheeks with her thumbs.

This is because of me.

If it wasn't for Fabian, he wouldn't be like this now. However, the revelation of what that bastard did to her had so rattled her that she allowed sorrow to consume her.

Once again, Brokk was the one who paid for it. She'd repeatedly pushed him away while in Doomed Valley, hated herself, and believed she could never love anyone as much as Fabian, but the whole time, her growing love for Brokk was breaking through Fabian's potion.

That potion hadn't broken completely, but it did crumble enough for her to find the ability to love again. That love had punctured centuries of her false beliefs about Fabian.

It was so strong that even before Fabian's hold on her broke, she'd grown to love Brokk more than she ever had her ex-fiancé. And their love was a wondrous thing that would help them heal.

She hadn't thought about sex since learning about Fabian; it seemed impossible to do so after what he did to her, but this garden, the water, and Brokk had reawakened her desire. The life flowing through here pulsed beneath her feet; it reminded her of their time together in Doomed Valley before the dungeon.

Their joining had caused power to pulse out of her as her body once again came alive beneath a man's touch. At the time, Fabian's potion still corrupted her mind, but her body had known the truth.

She belonged with this man, and only she could ease him. He would never ask her for it, never push her into something she wasn't ready for, but while a part of her remained raw and ragged, the rest thrummed with growing excitement.

Releasing his face, she gripped her skirt and pulled the dress over her head. She wore nothing underneath, which was the way she preferred to be when she wasn't fighting for her life.

Brokk still wouldn't look at her, but he'd figure it out soon enough. Stepping closer, she rested her fingers on his chest and inwardly wept when he flinched.

"I should go." His fangs distorted his voice as the muscles in his neck stood out.

Rising onto her toes, she kissed his neck. "Don't leave me."

When his eyes flew open, she wasn't surprised by the vivid red depths staring back at her. They burned brighter when they flashed over her naked body; she almost groaned when his thick shaft jumped against her belly.

"You. Are. Not. Ready." His words came out clipped and angry.

"I'll be the one to decide that." He stepped away, but she wouldn't let him leave. "You're not the only one who needs this."

"Too. Soon."

Every word sounded like it was being pulled from him as they grated out between his teeth. She kissed his cheek again and then his lips while she waited for him to give in, but the stubborn man remained unmoving.

Kaylia stepped away as she formulated a new plan. "If you won't give me what I want, then *I* will."

His eyebrows drew together in confusion as she stepped away and walked back toward the pool. On the other side of the crystalline water was a mossy bank.

Stepping into the water, she sighed when its pulse of life flooded her system and sent a current of power through her. It felt fantastic when she was wearing her dress, but naked—as she much preferred to be in nature—it filled her with its potency.

Her nipples hardened, and desire grew within her as an ache spread between her legs. She was coming alive again, and she *relished* it.

Kaylia waded through the knee-high water to the other side. She sat on the spongy ground and scooted back to lean against one of the trees while keeping her toes in the water.

Brokk remained rigid on the other side of the small pool; his red eyes fastened on her as she swirled her feet around the water. She took it as a good sign that he hadn't left yet.

Closing her eyes, Kaylia absorbed the magic of the water and land beneath her. The pulse of it crawling through her reminded her of the time in Doomed Valley when she was near the riverbank, basking in its powerful life force and aroused for the first time in centuries.

Then, she'd denied herself release, but she wouldn't now as the world flooded her with its energy, and she was determined to show Brokk she was ready. She was far from healed, but she was even further from broken.

The revelation of the potion rattled her confidence, but she was still *her*... more so now than a week ago because Fabian's hold on her had broken. As the energy of the trees, earth, and water pulsed around her, her body awakened again.

Unable to stop herself, she trailed her fingers down between her breasts and over her belly. Everywhere she touched, her body tingled with a need that had been buried beneath the onslaught of her distress and grief.

That need transformed into a demanding beast that refused to be left unsatisfied. When she slid her hand between her legs and grasped her breasts, she gasped.

Closing her eyes, she imagined her hand was Brokk's as it moved between her thighs. "Brokk," she whimpered.

She could bring herself to release and enjoy it, but she'd far prefer to have him touching her.

CHAPTER FIFTY-SIX

HE SHOULD TURN and walk away, but his feet remained planted in place while he watched Kaylia. When her legs parted and she moaned his name, every part of him became a divining rod, and *she* was the one it sought.

Even if he'd wanted to, he couldn't stop himself as he pulled off his boots and clothes.

I won't hurt her. I won't.

Those words became a mantra as he waded into the water and crossed toward the beautiful woman whose back arched as her breaths came faster.

"If you won't give me what I want, then I will."

Her words returned to him as he waded into the middle of the pool. It would *not* be her.

When he reached the bank where she sat, he stopped before her as her eyes met his. His mouth watered as his gaze ran over her body.

She'd regained some weight since returning, not much, but enough to fill her curves back out again a little. Small white scars crisscrossed her belly, and he'd seen others on her back.

They were fading, but he didn't know if they'd ever completely go away. They stood as a testament to her strength.

She was so aroused he could see the wetness between her thighs as she lifted her hands over her head and grasped the tree behind her to bare herself to him completely. He doubted she knew how exquisite a banquet she presented.

Brokk grasped her knees, spreading her legs wider before kneeling before her. He kissed her knee and rejoiced in the sound she made.

She lowered her hands to thread her fingers into his hair, drawing him closer. Moving slowly, he left a trail of kisses up her inner thigh until he reached the prize he sought.

She tasted better than he remembered; he savored her taste while fucking her with his tongue. Her fingers tightened in his hair, and she cried out while she came.

The dark fae part of him was already feasting on the sexual energy she exuded when he pulled away from her. Brokk settled his hands on her hips and lifted her from the mossy bank.

I'll be gentle.

He vowed this repeatedly as her legs circled his waist. She played with his hair, smiling as she wiggled into position over his shaft.

With one thrust, he settled himself deep inside her and groaned as his fingers dug into her. A sense of rightness encapsulated him as she kissed him.

He grasped her head as their tongues entwined. He belonged with this amazing woman who possessed a heart of gold and a will of steel.

She was his; she'd always be *his*. As they fucked and he fed and fucked some more, he knew only happiness. With whispered words of love, she came again as she eased his starvation and strengthened him once more.

CHAPTER FIFTY-SEVEN

THE LAST PLACE Brokk ever wanted to go again was Doomed Valley, but there he stood, staring up at the towering structure of the pyramid and the eye at the top. That eye with its elliptical pupil and golden iris stared back at them before shifting to survey the land.

Brokk felt the emperor could somehow watch them from, or communicate with, the eye and knew they were here. When it returned to him, he smiled as he gave the thing the finger.

Having lived in Doomed Valley for so many years, Brokk doubted the ophidians knew the human gesture, but *he* did. It made him feel good to tell that asshole to fuck off before he got the chance to destroy him.

From experience, Brokk was aware the ophidians were experts at setting traps. That was how they ended up in the dungeon, after all.

The ophidians might not be inside the pyramid anymore, but if they'd left it, they'd also left a deadly path to navigate upon entry. It was a path they'd all have to tread to ensure the ophidians didn't live within the building... if they ever did.

Standing to his left, Cole pulled shadows from the trees; they slithered across the ground before rising and slipping inside him. Beside him, Ryker leaned a little away from Cole.

Like him, Ryker was still too thin, but his beard was gone, and he'd regained enough weight to at least look formidable again. The ophidians would regret what they'd done to him.

"Have you heard the stories about the Shadow Reaver?" Brokk inquired.

"Those old bedtime tales meant to scare kids into behaving?"

"Yes, except they're not tales."

"I can see that."

After Cole called the shadows to him, they slithered across the ground and swirled around their feet. They stayed there for a few seconds, but when Cole whispered to them, they took off to the pyramid.

Brokk hoped Cole could keep his ability under control while he was away from Lexi. The last thing they needed was his brother spiraling into madness again while they were here.

He didn't voice his concerns; he couldn't let the others think Cole might have a weakness. While here, he'd keep an eye on his brother and, if necessary, send someone back to get Lexi before they lost Cole.

Cole wouldn't come here if he didn't think he could handle this. Still, Brokk couldn't help but worry and knew he wasn't alone when he met Varo's troubled eyes on the other side of Cole.

"The shadows cannot see into the pyramid," Cole stated. "It's too dark for them to enter."

Cole's distorted voice sent a shiver of unease down Brokk's spine. It had been months since he heard the shadows speaking from his brother, but at least Cole wasn't referring to them as *we*... yet.

"So that means we have to go in there," Brokk said.

"If we intend to learn what's inside, yes," Cole said. "More shadows are searching the jungle. If they find anything, they'll let me know."

"What are the chances the ophidians stayed in Doomed Valley?" Sahira asked.

"They don't think anything can take them down," Ryker responded. "They might have abandoned the pyramid, but they're still in the jungle, waiting for us, and they've set traps. They have no doubt they can take us down."

"And they're wrong," Orin said.

Brokk glanced back at the army of assorted immortals they'd assembled. Ryker had recruited more amsirah from Tempest, and more demons, dwarves, lycans, dark fae, witches, warlocks, brownies, sirens, and a giant stood with them. Tucker and Leland were among the group of amsirah and witches.

A number of vampires waited in Dragonia for night to fall before they too would join them. The only vampire to make this trip was Del; his amulet kept him from burning alive, and he refused to let his sister make this trip without him.

Cole could draw forth more shadows and block out the sun, but the brothers had agreed that wasn't the best idea. If necessary, Cole would block the sun for the vampires to join them here; until then, or sunset, the vamps would stand as extra guards for Lexi.

Some merfolk and other assorted immortals, such as a few berserkers and pixies, were in the crowd too. They'd all joined to fight against the Lord, but that battle provided mutual benefits to all of them.

With the Lord dead, their homes wouldn't be destroyed, and they wouldn't have to live in terror. They could have the rightful queen on the throne, not an insane madman.

Then, all the immortals had done what was necessary to save themselves by fighting the Lord. Now, they'd joined together because they were allies and had each other's backs.

They would help Ryker free Leonidas because they assumed

the amsirah would ally with them afterward and help their power and army grow stronger to stand against their enemies. But they were also here because some of their own, Brokk, Kaylia, and the many others who'd entered Dragonia and never returned, deserved to be avenged.

They were all different species of immortals, who had often refused to work together in the past, but they'd come together to present a united front that *no one* could destroy. This was how realms should be, and he'd helped make it happen.

"I'll transform into a wolf and lead the way," Cole stated. "I sense things better that way. I'll carry a torch in my mouth so the shadows can go ahead of me."

"You can control the shadows in wolf form?" Brokk inquired.

"I can."

"When did you discover that?"

"Not so long ago."

So, his brother had been experimenting with the shadows. It was probably best Cole learned everything he could do with them, but he'd seen his brother slip into the madness the shadows could create and wouldn't let it happen again.

While Lexi remains safe, he'll be okay. Brokk told himself this, but the words didn't reassure him as much as they should.

"Then lead the way," Orin said.

Cole's shoulders hunched forward as, with a shimmer of air and a crack of bones and joints that made Brokk wince, his brother shifted into a black wolf with silver eyes. Cole's paws were the size of his head as he became the size of a lion.

Brokk looked back at Kaylia, who stood behind him and Ryker. Her chin jutted forward in determination as her pewter gray eyes met his.

After what passed between them yesterday, he'd spent the night and this morning constantly searching her for signs of weakness. The dark fae part of him had fed from her repeatedly yesterday, but he'd only taken her blood once for the connection it formed.

He still wasn't back to full strength; that would take a few weeks, but his ciphers had darkened again, even if they weren't their deep ebony color yet. She'd strengthened him, but he couldn't feed on her like that again. He would take it easier with her from now on, but he was still worried he'd taken too much.

Maybe she shouldn't be here.

But as he considered it, he knew nothing was keeping her out of this. Just like there was no keeping him and so many others away.

Maverick had brought half his pack, Zeth led a horde of demons, and a lycan named Belda had brought her whole pack. Pip sat on Orin's shoulder while Puth led hundreds of brownies, and dragons circled overhead.

And they were all about to enter that pyramid... the place of his nightmares.

CHAPTER FIFTY-EIGHT

COLE OPENED his mouth to receive a torch when someone brought it forth. The fire curled up toward his head, but he managed to stay away from the crackling flames.

Around him, the torch created shadows that danced as they went out to do Cole's bidding. While the shadows moved out, Brokk and Orin worked to divide their army, leaving half outside while the other half entered the pyramid with them.

Kaylia kept her uneasiness hidden as she watched the shadows. She'd seen Cole lose control, witnessed him on the edge of destroying everything before, but she had faith he could keep it under control.

At least this time, they all knew what to do if he started spiraling out of control and could get Lexi at the first sign of something going wrong. When Cole prowled forward with his hackles raised, the shadows swirled around him.

Orin and Brokk flanked his sides while Varo and Maverick fell in behind him. Del walked beside her.

Kaylia didn't like the idea of being separated from Brokk but didn't have a choice. Once they entered the pyramid, Brokk and

Orin would have to fall back to give Cole room to navigate the narrow halls.

When darkness enveloped them, Kaylia gulped as she tensed. She'd become used to the stench of the dungeon while trapped there.

But some of that smell was prominent throughout the halls too. She'd been too afraid to notice it when the ophidians first carried her through these halls, or maybe she was too focused on trying not to move because every time she did, the silver netting would cause more pain for Brokk.

Now, the thick, musky scent permeating the air clogged her nostrils. The earth's dampness and the aroma of the snakes made her stomach turn, but she swallowed back the bile rising in her throat as she tried to block the disgusting odor.

The flames from Cole's torch flickered off the stone walls surrounding them and the ground before him. Its glow didn't travel much past him.

Thankfully, beside her, Sahira also held a torch. Its illumination revealed the layers of snakeskin stuck to the walls and floor as they searched above for some trap while Cole examined the ground.

Kaylia gulped as she resisted her impulse to vomit; this was one more detail she hadn't seen when they first went through here. Now, it was impossible not to notice the remnants of the serpents who had nearly destroyed them.

There was also a chance the smell and the skins hadn't been there before. Maybe the ophidians had fled this place, and they left a bigger mess than normal during their escape.

Up ahead, Cole stopped, and those at the front of the group shuffled as Brokk moved forward to examine whatever caught Cole's attention. Kaylia's heart battered her ribs as she resisted the urge to call him back.

"There's a trap here," Brokk said.

Grasping Varo's shoulder, Kaylia pointed ahead of her, and

he turned to let her pass. She slipped forward to stand behind Orin.

"I can cast a protective spell," she said. "It will help keep everyone up here safe."

When Brokk lifted his head to look at her, his blue eyes calmed her distress. "This trap's built into the floor. Will it keep us safe from that?"

Kaylia moved closer to inspect the wire Brokk had uncovered from under a layer of dirt. "No."

"A protection spell against other things wouldn't hurt," Sahira said from behind her. "We can't cast it over everyone, but we can cast it over you, and since you're in the front, you're the ones most at risk."

They hadn't brought all their army into the pyramid, but there were still too many immortals present for the witches to cast a protective barrier over them all. But Cole, Brokk, Varo, and Orin faced the worst danger and could be helped.

"Cast it." As soon as Orin finished speaking, Pip darted through the crowd, scampered up his leg, and settled on his shoulder. "I thought you were staying outside."

"Puth changed his mind."

"How much did you irritate him for that to happen?"

"I don't irritate. I'm not a dark fae."

Orin chuckled as he shifted his attention back to Brokk. "Can you disable the trap?"

"I'm not sure."

"Let me have a look." Ryker turned sideways to get through the crowd; he passed her to kneel beside Brokk. "I've dealt with some of their traps before."

While Ryker examined the trap, Sahira, Elsa, Leland, and Kaylia worked together to weave a spell over those at the front of the line. A protective bubble shimmered into place over them. It was invisible to the others, but she saw the colors marking their magic.

After a few more minutes, Ryker and Brokk succeeded in disabling the trap, and Cole moved forward. They crept deeper into the bowels of the place she'd never wanted to see again.

When they made it to the dungeons, she threw her shoulders back and braced herself to enter the hell they'd fled. *You're not a prisoner anymore. They don't have any control over you.*

Ahead of her, Brokk and Ryker also tensed, but their steps didn't slow as they walked through the doorway. Kaylia refused to let her step falter as she entered behind them.

The reek of fear, blood, and waste permeated the air. It engulfed her in a cloud of misery that threatened to sweep her back into nightmares.

Brokk dreamt of this place too. She'd sometimes wake to find him twitching in his sleep, and while she knew memories of the war he'd waged *for* the Lord and *against* him haunted his dreams, he'd told her it was the dungeon he dreamed of most.

In his nightmares, he lost her and spent much of the time calling into the darkness for her. Unable to break free of the bars, he remained trapped while screaming her name.

She understood that nightmare as it was one she often had too. When sleep finally came, she'd find herself back in the darkness, searching for him but unable to break free of the bars before the ophidians returned.

Then, she'd hear him scream, something she *never* heard when they tortured him in this place. Those screams would reverberate all around her as they came out of the darkness.

She'd often wake, unable to catch her breath and drenched in sweat. Sometimes, Brokk would also be awake and pull her into his arms while whispering reassurances.

Other times, he was trapped in his nightmare, and she would wrap herself around him in the hopes of easing his suffering. Sometimes, it worked; other times, he remained trapped until he woke.

The nightmares where she lost him in this place were far

worse than the ones where she was back on the rack or standing helplessly by while the ophidians beat him. At least then, even if it was horrible to relive those moments, she knew where he was.

She felt Sahira's gaze on her but didn't look at her friend as Cole set the torch down, shifted back into a man, and rose to survey the dungeon. His clothes all tore off when he transformed into the wolf, and now his ciphers were on display as he reclaimed the torch to walk with Orin and Varo to the end of the dungeon.

Brokk and Ryker didn't hesitate to enter the dungeon again but didn't follow Cole as other army members did. Kaylia, Tucker, and Leland didn't move either; they all knew this was an endless pit of desolation.

She couldn't bring herself to look at her cell. Being here was bad enough; she couldn't see inside that cage again. The torch-light didn't reveal much of the cells from where she stood, but she knew every inch of those small confines.

When Cole returned, he didn't speak as he rested his hand on Brokk's shoulder and squeezed it. Brokk nodded to him, and Cole handed him the torch before, with a cracking of ligament and bone, he transformed into a wolf again.

Brokk gave the torch back to him when he finished. A hush hung heavily as they exited the dungeon to explore more of the deadly pyramid.

CHAPTER FIFTY-NINE

THEY SPENT the next hour exploring the rest of the pyramid, dismantling traps, and creeping through the too-narrow corridors before making their way into a cavernous space in the middle of the structure. The tables created a circle around the center of the vast room.

Brokk didn't know what they used this room for, if it was a place for the ophidians to dine or a gathering spot, but nothing sat in the center of that circle. He saw no signs of plates or food here either.

The ophidians' stench filled the air, and shed snakeskins clung to the backs of the chairs, the corners of the table, and streaked the stone floor. Brokk's lips twitched toward a sneer before he suppressed it.

No one spoke while Cole carefully patrolled around the outside of the room and the tables. When he moved toward the center of the space, they crept up toward the tables.

Brokk tipped his head back to take in the point the walls around him formed. They were at the top of the pyramid; the eye was above them, looking over the land and probably aware they were beneath it.

Brokk searched for a place where the sun might enter but found none. Without the torches, darkness would encompass this place.

This cool, damp spot was where the ophidians could slither to avoid the jungle's heat. What they did here, he didn't know, but he doubted it was anything good.

Along the way, they'd discovered three other traps but no sign of the monsters they hunted. He'd realized this place wasn't the ophidians' home; it was where they kept the unfortunate souls they tortured and a gathering place for whatever foul deeds they planned to commit.

When Cole finished inspecting the room, he lowered the torch and transformed into a man. As he rose, he claimed the torch again before striding toward them.

"There's nothing here," he stated.

"Then let's get out of this shithole," Orin said, "and hunt these fuckers down."

Brokk was more than happy to do exactly that as the army retreated from the room and filed back down the stairs toward the entry. The walls brushed against his arms and shoulders while he descended; he kept waiting for them to close in on him, squishing them all between the rocks.

He'd planned to return to Kaylia's side, but she fell into line ahead of him; a few lycans, Sahira, Del, and Ryker, separated them. His skin itched with his compulsion to return to her, and he resisted his impulse to shove the others aside.

Pushing and shoving down these steep stairs could result in a domino effect that could send their fighters plummeting to the bottom. Taking out half of their army wouldn't be his best decision in life.

They were almost to the bottom when someone shouted from ahead of them. Brokk stopped and frowned as he tried to make out their words, but ten feet in front of him, the stairs took a sharp turn and vanished.

The walls, and the distance between him and whoever was shouting, suppressed the words. A murmur ran through the crowd ahead, making its way back to them.

And then one word broke through all the rest. *"Run!"*

CHAPTER SIXTY

As soon as Brokk recognized the word, a grinding, grating sound came from all around as the rocks creaked and jerked forward. Brokk's mouth went dry as he realized the walls *were* creeping in to crush them.

"*Run!*" he bellowed.

The crowd surged forward ahead of him, and he lost sight of Kaylia as she vanished around the curve. He wanted to sprint forward, grab her, and race down the stairs, but too many immortals separated them, and he could only go so fast with the crowd ahead of him.

Behind him, Varo's breaths were heavy as the walls moved closer. Behind Varo, Orin and Cole were the last two in the line.

He resisted looking back at his brothers. That small fraction of a delay could mean the difference between living and dying for all of them.

The possibility of living grew smaller as the walls pressed against his shoulders, squeezing him further between the thick stone. Ahead of him, Kaylia and the others came back into view.

Ryker was already having to turn sideways as the walls crept closer. The immortals at the front of the line were moving fast and might have already made it outside.

Kaylia leapt down three stairs and got hit by the closing wall. She would have tumbled down the steps if it hadn't been for Sahira grasping the collar of her tunic and ripping her back.

Behind him, he knew Cole must be sideways too and would get caught between the closing walls soon... as would Ryker. And if Ryker got pinned, it was over for him and his brothers.

Kaylia and the others vanished from view again. When he came around the corner, he saw her sprinting out of the stairwell. At least she was free.

She turned and looked back. Kaylia and Sahira rushed back toward them, but Del caught his sister around her waist and pulled her back as Maverick seized Kaylia.

Neither of them could do anything to help as Brokk had to turn sideways too. Ryker was almost stuck, the walls against his chest and back while he was still ten feet from freedom.

He's not going to make it, and neither will Cole.

Eight feet from freedom, Ryker threw himself to the side. He plummeted down what remained of the steps, bouncing off them before stopping near Kaylia's feet.

"Brokk!" Kaylia screamed.

Knowing he had to get out of the way now to give Cole a chance of surviving, Brokk threw himself down the stairs too. His elbow and then his head cracked off the stone.

Bright white stars burst across his mind; unconsciousness loomed as his body bounced and thudded off the stone. All his bones ached when he came to a rolling stop.

Brokk wished he could have a second to lie there and take stock of his injuries, but there was no time for that. His eyes flew open as Varo and Orin came to a bouncing stop a few feet away.

The walls ground together with a grating crunch that caused Brokk's stomach to plummet. Was Cole still in there? Were those *his* bones breaking as the walls crushed him?

He searched for his oldest brother but didn't see him anywhere amid the assortment of limbs. Arms swept around his neck, and Kaylia crushed herself against him.

"You're okay," she breathed.

"Where's Cole?"

Before she could answer him, his oldest brother rose from the front of the pile. He wiped away the blood trickling from a gash on his forehead and flicked it away.

"What happened?" Cole growled.

"It was a stone in the wall," a berserker responded. "I stumbled on the steps and pushed against it with my elbow. Thankfully, it was toward the bottom of the stairs."

It was at the bottom for you, Brokk thought but kept that to himself.

The man couldn't have known the trap was there, nor could Cole if it was in the wall. His brother looked at the ground while the rest searched above them.

Brokk squeezed Kaylia's arm. She kissed his cheek before releasing him.

Brokk bit back a groan as he pushed his aching and battered body up. His vision swam again, and he locked his knees to keep from going down while he waited for it to clear.

When he was sure he wouldn't collapse or pass out, he crushed Kaylia against him. Together, they walked out of the pyramid and into the humid air of the jungle.

Brokk closed his eyes as he inhaled the aroma of flowers, foliage, and the fresh air that didn't possess the stench of the ophidians. He wanted to ask Lexi to command the dragons to burn this entire Valley down, but he couldn't.

Most of the creatures who lived here were terrible, flesh-eating things, but it was still their realm, and they had a right to reside there. The ophidians had forfeited that right.

He'd like to see this whole place on fire, but they were the intruders here. They'd chosen to come to this lethal realm and couldn't punish the creatures here for their decisions.

"Destroy the pyramid," Cole said to the giant.

The woman smiled before lifting her fist and hammering it onto the top of the pyramid. The top half of the stone structure collapsed; she used her feet to stomp out what remained of its walls.

Brokk smiled, and Kaylia grinned while the giant reduced the pyramid to rubble. When the giant finished, she stepped back and wiped away the debris clinging to her hands.

Dust rained over them, but Brokk didn't mind. He enjoyed bathing in the ruins of his enemies.

Soon, he would drench himself in their blood.

CHAPTER SIXTY-ONE

MOVING SUCH a vast army through the jungle was slow going as they sought to avoid the monsters residing here and the numerous traps the ophidians left in their wake. They lost a couple dozen soldiers to two of those traps.

It was impossible to locate them all, but they were trying, as the ophidians didn't often use the same trap twice. Some emerged from the ground while others plummeted from the trees, and some exploded from inside the trees.

The lycans, in their wolf forms, prowled the jungle as they tried to sense those traps before more of them perished. The sun crept higher into the sky, and hope drew them onward as the shadows beckoned Cole to follow them through the thick vegetation.

Those dark figures ruthlessly pursued the enemy, and no one evaded the shadows. They would find the ones they sought.

Kaylia and the other witches didn't cast another protective barrier over the army. There were far too many to keep sheltered and more obstacles for a barrier to do them any good. Besides, it would only hinder them if the witches rendered their powers almost useless before encountering the ophidians.

It was almost noon, the sun was high in the sky, and the jungle crowded them in the familiar way she'd come to loathe. The energy this place emitted strengthened her, but it still reminded her of a tomb.

She'd come far too close to Doomed Valley becoming her burial place to be comfortable with its claustrophobic feel now. She, or some of those she loved, could still be as good as dead and didn't know it yet.

The possibility caused her to gulp as she tugged at the collar of her green tunic. She tried not to let that foreboding possibility become a malignant thought; it would only hinder what they had to do here.

Besides, there was nothing she could do to stop the guillotine possibly hanging over their heads. Death would unfold here. It was a guarantee.

~

ONE OF THE dragons dropped from the sky and, with a rush of wings, turned sideways to cut through the trees above. Brokk tilted his head back to watch as its wings sliced off leaves and branches from the trees before disappearing.

In front of him, Cole transformed into a man again and rose to his full height. They all watched as the dragon unleashed a blast of fire. From up ahead, something screamed.

"What was that?" Varo asked.

"In this hellhole, it could be anything," Brokk replied.

"Do you think it's the ophidians?" Maverick inquired.

"It could be," Ryker answered, "but it could also be one of any number of things looking to eat us."

"What a delightful place," Orin quipped.

The dragon rose into the air, and as it did so, it became tangled in a net hanging between the trees. The dragon released a scream the likes of which Brokk had never heard before, but that scream reverberated through his soul; he knew the agony the creature endured.

"It's one of *those* nets," he snarled.

The dragon screamed and thrashed against the silver netting as it sought to escape its confines, but the more the creature fought, the more entangled it became. If the dragon wasn't careful, it would kill itself as the edges of those nets could slice through an immortal.

The netting might already be cutting into the dragon as it descended from the sky. Overhead, the other two dragons who entered Doomed Valley with them bellowed as they swooped toward the trees.

They didn't dive low like their friend as they released a torrent of fire on the tops of the trees. Flames erupted from the treetops, but the humid air and damp vegetation prevented them from spreading quickly.

However, they burned long enough that the top of the trees broke off before tumbling into the oblivion below. Smoke choked the air as the dragons bellowed and their friend screamed. The tangled dragon vanished into the jungle.

"We have to help them!" Sahira cried as she started forward.

Brokk grasped Kaylia's arm, halting her when she went to follow her friend. "Not yet."

Orin also stopped Sahira.

"We can't leave them alone up there!" Kaylia cried.

"We're going to help them." Cole lifted troubled eyes to the sky when one of the dragons vanished through a portal. "We can't rush forward when we don't know what's ahead."

"Where did that other dragon go?" someone demanded from behind them.

Cole looked resigned as he lowered his gaze from the sky. "To get help."

His brother couldn't communicate with the dragons, but they would never leave one of their own behind. The dragon was going to get more of its brethren, and when they returned, they would make these creatures pay.

"If she hears about this, Lexi *will* return with them," Del said.

"I know. We have to be careful about how we proceed," Cole replied.

Around them, the shadows shifted as the ones still with Cole raced across the ground with a speed that made them almost invisible to the naked eye. They sped into the jungle in search of the enemy and to report on the dragon.

Brokk didn't know if the ophidians lay ahead or if the netting was another trap the monsters had set to spring on them. If it was a trap, then more of those nets could be waiting.

As the trapped dragon's cries filled the air, the other one swept low and torched more of the treetops. If there were more nets, hopefully, they would fall from the burning trees.

The smoke drifting through the jungle made breathing the cloying, humid air difficult. The acrid smoke burned his eyes, and he blinked away the tears forming there.

"Let's go," Cole commanded.

CHAPTER SIXTY-TWO

BROKK RELUCTANTLY RELEASED Kaylia as they started through the jungle again. One good thing about the smoke was that it chased away the bugs, and he spent a lot less time slapping away the bloodsucking fiends as they carved a path through the thick vegetation.

They moved slowly, trying to ensure no traps hung overhead or were implanted in the ground. Above, the other dragon continued to unleash its wrath on the jungle while the cries of its friend subsided.

It didn't take much time to learn the more someone fought the netting, the worse it was. Not resisting the enemy was difficult to accept, but when that netting felt like it was slicing away flesh, it became a little easier not to fight.

A shout from the left filled the air a second before another net shot up from the ground with a lycan and dark fae trapped within its brutal grasp. They screamed as they thrashed against their captivity.

The free dragon bellowed again, and another trap sprang. It launched into the air with a couple of dwarves trapped inside.

"The more you fight the net, the worse it is," Brokk shouted at them.

It's not much better, but it's better. He didn't speak those words; they'd figure it out soon enough.

"How do we get them down from there?" Maverick asked.

Before anyone could reply, a flurry of motion rattled the vegetation around them as something rushed toward them. The thick jungle made it impossible to see what was coming, but the low vegetation whipped back and forth, and branches broke.

Brokk stepped closer to Kaylia when an enthusiastic chatter started, and something clacked together. He reached over his head to unsheathe his sword as the sway of the vegetation came closer and closer.

Five feet.

He still couldn't see what was approaching but sensed the excitement radiating from the hidden creatures as the chattering increased.

"What the fuck is it?" Orin demanded.

Three feet.

Beside him, Kaylia lifted her sword and braced her legs apart as a horde of gremlins rushed from the underbrush. The hideous creatures leapt forward with shrieks and the clicking clatter of their teeth.

Those teeth still had pieces of flesh dangling from them, and many had bloated bellies that didn't slow them. Their ears flapped as they hooked their three-inch claws in preparation for tearing into something.

Their humanoid faces with big, red, bulbous noses twisted into murderous expressions. No bigger than three-feet-tall, they were still lethal monstrosities that would gladly devour them.

Brokk had no idea how these things broke free from the mirror realm, but he suspected the ophidians freed them in exchange for some help in the jungle. Which meant they were probably closing in on the serpents.

Brokk hacked through the first gremlin to reach him and ducked a second one. Kaylia sliced through one before kicking away another and decapitating a third.

Others weren't so lucky to avoid the beasts' wrath as the ravenous creatures pounced and took them down. Confusion reigned as immortals shouted in pain and alarm.

The shadows swept toward the creatures, encompassed some of them, and hauled them away. Clawing at the ground, the gremlins tried to keep from being taken, but they couldn't fight the shadows.

Smaller than all around them, the brownies managed to evade the attackers. The small creatures screamed as they leapt onto the gremlins and beat or stabbed at them. They were tiny but fierce.

Hauled into the jungle by the shadows, their enemies' shrieks mingled with those of their army until a cacophony of noise filled the jungle. Brokk hacked through another gremlin before lifting another and smashing it off a rock.

He'd released the repulsive gremlin when one of the big black cats, with fangs hanging over its bottom lip, sprang from the dense foliage. With its claws extended and its jaws open, it went for Kaylia.

CHAPTER SIXTY-THREE

BROKK SPUN and lifted his sword to bring it down on the monster, but it was already moving away. Kaylia had released her blade and thrown up her hands. With her palms up, she pushed outward like she was shoving something at the creature.

Waves of air rippled outward as the feline flew backward. When it soared past him, Brokk brought his sword down across its back, slicing through sinew and bone before it hit the ground and bounced toward a rock.

It lifted its head before collapsing onto the ground. One of the gremlins used the cat's massive body as a launching pad, raced across it, and jumped into the air toward Kaylia.

Its arms swung as three more of the tiny monsters sprinted toward Brokk. The shadows rose and engulfed two of them before ripping them apart; the third got through.

Brokk yanked his sword from the cat's back, but he didn't have time to get the blade up to deflect the creature. Releasing the handle, his weapon hit the ground as the beast slammed into his chest, knocking him back a step.

Brokk grabbed the monster around the middle and tried not

to cringe at its scaly body's cool, clammy feel. The gremlin's razor-sharp teeth snapped in his face as more screams rose.

A knife suddenly burst through the gremlin's chest, nearly poking Brokk in the nose before someone seized the creature's nape and ripped it away. Orin stood on the other side of the gremlin, a grin on his face.

"You're welcome," his brother said.

"You almost stabbed me in the nose."

"You're still welcome. Besides, it's not like you're as handsome as me, so don't worry about a little sword to the face."

Brokk didn't get the chance to tell Orin to fuck off before another cat leapt out of the jungle and onto Orin's back. Brokk scrambled to reclaim his sword as Orin hit the ground.

The cat's claws hooked into Orin's back and dragged him toward the jungle. Snatching up his sword, Brokk sprinted forward and plunged his blade into the side of the creature's head as another pounced on Kaylia.

Brokk's heart lodged in his throat when she staggered forward and went to her knees. Ripping his sword free of the one who collapsed on Orin, Brokk sprinted toward Kaylia and brought his blade down across the cat's back, severing its spine.

Before he could kick it off her, one of the giant, lumbering monsters that chased them into the white goo leading to the mirror realm broke free of the underbrush. It thrust its horn forward, spearing a witch before stampeding a warlock and dark fae.

The size of a human's tank, the earth quaked beneath the thuds of the creature's hooves as it pounded at full speed. Orin remained trapped beneath the cat as Kaylia tried to pull herself out from under the one that had fallen on top of her.

The cat's front legs pawed at the ground as it tried to drag itself away, but its back legs remained useless. And the beast was barreling toward them.

"Get her!" Cole shouted as he sprinted toward Orin.

A group of gremlins darted from the undergrowth and launched onto Cole's back. It was a mistake they only had a few seconds to regret before the shadows enveloped them, ripped them away, and tore them to shreds.

Brokk released his blade and seized the cat's head to drag it off Kaylia while a tanklike monster closed in on them. Every encroaching thud of its hooves vibrated the ground more until Brokk rose and fell a foot or two at a time.

He didn't look back to see how close it was getting as the cat twisted its head to the side and snapped down on his arm. He bit back a yelp as its teeth sank through his flesh.

Having dropped his sword, Brokk had no option but to continue pulling the thing away. When he finally freed Kaylia, she scrambled to her feet and staggered to the side as the ground heaved.

Needing to break free, Brokk delivered a series of blows to the feline's head before the beast finally released him. Hot air blew against his neck as he leapt to his feet and sprinted toward Kaylia.

As he ran, he teleported to within a few inches of her, wrapped his arms around her waist, and threw all his weight against her. He sheltered her head with his arm as he sought to protect it while they bounced across the ground and away from the beast looking to squash them.

Brokk tried to catch his breath, but remaining still was the equivalent of death in this place, so he rose. Extending his hand, his gaze traveled over Kaylia, but aside from some cuts and bruises, she was all right.

The armor-plated monster thundered past them, taking down trees and more immortals before running into the blaze the dragons had created. The flames swallowed it.

When it didn't immediately reappear, Brokk started to smile as he realized the stupid creature had plunged into its death. That smile never fully developed as a shadowy figure rushed from the depths of the fire and the beast reemerged.

Not one burn marred it as it tossed the charred remains of the witch from its horn. Pawing one of its hooves, it snorted as it eyed the immortals gathered around it, fighting for their lives.

"Shit," Kaylia breathed.

CHAPTER SIXTY-FOUR

BROKK ENSHROUDED himself and Kaylia in shadows as the creature barreled through a couple of lycans and a merman who weren't fast enough to get out of the way. He had no idea how to destroy these things if fire didn't affect them.

They didn't get far before two more tanks charged onto the scene. *This keeps going from bad to worse.*

Keeping Kaylia in his arms, he ran with her back toward where Cole had freed Orin from the cat. Cole, Orin, and Varo were now calling for a large group of their army to cluster together to fend off the gremlins, cats, and prehistoric tanks.

Sahira, Del, Ryker, Maverick, Tucker, and Elsa stood at the front of the group as the gremlins and cats approached. Their prowling movements didn't matter, as the tanklike creatures could easily divide the group.

Brokk and Kaylia had almost made it to the group when a thunderous bellow vibrated the air and drowned out all other sounds. Brokk looked up as a dozen dragons emerged from a portal in the sky and swept toward them.

He recognized the flex of yellow decorating Alina's belly before he spotted Lexi bent over the dragon's neck and her braid whipping out behind her. Alina turned to the side as she prepared to come at them.

He and Kaylia made it to the group as Alina swooped toward them. Brokk released the shadows and bent to claim a sword from a dead siren.

"*Fuck!*" Cole's voice came out a mixture of his and the shadows.

Brokk didn't know if that mixture meant the shadows were starting to take over or if it was a brief slip because his brother didn't want his fiancé here. Either way, he didn't like hearing it.

Smoke choked the air around them as the fire crackled only ten feet away from their backs. Its heat only added to the oppressive air of the jungle as more sweat broke out on his back, cleaving his shirt to him. When it beaded across his forehead and slid down his face, he wiped it away before it got in his eyes, but it was a losing battle.

The roar of the blaze drowned out almost all other noise as the tops of trees broke off and crashed to the ground. Sparks and falling debris rained down on them, and a couple of times, he had to slap them away before they caught on his clothes. One burned his cheek before the small blaze went out.

The fire, gremlins, cats, and tanks racing toward them kept them trapped. They had two options: open some portals and leave or stand their ground. Some of these monsters would escape through a portal with them, but they should be able to take care of them before they fled into the realms.

When Alina swooped low through the trees, their broken and scorched tops enabled her to get closer to the ground than the dragons before her. She unleashed a torrent of fire on their enemies.

The flames didn't affect the tanklike beasts but tore up the earth as it scorched a crevice across the land. It hit the sides of the giant monsters, lifted them, and flung them into the jungle.

The gremlins and cats screeched as they scampered to get out of the way, but many didn't elude Alina's wrath. The ones who did were taken out by the dragon following her and then the next.

The dragons were destroying their enemies, but they'd become trapped inside the growing inferno if they didn't move soon.

"Move out!" Cole shouted to be heard over the flames and destruction of the earth as the dragons' fire ripped it asunder.

CHAPTER SIXTY-FIVE

KAYLIA THREW her arm over her head to help protect it from the fiery branches breaking free of the trees and tumbling to the ground. Sparks and debris cascaded around them as they raced after Cole and into the jungle.

Moving fast wasn't their best option, considering they had no idea if more traps lay ahead, but they didn't have a choice. Besides, the jungle hindered their progress as it pressed against their sides, much like the closing walls had.

Kaylia shuddered at the reminder of how close they'd come to being squished to death within the pyramid. She wanted out of this Valley before they lost any more of their number, but she suspected they were closing in on the ophidians as their traps and monsters ramped up around them.

When a large shadow fell over her, she looked up in time to see the giant leaning over them and using her hands to shove trees and debris out of their way. Giants weren't immune to flames like Lexi; the fire had to burn the woman, but she showed no signs of stopping as she carved a larger path through the jungle for them.

Then the flames caught on the woman's shirt, raced up her

arms, and surged toward her face. Her cry was as loud as thunder; she tore her shirt away and threw it into the jungle, but it was too late as the fire had spread to her hair.

Staggering into the jungle, the giant pummeled her head to smother the flames before disappearing into the vegetation. A resonating thud rocked the jungle as the ground vibrated.

Kaylia's heart ached for the woman who had helped save them, but she didn't have time to mourn her loss as they raced through more of the fiery debris while chaos ruled around them. Three dragons soared so close overhead that the wind from their passing plastered her clothes to her.

She swore one of them brushed her head with the tip of its wing, but they weren't that close. A branch broke free of one of the trees and tumbled toward them faster than she believed possible.

Before it could hit them and severely maim or kill someone, Kaylia threw up her hand and created a blast of air to fling the branch into the woods. She was powerful, but her abilities were dwindling beneath her constant use of them today. She had to be careful not to drain herself completely before they faced the ophidians.

The sweat sliding down her neck cleaved her tunic to her nape. The flames were all around and rolling over their heads as they mingled with the oppressive temperature of the jungle.

They created brutal conditions that made her head spin and her throat burn with thirst. It took all she had to keep moving.

Just when she was about to collapse, the flaming trees and sparks gave way. The heat became less stifling as they plunged out from under the inferno and into a section of the jungle that wasn't on fire.

Cole almost ran into the teal-colored dragon trapped beneath the netting but skidded to a stop before he did. The net had cut off the end of the creature's tail. It lifted its head, and instead of bellowing, it released only a small, heartbreaking moan.

"Don't touch the net!" Brokk yelled when Cole went to grab it.

Cole hesitated with his hands only centimeters from the netting. Kaylia shuddered as she recalled what it was like to have that net against her, and she'd been lucky to have Brokk's body mostly protect her from its agonizing effects.

"Then how do we free it?" one of the brownies asked; she thought it was Loth.

Kaylia studied the netting and the dragon pinned beneath. The earth shook when one of the enormous beasts landed nearby and closed its wings before stalking forward.

Alina landed on the other side, and the witches gathered closer. "We can lift it off with a spell," Elsa suggested.

When Alina stopped a few feet away, Lexi slid from her back and landed on the ground. She stormed forward and examined the dragon trapped beneath the netting before stopping beside Cole.

"We agreed you would stay in Dragonia," Cole said.

"We did." When she rose on her toes to kiss his cheek, his expression softened, and he rested his hand on her hip. "But that was before Aladon was injured. How do we get this off?"

"We'll take care of it," Kaylia assured her.

Taking a deep breath, she grasped the hands of her fellow witches as they formed a circle around the dragon. With their hands entwined and the earth pulsing beneath her feet, power flooded her as they all strengthened each other.

They whispered to each other while deciding on a spell. When they finally agreed, Kaylia turned her attention to the dragon, who whimpered as its golden eyes surveyed them.

Her heart went out to the creature, and she swallowed the lump in her throat. She couldn't cast a spell if she couldn't speak.

Taking a deep breath, she savored the crackle of energy in the air and the warmth flowing through her as the witches all gathered their power. It had been so long since she'd felt united in this way; she hadn't realized how much she missed it.

She glanced at Sahira standing beside her and smiled. It wasn't only her who needed this; Sahira had never belonged in a coven, and now she did. But more than that, the witches were becoming one giant coven that worked with other immortals to improve the realms.

She'd never dreamed of such a thing happening but was incredibly grateful it had. Together, they were all stronger.

"Light as a feather, object there, Net, I command you to float on air."

Their voices rose and fell in unison as power swelled between them. It grew and crackled across the air until her hair floated around her. Static electricity crackled as it zapped around them while the net rose in the center of their circle.

When it was high enough, the dragon slid out from under it and scurried away. Blood trailed from its sliced tail as it moved across the ground.

Once it was free, the witches released hands, and the net crumpled to the ground. The nets that once held them weren't as big as this one. The ophidians had prepared for the dragons, meaning there were probably more of them throughout the jungle.

Her gaze went to the trees, but she didn't see any nets draped between their boughs; that didn't mean there weren't more. A familiar thrill went through her when Brokk's hand settled on her arm.

"Are you okay?" he asked.

"Yes."

The spell hadn't weakened her because so many witches were involved in it. Their joined strength had helped rebuild hers, but she still had to preserve her powers until they discovered the ophidians again.

When the wounded dragon took flight, some of its brethren

flew to its side. They nipped and cried as they reassured themselves that, while their friend was injured, he would be fine.

The other dragons split away from Aladon as a portal opened in the sky, and he vanished. The other dragons shifted their attention to the jungle and flew lower to torch more trees.

One does not fuck with the dragons.

Kaylia started to smile, but it fell away when the jungle erupted around them.

CHAPTER SIXTY-SIX

OPHIDIANS EMERGED from under the rocks scattered throughout this section of the jungle. Brokk only knew this because he saw three emerge from under a large boulder.

They probably didn't all come from under the rocks, but he was sure the majority did as surprised shouts filled the air. Upon hearing the cries from below, the dragons roared but didn't release their fire. If they did so now, they'd also kill a fair number of their army.

Instead, some of them swooped down to snatch up the ophidians. Their powerful jaws clamped down on the serpents, cutting them in half or wrenching off their heads.

The ground quaked as Alina and another dragon raced across it, barreling through ophidians, lifting them, and tossing them aside with their whipping tails. The serpents flew through the air or screamed while the dragons devoured them.

But the dragons couldn't get to them all as the ophidians heaved spears into the dragons' vulnerable places like their mouths and noses. The dragons' screams of pain mingled with those of their army and the ophidians.

And the ophidians weren't the only things rising from the

earth. At first, Brokk didn't realize there was a new menace until something hit Del in the chest and knocked him back a few steps.

Brokk hadn't seen whatever attacked his friend, but blood spread across Del's chest. When Del dropped his sword to grasp at whatever clung to him, Brokk realized it hadn't been a weapon of some sort to hit him, and that something was still on him.

More blood spread across Del's shirt as it sliced open. Whatever was on him was tearing at him with a wild frenzy.

"Dad!" Lexi cried.

Brokk grasped Kaylia's wrist when she moved toward Lexi. Twenty feet separated them from her; it was too much for Kaylia to cover without something attacking her. They had to move together.

"Not without me," he said. "We stick together."

Her pewter eyes were full of love when they met his. "Always."

Del managed to pry whatever was on him away and flung it toward the jungle. Brokk only knew this because he followed its bouncing trail across the ground, where it kicked up debris before crashing into a tree.

Once there, the tree shuddered, and a two-foot-tall creature became visible. It had a six-inch long, pointed nose jutting over top of the crooked, yellow teeth protruding from its mouth.

The thing staggered back to its clawed, hairy feet. When it moved, its hands dragged across the ground, and its potbelly jiggled. Green eyes, the color of bile, narrowed from beneath its prominent, rippled brow.

"Goblins!" Cole bellowed to be heard over the screams, clashing steel, and fists thudding against flesh.

It had been a while since Brokk encountered one of the creatures that could turn invisible. The dark fae cloaked themselves in shadows to avoid detection; goblins possessed a magic that made it impossible for mortals and immortals to see them.

The nasty bastards often sold themselves to the highest bidder during a war. The Lord had occasionally used them while waging his war against the humans, but not often.

Brokk *hated* working with the creatures. They were often fickle, and when things got tough, they would abandon whatever side they worked for without hesitation.

Aware this was common knowledge among immortals, they demanded half their payment upfront. With plenty of carisle already in their pockets, they didn't care if they ditched the other half in favor of saving their asses.

Working with goblins was always a crapshoot that could backfire... or bring down destruction on the enemy. In the tight confines of this jungle, the goblins could rain down a path of invisible devastation.

Something crashed onto his back. The creature's clawed fingers encircled his throat, but before they could slice his flesh, Brokk released Kaylia to yank the goblin over his head.

He smashed the creature onto the ground, planted his foot somewhere on its small, invisible body, and jerked upward. The goblin released an awful screech as he tore its arm free.

Whatever magic it used to cloak itself vanished. He used his sword to decapitate the tiny monster before kicking away its body.

As he did so, he realized they weren't the focus of the goblins' attention as Alina and the other dragon spun. Their jaws snapped at their back and stomachs; shrieks filled the air as the dragons tore them free and flung them away.

Some were visible again when they hit the ground, but others remained unseen. The dragons' talons tore up the earth as they sought to shake free of the creatures clambering over them, tearing at them, and spilling their blood.

Members of their army scattered to get out of the way of the dragons' tails and lumbering steps as the ophidians used the goblins' distraction to close in on them. It was difficult to fight off the snakes when the dragons were becoming as big of a threat as the other creatures the ophidians unleashed on them.

Alina screeched, and blood spilled from a gash in her throat. She shook her head back and forth as she sought to avoid the goblin carving into her.

CHAPTER SIXTY-SEVEN

"No!" Lexi screamed.

Fire erupted from her hands. She raced toward the Speaker, but as she ran, Alina leaned back and launched herself into the air.

Alina rolled as she frantically tried to rid herself of her attackers. Another dragon launched into the sky to flee the goblins, leaving the rest of them to become the center of the small monsters' attention.

Shadows rose and fell all around them, but without being able to see the goblins, they were useless against the terroristic monstrosities. They engulfed some of the ophidians in their dark embrace and tore them apart.

Blood and body parts from both sides littered the ground as swords clashed against each other, screams filled the air, the dragons roared, and bursts of fire took out more of the trees. Overhead, Alina stopped rolling and plunged back toward them. When she hit the ground, she yelled for Lexi, who had retreated to Del's side.

"I'm not leaving!" Lexi shouted back.

Cole's jaw clenched, but he didn't protest her words. This

wasn't the place for the last living arach, but Lexi would never leave them to face this without her.

Brokk ducked an ophidian tail that lashed at his head as something crashed into his leg. He grunted when goblin teeth sank into his thigh.

"Motherfucker!" he spat.

Gripping his sword in both hands, he plunged it straight down. When the goblin reappeared, he saw he'd sunk his blade through the top of its head.

"Are you okay?" Kaylia yelled as she kicked away another goblin.

"I was briefly a snack, but all is well now!"

Brokk shook the creature free of his leg as thunder rumbled. A second later, lightning bolts hammered the earth, flinging up chunks of earth that rained debris over them.

The bolts slammed into some of the ophidians, exploding their heads or launching them into the jungle. The dragons swept out of the way of the lightning as the noise of the erupting earth added to the chaos.

More lightning blasted into the ophidians as its radiance created a strobe-like effect over the jungle. Shadows rose to engulf more ophidians as the invisible goblins launched themselves at unsuspecting immortals.

The dragons unleashed more fire, and Alina remained on the ground, tossing aside or stomping on ophidians as she stalked toward Lexi. After a minute, she took to the sky again with a shriek; a trail of blood followed her.

As soon as she left, another dragon landed near Lexi. The shadows dragged the ophidians into the jungle, where their screams cut off.

Even as this was happening, Cole staggered back. His shoulders jerked from side to side like something was pummeling him, and then he went down beneath the weight of the goblins swarming him.

Orin sliced off an ophidian's tail as he raced toward Cole, but an invisible force knocked him off his feet, and his back hit the ground. Sahira used air to knock aside the goblins while Varo pulled Orin to his feet.

Zeth punched an ophidian, knocking him backward as he caved in his face. Beside him, his wife tore the tail off another.

The brownies shrieked as they swarmed over the enemy, using their tiny swords and spears to stab them. They also tore at them with fists and teeth until one of the ophidians raced into the jungle. The brownies leapt off and ran to find their next victim.

Maverick, Belda, and Leland worked with a group of witches and lycans to hold some more of the ophidians at bay. A group of ophidians surrounded Ryker and the amsirah; lightning pummeled the ground around them.

Chaos ruled in the jungle, and Brokk pushed Kaylia behind him when one of the snakelike creatures rapidly approached them. When the creature was almost on them, he recognized it as one of the monsters who had enjoyed putting him on the rack to drive spikes into his back.

He took deep, calming breaths as fury thundered through his veins. The worst thing he could do was lose control and let emotions rule him.

He would destroy this monster but had to remain clearheaded to do it. When the ophidian was near them, it suddenly stopped, lifted a bow and arrow, and fired from only ten feet away.

Thrown off by the abrupt change in tactic, Brokk flung himself backward, grasped Kaylia, and pulled her down beneath him to shelter her body with his. They rolled before he released her and leapt back to his feet.

By then, the ophidian was already bearing down on him with a dagger. The man's forked tongue flicked out of his mouth as his lips peeled back to reveal the lethal, hooked fangs dripping with saliva and venom.

The serpent was already too close for him to get his sword up between them, so Brokk released it and clasped the handle of the dagger the ophidian wielded. Rising on his tail, the ophidian used his towering height to bear down on him as he tried to sink the dagger into his heart.

The blade wasn't made of fae metal and wouldn't kill him, but it would weaken him, and he couldn't let that happen. Brokk gritted his teeth as he pushed back into the ophidian's impressive weight.

Saliva dripped onto Brokk's face as the man hissed at him, missing him by inches. Brokk shoved back against him, but the beast had to weigh at least three hundred pounds more than him, and he used that weight and height to bow Brokk's back toward the ground.

He was losing this battle.

CHAPTER SIXTY-EIGHT

His arms and back ached; he still wasn't up to full strength, but with Kaylia behind him, he had a bigger reason to fight than this man. Not to mention, he owed this man for some of his scars.

His muscles quivered as he pushed back against the ophidian; his gaze locked on the monster's yellow eyes. Their stares held for a minute before Brokk jerked himself to the side.

Unprepared for the movement, the ophidian fell forward as Brokk twisted the creature's arms up and plunged his blade into his belly. Blood spilled over Brokk's hands and pooled on the ground as he ripped the dagger upward.

Brokk yelled as frustration and rage rose within him. He was at the mercy of these beasts for months, and now he was slicing through one.

When the ophidian's intestines spilled over his hands, he bared his teeth at the monster in a macabre grin as it tore into his rib cage. Jerking the blade free, he twisted the slippery, blood-coated weapon to plunge it straight up under the creature's chin. It poked out the top of his head.

The man made an awful gurgling noise as blood slipped from

between his clamped lips. Brokk reclaimed the sword he dropped and, with one swing, cleaved the man's head from his shoulders.

When he turned to Kaylia, she had a hand on her head as she rolled to the side and pushed herself up. She must have hit her head on something while they were moving, as a nasty lump was already forming at her temple.

Then she looked up, and the color faded from her flushed cheeks. Her legs trembled as she rose, but then she locked her knees in place.

Her terrified gaze met his before she started running. At first, her movements weren't as graceful as normal, but that quickly changed as she bounded across the ground.

Brokk followed her as she ran toward where he'd last seen Lexi, but now she was fighting off the invisible goblins swarming over her and Cole. The shadows still worked to pull many away, and flames engulfed Lexi's wrists.

That wasn't enough to deter the goblins as blood dripped down Lexi's legs, and they tore at Cole. Streaks of blood criss-crossed his chest and belly.

From the corner of his eye, Brokk spotted Del staggering toward Lexi. Alina dive-bombed from the sky with her talons tucked under her belly as she screamed, "Move!"

Kaylia skidded to a halt. Del started retreating, but as he did, a group of ophidians slithered after him. Sprinting toward him, Orin wrapped his arms around Del's waist, and the two of them hit the ground before Orin's impact caused them both to disappear into the jungle's foliage.

Alina landed beside Lexi and unleashed a wave of fire on the goblins no one could see.

CHAPTER SIXTY-NINE

SCREAMS RENT the air as Alina torched the goblins. Their magic slipped, making the small creatures visible while they streaked through the jungle with fire trailing them. As they ran, the vegetation shriveled and dried as more of it caught fire.

Anarchy ruled the jungle as more goblins brought down their allies, dragons swooped down to destroy some of the ophidians and goblins, and more serpents flooded the area. Lexi sprinted from the flames, unhurt by them as her clothes burned away.

Silver, scalelike dragon markings etched Lexi's skin as it glowed beneath the sun's rays. Brokk wouldn't be stunned to see her take flight like the dragons as rage emanated from her.

She unleashed more fire on the goblins swarming over Cole, careful to keep it under control and away from him, as she torched the little fuckers. Together, she and Cole successfully destroyed the goblins trying to take them down.

Brokk hacked through the middle of an ophidian while Kaylia used some of the flames from Alina's blast to throw a ball of fire into the faces of the ophidians closest to her. Lightning continued to bombard the jungle, exploding those it hit and leaving craters behind.

Blasts of wind swirled up from the amsirah and witches; they flung some of the ophidians into the trees, where either flames engulfed them or dragons ate them. They bit the monsters in half and spat out what remained.

Body parts and blood littered the area as the fire spread around them. Brokk carved through more of the ophidians as he and Kaylia made their way toward Varo, who was fighting off a horde of goblins a few feet away.

Unable to see the hideous monsters, Brokk plunged his sword into the air, keeping it away from Varo. Blood stained the tip of his blade, the creatures wailed, and together, he and Kaylia freed Varo from the unseen mass.

Across the way, Orin, Maverick, Del, and Sahira fought off the horde of ophidians surrounding them. Brokk hacked through more of the ophidians and kicked off a goblin that latched onto his leg.

He couldn't see the creature, but its claws bit into his flesh as it slid down his leg. Swinging his sword down, he sent the creature flying in a spray of blood that showed bright red against the sky.

The goblin turned visible ten feet away from him as it tumbled through the air. A wave of dragons swept over the earth, one right after the other; they unleashed a torrent upon it, tearing it to shreds and flinging debris everywhere.

A lightning bolt shot straight past Brokk's head. It crackled against his ear, his hair stood on end, and a jolt of electricity vibrated against him before it struck the ophidian he hadn't seen approaching from behind. The bolt hit the creature and flung it into two more.

He nodded thanks to Ryker as the amsirah general lowered his arms. Dozens of brownies raced past him, screaming as they charged at more ophidians.

The small creatures clambered up their tails, scaled their backs, and tore at them with frenzied motions. They were relentless as they used their weapons, hands, and teeth to savage the ophidians.

When another ophidian spun and lashed out with its tail. Orin and Sahira jumped to avoid being whipped by it.

Zeth caught the offending appendage and, with a violent wrench, jerked the tail up. He lifted the ophidian ten feet off the ground before slamming him down.

Flames blazed from Lexi's hands as she set another ophidian on fire, and more goblins screamed as the shadows tore them in two. Swords clashed, and Maverick transformed into his wolflike state to clamp his teeth to the end of another ophidian's tail.

He lifted the serpent off the ground and whipped it back and forth. He finally bashed it into a tree and released it as a dragon dove to scoop it up. Beside him, Kaylia used more of the fire to send a flaming ball at the ophidians.

Smoke drifted through the jungle, the dragons roared, trees splintered apart and crashed to the ground with resounding thuds, flames crackled, but a strange calm descended over the land. The ophidians were retreating, and Brokk had no idea what the goblins were up to, but they must have fled as no one was getting attacked anymore.

Brokk turned to Kaylia as, over her shoulder, Ryker, Tucker, and two other amsirah fighters plunged into the woods after the ophidians. This battle was winding down, but they still hunted their king.

Brokk was tired of fighting; he was battered and bloodied but couldn't let them go alone. "Stay here," he said to Kaylia.

Before she could respond, he plunged into the jungle after Ryker and his men.

CHAPTER SEVENTY

KAYLIA DIDN'T HESITATE; she would never stay behind while Brokk went after Ryker and the ophidians. Running into the jungle after them, she ignored the slap of the vegetation against her, the crackle of the flames leaping through the trees, and the fiery debris falling around her.

Some of it landed on her clothes, and when it did, she pushed aside or slapped away the sparks before they could worsen things. She battered at the foliage trying to suffocate her within its thick depths and keep her from Brokk.

Before, it always felt like the jungle was moving around her, changing and shifting while holding them back, but now she was certain of it. She didn't know if it was malevolent or trying to help as it snagged in her hair and clothes and entangled her wrists; she didn't care to find out.

Her lungs burned, and her skin felt like it did when the ophidians flogged her as the branches and leaves whipped at her. Sweat soaked her clothes, adhering them to her and turning them into a cloying monstrosity bent on taking her down.

Kaylia was only seconds behind Brokk but couldn't see him through the thick vegetation. She heard him though, somewhere ahead… or maybe it wasn't him… maybe it was something far worse.

The possibility didn't deter her. After everything she'd endured, the only thing she feared was losing someone she loved, especially Brokk. Whatever else was out there could come at her because she would destroy it.

The others had followed her into the jungle; she didn't know how many trailed her, but their voices came behind her as they tried to find her path.

She knew Lexi, Cole, Varo, Orin, Maverick, Del, and Sahira would be back there, but how many more would continue fighting after the battle they'd waged?

They'd all done so much already, but there was still more to do. She couldn't blame them if they left, but she hoped the union they'd all created would continue to bind them.

Just when she was sure the jungle would never release her from its grasp, she emerged from the trees and skidded to a halt before she slammed into Brokk's back. When he glanced at her, she saw the sad resignation on his face, but instead of telling her to leave, he held out his hand.

When their fingers entwined, she sighed in relief. The jungle may be determined to never let them escape, but he was here with her, and they'd endured far worse than this place.

And now, they had a new hazard to face, as before her rose a mountain of rocks that didn't tower as high as the pyramid but were as daunting.

Overhead, much like they had with the pyramid, the towering trees shaded the stones, but the sun beat down on the fifty-foot-wide, flat stone at the very top. She imagined that's where some of the ophidians basked in the sun.

The tails of some of the ophidians vanished into the crevices between the pile of rocks. Once those tails were gone, no sign of movement stirred from within the rocks as more of their army crashed through the jungle to emerge into the clearing surrounding the mountain.

A few seconds later, Cole, Lexi, Varo, and Del emerged from the trees. Orin, Sahira, Zeth, Vorn, Elsa, Leland, and Maverick soon followed them. Pip sat on Orin's shoulder while more of the brownie army emerged.

The dragons flew in an arch as they circled the mountain. The sirens briefly debated joining them, but in the end, they were too afraid of being accidentally eaten to take to the sky too.

Alina and two others descended to stand with Lexi as the last of their army joined them. From what Kaylia could tell, despite the brutality of what they'd endured since returning to Doomed Valley, none of their remaining army had left. Many had died, but the survivors were united in this fight.

Her eyes stung, and her chest constricted, but now was not the time to get emotional over everything they'd achieved. They were together even if they still had what remained of these monsters to destroy.

"What is this?" Cole asked.

"I think it's their real home," Ryker said. "They all entered into the holes between the rocks."

"We can't follow them in there," Orin stated. "That would be pure stupidity."

"We can use fire to chase them out," Alina suggested.

"And what if my king is in there? They won't care about leaving him to burn." Ryker studied the rock formation before focusing on the dragons near Lexi. "Can you tear it apart?"

All eyes turned to Alina as she started to smile. "We can."

Alina propelled herself into the air while the other dragons remained to stand guard over Lexi. Alina rose high with her wings spread and the sun a background against her powerful body.

She released a series of sharp cries before turning, tucking her wings against her side, and diving toward the rocks. When she was almost to the structure, she unfolded her wings to slow her ascent and hovered in the air as three more dragons descended to join her.

Together, the four of them tore off the top rock and flew it over the jungle, where they released it before returning; more dragons descended to lift and carry away pieces of the mountain.

Together, the dragons steadily worked to carry off more and more stones. They broke down the mountain and tore away the ophidians' home.

As they did so, they revealed the hidden chambers the ophidians slithered through. Many of them were about five feet high, some were higher, and a few were barely large enough for them to slither through on their belly.

Soft debris filled some of those chambers, making it clear they slept there. The pyramid was where they played; this was where they *lived.*

As more of the rocks broke away, leaves and branches rattled on the other side of the clearing. Kaylia suspected it was goblins fleeing the structure, but the creatures didn't try to attack them again. They hadn't been paid enough to stick around and were abandoning ship.

The ophidians must not have opened a portal yet; they probably still believed they had the upper hand. She doubted they'd ever considered that something might dismantle their home piece by piece; their arrogance, and mistake, would get them killed.

CHAPTER SEVENTY-ONE

THE DRAGONS WERE HALFWAY through tearing the rocks apart when the emperor emerged from beneath the pile. Kaylia hadn't seen the hole in the side of the rocky mountain until he slithered from it with a man in his arms.

"Leo," Ryker breathed.

Although she had met the amsirah king before, she wouldn't have recognized him until Ryker spoke. When she last saw King Leonidas, he was a robust man with auburn hair, a thick red beard, and twinkling brown eyes. His laughter had been contagious.

Now, he was a gaunt shell of his former self. His skin was so pale she doubted he'd seen the sun since the ophidians took him from the ghouls.

He blinked against the light as he ducked his head and his broad shoulders hunched forward. He stood like he'd been in that crouched position for too long and couldn't reach his full height.

Pieces of silver netting bound his hands; it also encircled his ankles. He was so thin that all his bones stood out against his naked form.

"Motherfucker," Ryker snarled.

Leo lifted his head and squinted his eyes before closing them and lowering his head again. "Ryker."

Leo's voice came out as barely more than a croak as he tried to scan around him again before giving up. Dirt smeared his naked body; she wondered if they gave him buckets to bathe in too.

"Leo." When Ryker stepped forward, the emperor rested a blade against the king's throat.

"Stay where you are," the emperor commanded.

His voice haunted her nightmares and sent a shiver down Kaylia's spine, but it also ignited a fury that could torch the rest of this hellhole. The emperor made her skin prickle with alarm, but she'd gladly tear off his tail and bash him to pieces with it.

Leo sucked in a breath as the blade bit into his skin and blood trickled from the gash. When one of the dragons dove down, Lexi waved it away.

Terror flashed across the emperor's face before he relaxed again. *So, he's afraid of the dragons.*

If Kaylia didn't think it would be too easy a death for him, she'd love to see the emperor get eaten by one of them. She wanted to hear him scream.

The dragon returned to circling in the sky as what remained of the ophidians emerged. They slithered over to their emperor and formed a circle behind him. Only fifteen of the monsters remained, far too many for her liking.

"We're going to leave this realm," the emperor stated, "and you're going to let us."

When Ryker stepped forward, Leonidas hissed in a breath as the emperor pressed the blade deeper into his throat. More blood trickled from the wound he inflicted, and Ryker froze.

"You're not taking our king with you," Ryker stated.

"And who is going to stop me?" the emperor demanded.

Leo's vision cleared enough for his eyes to find Ryker. "*Kill me if they try to take me.*"

Kaylia's heart clenched, and Ryker blanched at his king's command. She knew what they'd endured in the dungeon, and while she couldn't see Leo's back, whip marks and gashes marred the front of him.

His haggard appearance, grimy skin, and disheveled hair told what he'd endured here. He was the ophidians' prize possession; he was kept here instead of the pyramid so they could always monitor him, but he hadn't avoided their cruelty.

She understood why he'd far prefer to perish than remain under these monsters' thumb. She'd survived months with them; he'd endured a year.

"Shut up!" the emperor hissed.

When Leo threw himself forward into the blade, the emperor grasped his hair and yanked it back. The tip of his tail encircled Leo's waist, locking him in place.

"I'll give you back your king." The emperor pinned Lexi with his unrelenting stare. "But she'll have to agree to let us leave. The dragons won't follow us into our portal."

He glanced at the dragons and then focused on Lexi again. Lexi glared at him before shifting her attention to Brokk and Ryker.

"We are here for you," she said. "You have to make the choice."

Brokk hesitated before replying. "This is Ryker's decision to make."

When they all looked at her, Kaylia pondered it before nodding her agreement. She wanted nothing more than to see all the ophidians dead, but they'd come here to rescue Leo too.

Ryker and Tucker had already sacrificed and endured so much that they deserved this break. They *would* kill the remaining ophidians.

"I want them dead, but the amsirah have been through far worse than us," Brokk continued. "This is their choice to make."

Besides, none of this mattered; even if the dragons didn't follow the emperor through the ophidians' portal, the shadows would. The emperor must believe Cole couldn't follow him through a portal.

He was dead wrong.

Kaylia resisted the impulse to rub her hands together as she practically salivated over the man's ignorance. The ophidians could leave, and once they did, they would die.

The shadows didn't move; Cole must be keeping them at bay, but she knew they were there... watching and waiting to strike. It was what they did, and they did it well.

Still, they all had to play the game until it was time for them to hunt. The only problem was Ryker might not know the full extent of the shadows' powers or Cole's.

She doubted anyone did... including Cole. So, Ryker could choose to kill the ophidians instead of having the emperor go, but she believed he would choose his king above all else, and he didn't prove her wrong.

"Let him go," Ryker said. "No one will stop you from leaving."

"It doesn't matter what you say." The emperor's malevolent gaze focused on Lexi. "It's her word I seek."

CHAPTER SEVENTY-TWO

LEXI SMILED as the dragons roared. "You have my word that if you let King Leonidas go, the dragons won't bother you."

But the shadows will. Those unspoken words hung in the air amongst those who knew what Cole could do.

"That's good to hear," the emperor stated. "I will give him to you. Open the portal."

One of the other ophidians opened a portal to another realm. It shimmered beyond the emperor's back.

"Go," the emperor commanded.

It astonished her that he let his followers flee before him, but perhaps being a decent ruler was the only good thing about this foul man. Kaylia couldn't tear her gaze away from Leo's thin, filthy face, which was mostly obscured by the thickness of his beard.

Leo's expression showed no signs of happiness despite the emperor stating he would release him. An uneasy feeling twisted in Kaylia's stomach; while he held Leo like that, they could do little.

With his tail encircling Leo, it would be difficult to separate them. If the shadows ripped the emperor away, he might slice off

Leo's head as they did so. It was a risk they couldn't take, but after what she'd suffered at the hands of these monsters, this seemed almost too easy.

When the last of the emperor's followers vanished, the emperor unraveled his tail from Leo and shoved him forward. Too weak to catch himself, and with his ankles bound, Leo couldn't stop himself from falling forward.

Ryker was already running toward him when the emperor's tongue lashed out. The forked ends drove through the king's neck and erupted out the other side.

It all happened so fast that Kaylia barely saw his tongue before it retracted into his mouth. She didn't realize what happened until Leo hit the ground, and his head bounced down the rocks to land ten feet away from his body.

"I never said how you'd get him back," the emperor stated.

CHAPTER SEVENTY-THREE

KAYLIA SUPPRESSED a scream of frustration as a bellow tore from Ryker. The lightning pummeling the rocks lit up the sky as it hammered them apart.

It filled the air with electricity that crackled against her skin. Kaylia lifted her hands to shield her eyes from the brilliant flashes.

It was too late for Ryker's wrath; the emperor was already retreating into the portal. With another bellow, Ryker reined in his power and stood, his shoulders heaving as grief etched his face.

Kaylia lowered her hands, and her gaze fell on Leo's broken body. She wasn't surprised the emperor had gone back on his word; he was a monster after all, but she hadn't expected her crushing disappointment.

They'd fought so hard to find this man; now all they had were pieces of the amsirah king. Their realm had been in turmoil for years; this was about to make it worse for Ryker and the other amsirah.

The emperor's tail vanished into the portal, and it started to close, but not before the shadows surged forward in a wave of black. Excitement radiated from them, and their chatter filled the air as they vanished into the portal.

A startled scream came from the other side, and the portal stopped closing as the emperor's tail reemerged. The shadows dragged him from whatever realm he'd been trying to flee to.

The emperor howled as his fingers clawed at the rocks, his nails tore away, and his screams echoed throughout the jungle. The shadows lifted him into the air as more of them flowed through the portal.

The screams of the other ophidians drifted from the other side before going abruptly silent. Kaylia smiled as the shadows returned; they wouldn't have left any survivors.

"You gave me your word," the emperor sputtered.

"I did," Lexi acknowledged, "and the dragons aren't bothering you."

When the shadows released the emperor, he hit the ground with a thud. "We never promised the shadows wouldn't," Cole said, his voice distorted by the shadows inside him.

Lexi rested her hand on his arm, seeking to connect with him as the shadows slithered into his eyes. As they returned from the portal, more shadows slid away from the emperor and coiled back toward Cole.

Kaylia gulped as she watched them. They were not to be fucked with; together, they were the most lethal union in all the realms. She was glad she was on their side and prayed to Hecate that nothing ever caused the couple to turn on the realms they protected.

"He's all yours," Cole said as he turned toward Kaylia and Brokk before focusing on Ryker.

Kaylia didn't move. She yearned to watch the emperor plead for his life as he died, but it was one thing to kill someone who was fighting them. It was another to kill someone when they were hanging before them, surrounded by shadows.

Besides, no matter all the *atrocious* shit he'd done to her and

Brokk, this man wasn't theirs to kill. Her attention shifted to Ryker, who remained standing closer to the rocks, his gaze on Leo's head.

She'd never seen anyone look so defeated before. Ryker had spent the past year searching for his king... his *friend*.

He'd been determined to free Leo and bring him home, and that quest had ended in heartbreak. Defeat carved every inch of his face.

The expression on the other amsirah's faces was despair, but they didn't emanate the same devastation Ryker did. Leo had been their king and leader; he was Ryker's friend and someone he'd loved.

Then, Ryker stalked toward the emperor. The tip of his sword, resting against the ground, clanked and clattered as he climbed the rocks to stand before the ophidian.

Without saying a word, and his face completely blank, he lifted his sword and severed the emperor's head before lowering his weapon and walking over to Leo's head. He stood, staring at Leo's open mouth and wide eyes, before bending to lift the head.

With the head held securely between his hands, he climbed the rocks, set Leo's head carefully down, turned, and with tender hands, turned over his body. Though she knew how incredibly painful it was, Ryker grasped the netting around Leo's wrists and started unwinding it.

A lump lodged in her throat, and she stepped toward him to tell him to stop, but Brokk grasped her wrist and whispered, "Let him do this."

Kaylia started to argue before closing her mouth. He was right; no matter how awful or badly it hurt, Ryker wouldn't leave this mark of the ophidians on his king.

Ryker had to stop often, and every time, she thought he might have to walk away, but then he'd return to the bindings again. When he finished with the wrists, he moved to his ankles.

Sweat dripped from his brow, his face grew florid, and his

hands shook as the muscles in his neck protruded, but he didn't stop until the last of the binding fell away. A sense of relief fell over those watching when it finally ended.

Kaylia's shoulders slumped forward as a single tear slid from her eye to drip off her chin.

Ryker rose, lifted Leo's head, and settled it on his chest before sitting beside the body of his friend.

CHAPTER SEVENTY-FOUR

As the army dispersed to search for survivors or rescue those caught in the traps, Ryker remained sitting on the rocks. Brokk, Kaylia, and the rest of the amsirah remained behind.

At first, his brothers, Sahira, and Lexi, stayed with them, but when Alina brought word that the giant still lived, they left to see what they could do for the woman. Gibborim and another giant had entered Doomed Valley a few minutes ago and carried the woman out.

The dragons had also all retreated, but he and Kaylia remained with Ryker and the amsirah. They should leave this place of death and misery; the ophidians weren't the only threat here, but Brokk would give Ryker some time. His friend had earned that and more.

While they waited, his injuries healed. He still wasn't recovering at the same speed he did before the jungle, but it was getting better.

As the sun started to set, and more creatures awoke in the jungle, Brokk climbed the rocks to sit beside Ryker. The general had one leg drawn up to his chest and his arm draped over his knee.

After a few minutes, Brokk spoke. "You couldn't have stopped it. No one, not even the shadows, could have stopped what happened."

"I had one mission, and I failed."

Brokk knew his words didn't matter, but he had to say them, and maybe, one day, Ryker would come to believe them. "You *couldn't* have stopped what happened here. You had hundreds of other immortals on this mission with you. We *all* failed."

Ryker didn't speak as he watched the myriad of colors spreading across the sky. Brokk looked to Kaylia as shadows spread around her; he had to get her out of here.

"They were collecting a ransom on him; I never thought they'd kill him," Ryker muttered.

"Neither did I. He was a good king."

"He was a *great* king. He was my friend and...." Ryker's voice trailed off as he glanced at Leo's body. "He was more of a father to me than my father ever was. He taught me everything I know about fighting for what's right. He's dead because I failed him."

"We *all* did."

Ryker glanced at him before he shifted his attention to the sky again. His nostrils flared as anger boiled beneath his surface.

After another minute, Ryker spoke again. "The shadows can go through portals."

"Yes, and they communicate with my brother."

Ryker ran a hand through his hair, tugging at the ends of it. "Shit."

"Yeah... it's... *interesting*."

"And frightening."

"Yes."

And Ryker had never seen Cole spiral out of control as he had. That was *terrifying*.

"I don't know if Prince Ivan will swear fealty to the queen. He's a selfish, greedy *idiot*."

"Prince Ivan is…?"

"Leo's brother and our future king. Leo had no children; in our realm, birthright is what decides our leaders and rulers."

That was far from the best way to decide who had the right to determine the course of a realm, but Brokk didn't say it. He was sure Ryker already knew that.

"That means Leo's brother will become king, and I have no idea what he'll do when it comes to Lexi or our realm. He'll likely try to shut Tempest off from the other realms, as he always told Leo to do that. He believes the king should have complete control over his realm."

"Shit."

"Yeah."

"That never works out for anyone who's not a king."

"No, it doesn't. Our realm will suffer because of it."

"That also takes a lot of power to do. Do you think he'll find it?"

"I don't know."

"What will *you* do now?"

Ryker glanced at Leo again before shrugging. "I'll return home. I have no reason to stay away anymore and nowhere else to go."

Brokk suspected the reason he'd stayed away from Tempest was more than seeking to get his king back, but he didn't question Ryker about it. They'd grown close over these past few months; it was impossible not to get to know him better when they were trapped together, but they weren't the kind of friends who shared intimate details of their lives.

"You're always welcome in Dragonia. Even if Ivan doesn't swear fealty to Lexi, *you*, Tucker, and any other amsirah looking to escape *are* welcome there. We could always use more allies… especially if those allies are also friends."

Ryker's small smile didn't reach his silver eyes. "Thank you, and if you ever need me, you know where I'll be."

"The same goes for you, my friend."

"It's time for me to return. I have a duty and all that. I'm my father's only child, and he's been commanding me to return. I doubt anything will ever happen to him, but I am his sole heir."

Brokk wasn't sure if Ryker realized it, but his expression made it clear he didn't want anything to do with it. While he understood duty, Brokk had never had the pressure of being the firstborn son or the only one.

Cole couldn't have inherited his father's throne, but more was always expected of him than Brokk or his brothers. It was a duty he never wanted.

"Remember what I said: if you ever need us, you know where to find us," Brokk said.

"And you know where I'll be."

Ryker rested his hands on his knees before rising. Brokk stood beside him.

They clasped hands and held on for a little longer than customary. They'd spent a *lot* of time together these past months; it would be strange not to see Ryker every day.

"I'm sorry to see you go," Brokk told him.

"I'm sorry to go."

And he meant that; Brokk could see it in his silver eyes. Whatever awaited Ryker in Tempest, he wasn't eager to return to it.

Brokk's gaze went to Kaylia, and his heart warmed, but even if he didn't have her, he'd still look forward to returning to Dragonia to be with his family and friends. Ryker didn't have that.

Ryker released his hand. "I will see you again."

"I hope so."

Ryker turned away and waved the other amsirah over. Together, they tenderly lifted their king's body and carried him through the portal Tucker opened.

Brokk descended the rocks to Kaylia and pulled her into his

embrace; he savored the warmth and reassurance of her before opening a portal.

Neither of them would ever return to this doomed land again.

CHAPTER SEVENTY-FIVE

OVER THE NEXT MONTH, Brokk grew stronger as he and Kaylia healed. Nightmares plagued them both, but when they woke from memories of the thick jungle, forgotten dungeon, and war, they turned to each other and found solace in their love.

He'd steadily put weight back on, and his ciphers had finally returned to their deep, black hue, though scars still crisscrossed his stomach and back. He suspected that, like the scar over his heart, these would take a lot more time to fade... or never would.

That knowledge didn't bother him. He didn't need a reminder of his time in the dungeon, but they were a mark of all he'd endured there.

Last week, he'd also revealed all the ciphers he kept hidden across his chest to Kaylia. He'd never shown them to another before.

Not only did he have ciphers across his shoulders and back, but he also had them on his chest down to his waist. She'd marveled over them while running her fingers across the markings before bending to kiss the white, starburst scar over his heart.

"You're magnificent," she'd told him.

"Not so much as you," he replied, drawing her up for a kiss.

He had no doubt she was the woman he'd spend eternity with, but he hadn't broached that subject yet. When they returned to Dragonia, Lexi and Cole's wedding planning resumed.

There was plenty of time to discuss their future later; now, everyone focused on Cole and Lexi. By the end of the week, his brother would be married, and Brokk was determined to see it happen, as was everyone else in the palace.

Lexi and Cole had originally planned a smaller affair, but now, with their growing number of allies, such a thing was impossible. They couldn't risk insulting anyone by not inviting them.

They were too excited about finally getting married, and neither cared that it wasn't exactly what they'd anticipated. Besides, most of their allies had also become good friends, and they were happy to have them there.

Now, while Brokk worked with his brothers in the Gloaming to finish the final details of the realm's rebuild, Kaylia remained in Dragonia to help Sahira, Pip, and some other brownies put the final touches on Lexi's wedding dress. After what happened with Amaris, they weren't letting anyone else in that room.

As he ascended the front stairs to the dark fae palace, the doors swung open, but no one stood on the other side to greet them. Helots still worked within, but the palace had opened the doors for them, not another immortal.

The dark fae's palace wasn't as bright and airy as the arach one, and it held on to its many secrets. It was the only home he'd ever known, and he'd loved growing up here, but things had changed.

Now, his home was wherever Kaylia was, and, for now, that was Dragonia. However, the familiar sound of their footsteps rebounding off the walls brought back childhood memories as he ran through here, laughing with his friends and brothers.

Often, he'd walked this hall with his hand in his father's as the king proudly told him the history of their land and the palace. Of course, he hadn't known all the secrets of this palace, and no one ever would as there were rooms none of them had ever entered.

This place liked to keep its secrets guarded, but he knew every square inch of this strange, mystical home... or at least the spaces it allowed him to enter.

When they entered the great hall, the doors closed behind them. Elvin, the only dark fae Cole had allowed to remain on the council, sat at the table already. The candle's flames played off his black hair and dark skin as he flipped through the papers before him.

The Gloaming was a realm where the most powerful dark fae families were allowed a say in the king's actions, and if one of them fell, a relative would fill their seat. Considering that most of the last council had tried to undermine or kill Cole, he'd decided to bar any of their surviving relatives from sitting on it and formed a new one.

Presently, only those he trusted most sat on the reassembled council. Elvin, Brokk, Varo, and Orin made up the new council... for now.

Cole had already promised Varo and Elvin that other members would sit here, but the new council would be elected to make sure the dark fae of the realm felt more represented at this table. If Cole decided they weren't trustworthy, they would be removed.

Brokk didn't think that would be an issue. Cole had more than proven he was fit to rule this land and the realms. The dark fae no longer saw him as a weak half-blood they could overthrow; they knew death awaited them if they tried.

While Varo sought to get off the council, Brokk and Orin would remain. Neither would go along with their brother's decisions because he was the brother. Varo wouldn't either, but he didn't want a leadership role.

They all settled at the table to discuss the current events in the Gloaming. The crops in the recently replanted fields were coming in nicely, and until they were ready to harvest, Dragonia would continue to supply the dark fae with wheat and corn.

They'd secured a lot of livestock already. They were housed in the rebuilt barns, and they'd already implemented a breeding program.

Brokk tried not to fall asleep as Elvin shuffled through the numerous papers before him. So far, being on the dark fae council was one of the most boring experiences of his life, but it was an important role, and that's why he'd chosen to stay on it in the future.

At least he told himself he was doing good as he stifled a yawn. Orin wasn't so discrete about it as he stretched, glanced at the doors, tapped his fingers on the table, and shifted constantly.

A loud knock on the hall doors drew their attention to them. "Come in," Cole commanded.

The head of a frenzied-looking helot poked around them. "I'm sorry to bother you, Milord, but your uncle is here. I told him you were in a meeting, but he insisted on seeing you now."

Cole's brow furrowed as he rose from his seat. Orin leapt up from his chair, and Brokk tensed before rising with Varo and Elvin.

Maverick rarely came to the Gloaming, and they'd spoken with him a few hours ago in Dragonia. *Did something happen while we were gone?*

CHAPTER SEVENTY-SIX

"Send him in," Cole commanded, his voice sharper than normal.

The helot bowed and stepped out of the way as Maverick strode into the room. Six foot nine with broad shoulders and a powerful build, the alpha lycan showed no signs of the near-death experience he endured when thrown into a fire.

His dark, wavy brown hair had grown out to frame his broad face. Brokk saw no unease in Maverick's chestnut brown eyes, but something had brought him here.

"I'm sorry to interrupt," Maverick said as the helot shut the door. "But I didn't think this should wait."

"What is it?" Cole inquired.

"It's for Brokk."

Maverick strode over to him and slid a piece of paper into his hand before squeezing Brokk's shoulder. "Be careful."

Maverick released him and walked over to Cole. "Sorry to interrupt."

"You're always welcome here."

"I'll see you in Dragonia."

When Maverick left the room, Brokk's attention shifted to the paper. His heart raced as his throat went dry. There was only one thing Maverick would have found important enough to interrupt this meeting for him.

Brokk unfolded the paper. On it were three simple sentences...

The human realm.

Trowbridge Tavern... what remains of Boston.

Last seen: today.

Brokk's heart hammered in anticipation. Weeks ago, Maverick sent some of his pack to search for Fabian or his brother. They'd found him.

"Excuse me, but I have to go," he said, shoving the paper in his pocket.

"It's him, isn't it?" Orin inquired.

"Yes."

"We're coming with you."

CHAPTER SEVENTY-SEVEN

BROKK HAD VOWED NEVER to return to Doomed Valley, but he needed something there. He hadn't told his brothers where he was going when he told them to return to Dragonia without him.

They weren't happy about it; they most likely suspected that he'd go after Fabian on his own or do something stupid, and while returning to the Valley wasn't his brightest idea, it was necessary. Eventually, they relented when he promised to meet them soon and went on without him.

He didn't want them coming with him to find Fabian; that bastard was *his* to kill. However, he'd do everything he could to protect Kaylia and wouldn't turn down their help when it came to that.

Fabian was an old, powerful warlock who wouldn't go down easily. Brokk had regained his strength since leaving Doomed Valley, but something could go wrong, and if it did, his brothers would destroy the man.

In the end, Fabian's death mattered most.

Stepping out of his portal and onto the mountain of rocks where the ophidians once resided, Brokk donned the metal gloves he'd taken from a suit of armor in the palace. He stopped near the strands of netting Ryker had removed from Leo's hands and feet.

Bending, he braced himself for the strands to still pack a punch as his hand settled over them. Vibrations ran up his fingers and arm as a tingling sensation spread through him.

The strands didn't hurt as much as if he'd grabbed them with his bare hands, but he still felt the power in them. If all went well, Fabian would too.

He placed the strands into a metal box that he slipped into a pouch before pulling the string tight. After removing the glove, he secured the pouch to his side, opened a portal, and left Doomed Valley without looking back.

A few minutes later, he emerged in Dragonia to discover his brothers waiting for him. "Did you get what you needed?" Cole asked.

"Yes," Brokk answered.

"Good."

Brokk's attention shifted to the palace and the dragons circling overhead. Kaylia was inside that palace, blissfully unaware of what he'd learned.

"Are you sure you want Kaylia involved in this?" Orin asked.

"Not at all, but if anyone deserves to confront Fabian about what he did, it's her. He chose for her; I *won't* do the same."

"Fair enough."

Together, they made their way up to the palace, and while his brothers waited by the entrance, Brokk went to find Kaylia. If the women were still working on Lexi's wedding dress, they would be in the sewing room.

Thankfully, he didn't have to look long as that's where he found her, laughing with Lexi, Sahira, and the brownies. They all sipped champagne while they relaxed in the overstuffed chairs inside the room.

Two brownies had joined arms and danced on a tabletop,

singing as they kicked their feet high. When they finished, two more jumped onto the table to perform another dance. Pip's melodious voice filled the air as the brownies hooked arms and spun in a circle.

When they finished, they collapsed on their asses, lifted thimbles from the table, and drank. Inelegant burps and more laughter followed.

Kaylia's face was aglow with happiness, and her eyes twinkled as she watched. She was so happy and relaxed, so carefree for the first time in months; he'd prefer not to intrude on this bubble of happiness and remind her about Fabian, but she had to know.

She deserved to go after that fucker more than him, and this couldn't wait. They risked Fabian moving on if they didn't go after him soon.

When Pip started a new song, Lexi set her glass down and rose. She bowed to the two brownies on the table before they jumped off to settle on one of the chairs with four others.

Lexi started to spin but stopped when she spotted him in the doorway. Her brilliant smile widened at first before faltering.

"Is everything okay?" she demanded.

He hated taking away her joy too, but if all went right, he'd never have to come to them with this again. "I have to speak with Kaylia."

Kaylia placed her glass down and rose. "What is it?"

The laughter vanished from the room as they all watched him. "I'm sorry I interrupted you."

"No need to apologize," Lexi said.

When Kaylia reached him, he stepped out of the doorway, and she followed him into the hall. They walked a ways before he turned to face her and clasped her hands.

She wanted Fabian dead too and was impatient to find him, but the man had manipulated and used her; he'd ruined *centuries* of her life, and now there was a chance she'd see him again. No matter how much she'd prepared herself for this, it would still be difficult for her to hear.

There was no easy way to break this news to her, so he dove in. "There's been a sighting of Fabian."

Some of the color drained from her face as her eyes sparked with determination. "Where?"

"The human realm, in a tavern, in what used to be Boston."

"I'm coming with you."

He buried his uneasiness as he leaned forward to kiss her forehead. "Do you have to say goodbye?"

She glanced back at the door. "They'll worry if I don't. Give me a minute."

Brokk released her hands, and she returned to the room.

CHAPTER SEVENTY-EIGHT

BEFORE THE LORD'S war devastated the human realm, Brokk frequented human establishments. He liked to watch the mortals going about their days, completely oblivious to the immortals who moved amongst them.

He'd often fed on the blood and sex of the mortal women. They weren't as powerful as an immortal and didn't sate him as well, but he'd still enjoyed them.

Back then, the human cities teemed with a vitality that was sucked from many of the immortal realms—years of being ruled by insane assholes who couldn't control the power of the arach throne had dulled life in the Shadow Realms.

Unlike immortals, people were always hustling around, trying to get everything done quickly. Everything was so important to them, but they had such short lives that they had to pack as much as possible into those small timespans.

Unfortunately, many chose the wrong things to fill their lives with. Still, they'd been fascinating to watch as they lived in a bubble of blissful ignorance.

Now, the cities he once loved were shells of their former

selves. Many of the once grand skyscrapers had fallen beneath the dragons' fire and the Lord's fury.

Dilapidated buildings stood in place of the once-towering structures. Of the buildings that remained standing, none had survived unscathed. All of them were missing windows and the top part of their structures.

People still resided in them, but they lived on the lower floors, and he doubted it was safe. Most of the remaining buildings looked as if a breeze would topple them.

The majority of the humans who survived the Lord's war on the cities chose to remain living in them, but those who did resided mostly in the smaller apartment buildings or stores. While they had sustained damage too, they remained mostly untouched by the war that ravaged this place.

Over time, the humans cleared some of the streets of debris and bodies. Many sidewalks remained clogged with chunks of concrete, bricks, rebar, and other assorted materials used to create the skyscrapers that once blocked the sun.

At one time, people hurried down those sidewalks as they rushed to and fro. Now, they scurried down the street with their shoulders hunched forward and their heads tucked in as if waiting for a new attack to start.

Before, he'd rarely seen a weapon amid the mortals; now, they all carried weapons that would do little good against the dragons who had leveled their homes. Still, they stalwartly remained in this place of despair and destruction.

Brokk understood why these humans remained. This city was their home; it was what they knew and loved.

They'd already lost so much that many couldn't part with what had become an integral part of them. Their memories and loved ones were here, their things, their hopes and dreams, and they couldn't bear to part with them.

Besides, life wasn't so great outside the city either, but at least in the towns and villages beyond these concrete tubes, people were building new homes, returning to the land, and restarting their lives. Here, amid these concrete tubes, he didn't sense much hope.

They were turning the parks into gardens, and livestock also moved amongst the debris. Some rebuilding was going on, but they still seemed so broken.

Ahead of them, a rooster hopped onto a pile of rubble and started crowing. A woman darted into a store when a lycan strolled past her. She watched from behind a dirty plane of glass as the lycan continued down the cluttered city street.

Much to Orin and Cole's annoyance, Sahira and Lexi had refused to remain behind. They weren't going to let Kaylia face this without them.

Against Cole's wishes, Lexi left the dragons in Dragonia. He'd prefer to have them for extra protection for her, but Lexi was afraid to traumatize the humans by having the dragons arrive to circle the city.

The last time dragons entered this realm, they'd unleased a lot of destruction. The humans wouldn't understand that they weren't here to start burning things to the ground again.

Seeing them would have thrown all the humans into a panic. He didn't blame them for it, but they couldn't have that kind of confusion running through the streets while hunting for Fabian.

Brokk suspected the man had probably kept tabs on Kaylia over the years. No one went to those depths to fuck with someone just to walk out of their lives and never look back.

If dragons arrived, then Fabian would most likely suspect Lexi was with them. And if he was following Kaylia's life, he'd know about her connection to the queen. He'd probably take off at the first sign of an arach.

And if he somehow got word that any of them were here, he'd probably do the same, so they kept the shadows around them while they moved. They were careful to avoid the frightened humans scampering down the road.

Kaylia could have cast a glamour over them to make them look different, but she worried Fabian would see through it. And since the presence of the king of the dark fae and the queen of Dragonia wouldn't go unnoticed by the immortals, the shadows were their best way to go undetected.

"It's up ahead on the right," Orin said.

Despite him and Cole having spent time in this city before the war, Orin was the only one who had ever been to this tavern. Varo had never really enjoyed the big crowds and noise of the human cities and hadn't wandered into them as often as his brothers.

When they arrived at the tavern, the thick drapes within covered the front windows, but music and voices drifted out of the establishment. Painted in gold, the tavern's name stretched across the front window, The Trowbridge Tavern.

Brokk shifted the pack he wore as anticipation hammered inside him. *This could be it. Fabian could be in there.*

CHAPTER SEVENTY-NINE

HE TOOK a deep breath to calm the rapid beat of his heart and pulled the pack closer. It contained the metal glove he'd require to remove the netting strands from his pouch. He'd strapped the glove inside so it wouldn't shift and make a sound when he moved.

"I'll step out of the shadows," Orin said. "I haven't been here since the city fell, but it won't be strange for me to enter this place. Varo can come with me, and between us, we'll keep the door open long enough for the rest of you to enter. That will let us see what's going on inside before exposing all of us."

"Go ahead," Cole said.

Orin looked around to ensure nobody was watching before releasing the shadows around himself. Seconds later, Varo did the same.

Cole moved ahead of Orin and pressed himself against the wall as his brother opened the door. Before Orin could step inside, Cole did. The rest of them followed, and the door slid shut behind Sahira when she entered after Varo.

It took Brokk's eyes a couple of seconds to adjust to the dim tavern, but once they did, he searched the occupants as Varo and

Orin made their way to the dark, wooden bar. He didn't see any sign of Fabian, but there was a cluster of warlocks and other assorted immortals in a few of the booths.

He suppressed his disappointment as his fangs pricked. He'd been looking forward to finding Fabian and making him pay for what he'd done.

That didn't mean they still couldn't find him. Someone here had to know where the douchebag was.

Standing behind the bar, a tall lycan used his towel to dry a glass while watching Orin and Varo approach. More immortals sat at the stools lining the bar, sipping their drinks while staring at the wall.

An air of despair hung over the place, and while the immortals in the booths talked, they leaned toward each other as they lowered their voices. A dull whisper of words filled the air, but no laughter.

Some of the immortals turned to inspect Varo and Orin, but they all turned away again. Only a dwarf at the end of the bar remained focused on them; a battle-ax lay on the bar before her, but she didn't touch it.

"What can I get you?" the bartender asked.

Brokk pondered if he'd told Maverick that Fabian was here.

"Two glasses of whiskey," Orin said as he rested his elbow on the bar and turned to survey the crowd.

About thirty immortals sat at the booths lining the walls, and another ten had settled onto the barstools. Three humans sat at a high-top table five feet away; they didn't seem fazed by the immortals amongst them.

By now, they'd adapted to living with those from the Shadow Realms. Plus, many immortals here weren't easily distinguishable from a mortal. Lycans were taller, and the vampires had small, visible fangs that could be hidden.

The witch wore a dress with a pentagram, but so did many

mortal women. The warlocks were almost impossible to distinguish, but Brokk knew who they were.

However, the orc in the corner didn't exactly blend, and neither did the dwarf or the two pixies bobbing up and down near the stage. Sitting there was a mortal woman who played her guitar and sang about a California hotel.

Brokk continued searching the bar, but things didn't change, and he didn't see anyone resembling the sketches Kaylia and Maverick had created. When the lycan returned with Orin and Varo's drinks, he placed them in front of them.

Resting his elbows on the bar, the man leaned closer to Orin before speaking. "If you're here for the reason I think you are, he's out back with a nymph. From what I know of him, he'll return soon. Get him out of here as soon as possible and with as few problems as possible."

Kaylia suppressed a small snort of laughter; Brokk's mouth twitched toward a smile as bloodlust flooded his veins. Fabian was here and would soon be *his*.

Orin sipped his drink before setting it on the bar. "Of course."

The lycan turned away and walked down to the dwarf with her battle-ax. Brokk didn't have the patience for Fabian to make his return.

He started toward the hallway leading deeper into the building but stopped when a tall man emerged from the shadows. He was still buttoning his pants and grinning as he sauntered toward the other warlocks.

Red clouded Brokk's vision, and his eyes narrowed on the man he planned to kill today. It wouldn't be an easy death.

CHAPTER EIGHTY

THE SECOND FABIAN emerged from the back, it felt like everything plunged out from under Kaylia. He hadn't bothered to cast the glamour of his brother over himself; that was how much he believed he could roam the realms as himself without any concern of her finding out about him.

Her hands fisted as she watched him saunter over to the warlocks with a shit-eating grin on his too-handsome face. She'd love to punch the smile off his face, smash his teeth down his throat, and gouge out his eyes as she ruined all his perfection, but they had to be careful.

As Fabian settled in the middle booth occupied by his friends, he lifted his drink and sipped it while listening to the conversation. He hadn't noticed Varo or Orin yet.

Kaylia's teeth ground together as she eyed the group. Those warlocks might be a problem, but she wouldn't let them stop her from making Fabian pay for what he'd done to her.

She had no idea what she'd do once she got her hands on him, but she was eager to find out. Her fingers curved into claws as she itched to tear him apart.

When Brokk started toward the table, Cole clasped his arm to hold him in place. Brokk glowered at him as Cole pointed at the warlocks.

"We have to go slow," Cole mouthed.

Sahira's fingers waved, and she murmured some words that the music covered. Sensing the magic, the witch looked around the room, but the warlocks were too focused on each other to pay attention to it. Eventually, the witch shrugged and returned to her drink.

When she finished with the spell, Sahira whispered, "Can Orin and Varo see us?"

"No," Cole said. "The shadows around us are mine."

"They can hear us," she said. "I included them in the silencing spell. Those warlocks will give us trouble if we try to take Fabian out of here. Some of the other patrons might too, but that seems unlikely."

"I don't care," Brokk said.

"Let them try," Orin said, staring at Varo like he was conversing with him. "We have the Shadow Reaver and arach queen. None of those warlocks can create fire or manipulate shadows into tearing off someone's head."

"I'm stating a fact," Sahira said. "Do we have any plan to get him out of here... other than brute force?"

"To scare the *shit* out of him first." Brokk's attention shifted to Kaylia. "Or do you have something you'd prefer to do?"

"I want him out of here," she said, "and dead."

"You have my guarantee on that."

"Are we going to kill the other warlocks too?" Lexi asked.

"Only if they give us trouble," Cole answered.

Orin finished his drink and set it on the bar. "Let's get this party started."

Sahira sighed. "Brute force it is then."

With a smile in place, Orin strolled toward Fabian's table. Nowhere near as amused or excited to jump into a fight, Varo walked behind him as they crossed the scarred wooden floor.

Kaylia's heart hammered, and her throat went dry as they approached the man who'd poisoned her, used her, and torn her life apart. Every part of her longed to leap forward and batter him into a bloody pulp, but they had to try to avoid conflict—she just wasn't sure that was possible.

CHAPTER EIGHTY-ONE

ORIN STOPPED beside the table and casually rested the tips of his fingers on the back of the booth behind Fabian's head. "You're Fabian, aren't you?"

It felt like someone punched Kaylia in the gut when Fabian's head tipped back to reveal his brown eyes. She'd always considered them warm and beautiful, but now an icy gleam shone in them as he surveyed Orin with open disdain.

"And you're a… nobody."

Orin rested his stump over his heart. "You don't know who I am? I'm amazed. My reputation usually precedes me."

When the warlocks noticed Orin's missing hand, a sneer curved the corners of their mouths. Beside her, Sahira stiffened as anger emanated from her.

"I already told you, you're a nobody," Fabian said. "Your older brother is the one with all the power."

Orin tapped his chin. "That's true; Cole does have a *lot* of power. So does his future bride, but so do I and my other brothers."

The warlocks all started laughing when they looked at Varo.

"He's part light fae; a puppy invokes more fear than him!" one chortled, and the others laughed louder.

Little ever bothered Varo, but this caused his eyebrows to rise as he and Orin exchanged a look before they both grinned.

"What kind of puppy do you think you'd be?" Orin asked him.

"Probably a golden retriever," Varo replied. "They're pretty friendly, and I am food motivated."

"I was thinking more like one of those beast dogs the dagadon had. They liked to eat a *lot*."

"As long as someone gives me some treats, I'll be happy."

The warlocks looked unamused by the brothers' banter.

"Why are you here?" Fabian demanded.

Orin rubbed his chin as he pondered these words. "Now, that's a good question, but I must ask, why are *any* of us here?"

"*Very* good question, brother," Varo murmured.

"I thought so too."

They were still smiling at each other when Fabian started to rise. The music stopped when Orin grasped his shoulder and shoved him down again.

Fabian's face twisted in fury. When the fingers of another warlock started to move to cast a spell, shadows raced out from around Cole and encompassed his hands. They pinned the appendages to the table.

The warlock yelped and tried to rip his hands free, but the shadows wouldn't relent. The others looked around, but none tried to bolt... yet.

Brokk moved swiftly to stand behind Fabian; cinching his arm around Fabian's neck, he yanked back the head of her ex-fiancé to expose his throat.

The grunts and struggles of the warlocks drew the attention of the other patrons. When the shadows melted away to reveal the four brothers, her, Lexi, and Sahira, they all gawked at them.

"She's here!" one of the other warlocks yelled.

Kaylia thought that was odd to shout, but it was all unraveling so fast, that she didn't have time to contemplate it. When two of the other warlocks went to rise, Varo stopped one and Cole the other.

Some of the other immortals slipped out the front door while the others leaned back to sip their drinks and enjoy the show. When Fabian's eyes landed on her, he didn't look surprised as he smirked.

Her skin crawled. *Something isn't right here.*

"Kaylia, my love, I—"

"*Don't!*" she snapped. "Don't."

There was so much she wanted to say, but no words came out as she stared at the man she'd once believed herself to be in love with. Without the potion to bind her to him, she recalled why she'd *never* desired anything from him.

He was smarmy, he always had been, and the centuries hadn't changed that. A glance at his hands told her they remained immaculate as ever. If he'd had someone to fight this battle for him, he would have had them do so.

"We're leaving," Brokk stated, "and we're taking him with us. Cole, hold him."

Cole didn't move, but the shadows slipped up to encase Fabian in a tomb of black that denied him movement. Brokk set his pack on the ground to remove a metal glove and pouch. Once they were free, he pulled on the glove and dipped his hand into the pouch.

"Where did you get those?" Kaylia demanded.

"Doomed Valley," Brokk replied.

"You went back?"

"Just to retrieve these."

Brokk returned to stand behind Fabian. The shadows retreated when Brokk clasped Fabian's wrists in both his hands.

From somewhere down the hallway, a door crashed open. Boots thudded against the wood as dozens of footfalls ran toward the barroom.

"Watch out!" the bartender shouted.

CHAPTER EIGHTY-TWO

A SECOND LATER, a dozen more warlocks, five lycans, and two dark fae entered the main bar area. They skidded to a halt at the end of the hallway, but when their gazes fell on the seven of them, they didn't seem shocked.

They looked more than prepared to face all of them. *They've been waiting for us.*

Brokk glanced at Cole before his gaze settled on Kaylia. When her troubled eyes met his, he saw the same understanding in their gray depths that had come over him.

We've walked into a trap.

And there are no dragons to help.

Brokk realized that's why they chose the human realm for this trap. They must have suspected that, if Lexi came, she would leave the dragons behind to spare the humans some trauma.

The look on the bartender's face told Brokk he hadn't been in on this as his eyes darted from the newcomers to Brokk and his family again. The immortals who had settled back in their seats when the confrontation with Fabian started, looked interested again as they sat up in their booths.

Some glanced at the door as they debated making a run for it, but they didn't move. They probably feared movement would draw an attack, and they were probably right.

The dwarf at the bar rested her hand on the battle-ax as she eyed the immortals who had just entered. The bartender set down a bottle of whiskey with a small thud.

Shadows raced across the room, but before they could attack the warlocks, the men's fingers all moved to emit a blast of air that hit Brokk like a truck. Lifted off his feet, Brokk flew into the wall.

The glove fell off, and the netting slipped from his fingers before he hit the dark wood paneling with enough force to dent it. The impact also broke one of his ribs.

Orin, Sahira, and Kaylia flew toward the front door while Lexi landed on Fabian's table. Flung a few feet away from her, Cole and Varo landed in the booth next to Lexi's.

The eruption of wind did nothing to dissuade the shadows from their lethal pursuit of the men who had entered. When they reached them, the shadows swarmed over an invisible barrier erected to keep the warlocks and their cohorts safe.

More of them raced toward Fabian and his friends, only to find another protective barrier in place. The dim light of the room didn't allow for many shadows, but even thousands couldn't penetrate the warlocks' protective barrier.

An inhuman snarl filled the air as the warlocks grabbed Lexi by the arms and hauled her toward them. Brokk tried to peel himself off the wall, but moving was impossible.

Pops and cracks filled the air as Cole half transformed and somehow pried himself free enough to roll toward Lexi, but as he moved, a wall of air slammed between them. It hit so hard it cracked the back of the seat.

Cole's hands ran over the wall as he battered it. Brokk didn't feel it, but another wave of air must have emanated from the warlocks as Cole was shoved back onto the table.

He lifted his hands a little to fight back against the air bearing down on him. If he lost, it would crush him.

Cole's bellow shook the walls as fire erupted from Lexi's fingertips and surged up her arms. It burned away her clothes while racing over her body.

The warlock holding her yelped and released her, but the one sitting beside him pulled something from his seat and lunged forward. A second later, a heavy metal blanket settled over Lexi, extinguishing her flames as the second warlock pulled it tight.

Lexi struggled in their grasp, but the thick blanket kept her fire smothered as another warlock produced a set of chains. When the warlock with burnt hands carefully started to wrap the chain around Lexi, she kicked out, catching the asshole in the chest and knocking him out of the booth.

He hit the ground with a thud and a rattle of chains as his face twisted into a sneer. "Bitch!"

The bartender shouted something and leapt onto the bar as he transformed into a wolf. Sprinting across the room, he jumped up and went to pounce on one of the warlocks but crashed into the protective bubble.

With a yelp, he flew sideways, where he bounced off a table before skidding across the room and crashing into a wall. Before he stopped, one of the dark fae stepped from the protective bubble and fired his crossbow; the bolt hit the lycan in the heart.

Still in wolf form, the man lay there, panting and unable to move. The shadows raced for the dark fae, but by the time they got to him, he'd already stepped into the protective bubble again.

The dark fae lowered his crossbow and strapped it to his side. Brokk glared at the traitor; the man looked vaguely familiar, but he couldn't quite place him. Not like it mattered; the man was as good as dead, and Brokk had no intention of giving him a proper burial.

When the warlock with the chain rose and started toward Lexi again, Brokk strained to free himself from the air pinning him to the wall. His fingers twitched as he sought to take control of the air and turn it against those seeking to harm them, but he couldn't wrest power from the warlocks keeping them imprisoned.

CHAPTER EIGHTY-THREE

THE DWARF at the bar suddenly stood, lifted her battle-ax, and flung it across the room. It turned end over end as it whipped through the air.

It must have hit the protective bubble just right as it pierced through before smashing into the warlock who'd thrown the blanket over Lexi. Strangled sounds emanated from the warlock as he clawed at the weapon embedded in his skull.

His head was nearly cleaved in two as he wobbled around before falling back in the booth and vanishing beneath the seat. A small thud told Brokk he'd hit the floor.

Some of the other patrons used this distraction to dash across the room and flee out the front door. The dwarf dove behind the bar, but it wouldn't do much to protect her.

The blanket started to fall away from Lexi, but the warlock next to Fabian leapt over the table and yanked it down again. Lexi thrashed and kicked before throwing her head back and bashing it off the warlock's face.

The man yelped, and his grip slackened for a second before he pinned her against his chest. A black lump was already forming on his cheekbone; Lexi's blow had broken it.

Called forth by Cole, more shadows poured through the windows. A lycan, who had entered with the warlocks, sprinted across the room and yanked the heavy drapes closed.

More darkness engulfed the room and eradicated many shadows, but the lamps hanging from the walls cast enough light to feed Cole. As they swamped him, the lycan wasn't fast enough to evade the shadows' wrath. His screams filled the air as the shadows tore him apart.

As they moved toward Cole, more shadows swept across the floor and over the ceiling. Brokk would have preferred to see far more of them, but any number was better than none.

That number dwindled as the warlocks near the hall moved together under their barrier to demolish five of the lanterns closest to them. More shadows disappeared.

As the remaining shadows funneled into Cole, they turned his skin darker, and his eyes burned silver while the whites turned black. Power thrummed in the air, and Cole's hands moved further upward against the wall of air encasing him.

Across the room, the warlocks' fingers moved faster; Brokk suspected they'd destroy Cole if they could. But the shadows had fueled his brother's strength, and his muscles bulged as he held off the crushing air.

Swaying back and forth against the wall of air imprisoning him, Brokk gritted his teeth as he sought to tear free of its grip. The warlocks had shifted most of their attention to Cole, and Brokk sensed a weakening in the spell holding him in place.

His teeth scraped together as Brokk succeeded in ripping one hand off the wall. He pushed further against the barrier, using his ability to control air to move it further away from him.

He'd been imprisoned once and would *not* allow it to happen again. These bastards would not cage him as the ophidians once did.

Brokk glanced at where Kaylia lay on the floor; her face strained as she sought to break free. He had to get to her.

As Cole managed to sit up, Orin and Varo partially lifted themselves, and Fabian leapt up from the table and raced across the room. Shadows pursued him but could only go so far before darkness cut them off. They hissed as they bobbed and weaved at the edge of the light.

Orin grabbed for Fabian's ankle but missed as the warlock jumped over him and landed beside Kaylia. Brokk yanked harder against his prison as Fabian scooped Kaylia up and clasped her against his chest.

A second later, the warlock placed the gleaming tip of a knife against her throat. Red exploded across Brokk's vision as his fangs lengthened and a primitive sound issued from him.

Kaylia sucked in a breath as the blade pricked her skin. Disgust and something more washed over her face as Fabian slipped his arm around her waist and pressed his cheek to hers.

Her skin paled before taking on a greenish hue. She looked about to vomit as she tried to move away from the man who had abused her so horrifically, but she couldn't avoid the knife.

Brokk would give anything to get his hands on Fabian. He'd tear him apart, strangle him with his intestines, and let him heal to do it all over again. What Fabian did to Kaylia was unforgivable, and Brokk would make him pay for it, but first, he had to get free.

Most of the shadows remained concentrated within Cole as they sought to help his brother get free, but the others continued stalking Fabian. He edged a little further into the dark before focusing on Brokk.

Brokk's upper lip curled into a sneer that revealed his fangs when Fabian smiled at him. Oh yes, he was going to enjoy destroying this monster.

"We've all heard about the witch who returned from Doomed Valley in love with a vampire." Fabian shifted his attention to Kaylia as he nuzzled her cheek with his nose. "I must say, I'm a little disappointed you moved on so quickly from me. How heartless of you, my love."

Kaylia's face flushed as her jaw clenched.

"Look at how far you have fallen from *me* to a *vampire*. I truly did ruin you, didn't I?"

Kaylia's nostrils flared, and a muscle twitched in her cheek as her chin rose. "He's a hundred times the man you ever were and a *far* better lover, you limp-dicked asshole."

As Fabian's eyes narrowed, a titter of laughter came from some of the remaining occupants. Kaylia rose onto her toes when he dug the blade further into her skin, but she didn't issue a sound as a trickle of blood ran down the blade.

Brokk jerked against his prison, tearing his other hand free as he got closer to breaking away.

"Stop!" Fabian commanded.

It wasn't the word that stopped him, but the small whimper Kaylia issued. Brokk froze as he met the warlock's gaze again.

CHAPTER EIGHTY-FOUR

Fabian took a deep breath before speaking again. "We won't kill the arach queen, but this bitch means nothing to us. Tell your brother to back down, or I *will* kill the witch, and then, I'll cut through the other witch."

Orin growled when Fabian flicked a pointed glance at Sahira. Kaylia's chin rose a little higher as Fabian pressed the blade deeper.

Rivulets of blood ran down the blade and dripped off Fabian's hand. Kaylia kept her gaze on the ceiling and her jaw locked as she sought to elude Fabian's torment.

Brokk looked at Lexi, who struggled against the warlocks trying to subdue her. He didn't know what they planned for Lexi, but they couldn't let them take her from here.

Fabian claimed they wouldn't kill her, but the man was a liar. He was the lowest form of life, and his words meant nothing.

However, if the warlocks intended to kill Lexi, they could have done so by now. They likely planned to use her to get past the dragons and to the throne; *then*, they would kill her.

And they'd slaughter the rest of them before leaving this

place. Right now, they were only still alive because they could be used to keep Lexi subdued.

When the shadows hissed, some of their enemies glanced uneasily at each other. More shadows crept out of Cole to slither over the walls and dangle from the ceiling.

The shadows couldn't pierce the protective bubble the warlocks had erected, but they searched for a weakness as they moved over the invisible structure. The warlocks beneath watched them as the shadows grew louder and their movements more frantic.

Brokk didn't know what they were doing until he realized their distraction was causing the air holding him in place to weaken. He subtly lifted one of his feet before lowering it to the wall again; he didn't want the assholes closest to him to realize he could move better.

As a murmur of unease ran through the tavern, Kaylia hissed in a breath. Her sound of pain drew Brokk's attention back to her as the dagger went deeper into her flesh.

"You may not care about her," Fabian said to Cole, who had succeeded in pushing the air away to sit on the table. "But what about your brother?"

He lifted Kaylia and edged forward to stand on Orin's remaining hand. "I can kill her and then *him*. Does your fiancé, who we will *not* kill, mean more than *both* their lives?"

Yes, she does.

Even Brokk knew that, and it wasn't because of Cole's love for Lexi but because of what she meant to the realms. Whatever these assholes planned for her, it had to do with power, and if they'd gone this far to get it, they would do anything to see their plan through.

And so many would suffer if they succeeded here. They may not kill her today, but to take power from her, she'd have to die.

Unless... Brokk swallowed as an unsettling idea occurred to him. *Unless they intend to do to Lexi what they did to Kaylia and take control of her with their magic and potions.*

Lexi was extremely powerful but also young and didn't know the true depth of her abilities. That made her more susceptible to these monsters who knew exactly what they could do.

Kaylia succumbed to Fabian's magic because she was younger than him and unprepared. Lexi was prepared for that, but would it be enough to keep her free of their control?

She was also already in love with Cole, so he doubted a love spell or potion would work, but he didn't know for sure. Besides, they could easily have something else planned for her.

The shadows stopped moving, but it wasn't because the growing risk to his family had subdued Cole; Brokk knew he was trying to lure these assholes into believing their threats had worked.

It was only a matter of time before blood drenched this bar.

Cole had mostly transformed into his male form as he regained some control over his emotions, but his eyes remained a burning silver against black. Only a fool would consider him tamed.

One of the warlocks across the room said something to a lycan. The man strode toward the dwarf, who glowered at him from behind the bar. She lifted a bottle and heaved it at the massive man stalking her.

The lycan threw up his hands to protect his face while the dwarf lifted and threw more bottles. They bombarded the man and broke apart to shower him in glass.

From the hall Fabian first emerged from, a nymph strolled out. She froze when she saw the scene in the bar and, with a squeak, turned and fled. A door crashed shut a second later.

"We have to get out of here," Fabian said, "before one of the cowards who left here goes for help. Grab the queen."

The sound Cole unleashed made the hair on Brokk's nape rise. These assholes had to know they weren't getting out of here alive with Lexi, but they seemed oblivious to the danger stalking them, hanging over their heads, and waiting to pounce.

The dwarf switched from bombarding the lycan with bottles of alcohol and flung one across the room. The woman's aim was something to behold as the bottle crashed into Fabian's head, knocking it to the side and causing the knife to slice across the bottom of Kaylia's chin.

Brokk roared as he fought against the air pinning him to the wall. He kicked against the paneling but still couldn't get free as Kaylia's blood spilled across the ground and Fabian jerked her back against him.

CHAPTER EIGHTY-FIVE

BLOOD POURED from under Kaylia's chin, but with the knife no longer there, and Fabian's hold on her was loosened by the blow, she twisted in his grip. As she did so, she drove her elbow into his ribs.

He grunted as the impact knocked the air from him and bent a little forward. Before he could recover, she turned enough to unleash a series of blows that caught him under his chin and in the throat before pummeling his rib cage.

Not only did she have her hatred of this man and everything he'd done to fuel her, but she also had her fear for Brokk and her friends. Those things combined to unleash a primal rage determined to destroy this man, who was a worse monster to her than every creature in Doomed Valley.

Most of the things in the Valley were animals just trying to survive. The ophidians were ruthless, but Fabian was a living nightmare who needed to *die*.

Her attack on Fabian provided the distraction the others needed to tear themselves free. From the corner of her eye, she saw Brokk peel himself off the wall as Cole transformed into a wolf and attacked. Screams of terror and pain filled the air but Kaylia remained focused on Fabian.

Launching at him, she gripped his throat as the impact of her weight staggered him to the side. She pushed her thumbs into his windpipe to cut off his air supply.

Her plan was interrupted when he swung the blade at her. Throwing her arm up, she knocked the arc of the knife aside before he could impale her in the back.

Gripping his throat again, her fingers constricted around it as the blood rushing through her ears made it difficult to hear anything. A haze of red pinpointed her vision onto Fabian.

Every cell in her body was hyperaware of him as memories of what he'd done bombarded her. The feel of him reminded her of all the times she'd allowed him to touch her... something she *never* would have done without a potion.

This *fucker* had used her and left her life scattered and broken. He'd probably spent centuries laughing about it while she cried.

He'd only reemerged now so he and his buddies could set this trap for Lexi. She didn't know if they'd originally expected Lexi to come with her or planned to use her and Brokk as leverage against the queen.

Once Lexi did arrive here, they'd probably planned to take a couple of them too so they could keep Lexi in line. They most likely intended to slaughter the rest.

Kaylia would never be a prisoner again; she wouldn't be leverage against her friend, and she certainly wouldn't let this beast touch her again. She'd die before any of that ever happened, but she'd far prefer to have *him* die.

Grunts and shouts pierced through some of her fury, but they remained muffled and distant despite coming from the same room as her. Fabian beat at her arms before clawing at her hands as he tried to break her hold; her fingers dug in until they pierced his flesh.

A strange, teeth-bared, almost maniacal smile propelled the corners of her lips up as Fabian's blood spilled over her fingers and ran down her arms. She felt savage and out of control, but she didn't want any control; she wanted death… *his* death.

When the high-pitched screaming started, she knew something had caused the barrier protecting the warlocks to fall. Those cries could mean only one thing—the shadows were tearing their enemy apart.

From the corner of her eye, she saw Orin roll to the side before rising. Distracted by the shadows and most likely dying, the warlocks lost their ability to use air to suppress the others.

When Orin raced toward Cole and Lexi, she lost sight of him. She prayed to Hecate that Brokk was okay but didn't dare take her attention off Fabian to look for him. A second's distraction could mean her death.

Kaylia's awful smile grew as she met Fabian's wild, terrified eyes. He looked like he was staring death in the face, and if she had her way, he was.

Fabian's punch to her gut knocked the breath from her while lifting her off her feet. Kaylia's fingers dug deeper into his flesh as the past three hundred years of sorrow, guilt, and discovery rushed over her.

She'd spent too many years engulfed by grief, anger, and emptiness. All that loss caused her to shut down as she contemplated dying.

When she finally found true love with Brokk, she'd questioned it, hated herself for it, and pushed him away. She'd spent too long avoiding the miracle of what developed between them, and it was all because of *this* monster.

Fabian brought his hand down across one of her arms, knocking her grip free of his throat. Determined not to let him get the upper hand, Kaylia lunged into him. He staggered into the wall as she hooked her fingers and raked them down his face.

Screaming, he slapped a hand to his cheek when she gouged

one of his eyes. Her awful smile returned as Kaylia leaned into him, pinning him against the wall.

Against her side, she felt the fingers of his other hand working to create a spell. Before he could succeed, she grasped it and snapped two of his fingers backward. She cut off the howl he emitted by using the side of her hand to deliver a sharp blow to his windpipe.

Choking, he gagged as he tried to draw in air. From somewhere to her left, a spray of blood hit them, more screams filled the air, and a burst of fire illuminated the tavern. That fire meant Lexi was free of the blanket.

With some of his disbelief fading over her vicious attack, a snarl curved Fabian's lips as blood dripped down his face and his eyelid drooped. Much to her amusement, he wasn't so perfect now as she gripped his throat with both hands again.

He lifted his hands between her arms, knocking them apart and tearing her grip on him free. At the same time, he shoved her back a few steps.

Kaylia stumbled before catching herself. She thought he would come after her, but he turned toward the front door.

The coward is trying to flee. That's not going to happen!

Pulling the dagger strapped to her side free, her grin returned as she went after him. Her arm moved with a speed she'd never experienced before as she sank the dagger into his side and pulled it out.

He twisted toward her while stumbling forward. When she lashed out at him again, he tried to slap her arm away, but she used her free hand to punch him in the face.

The blow caused him to stumble before crashing into the wall. As he pushed himself off it, Kaylia threw her weight into him, pinning him there as she unleashed her fury.

With rapid movements, she stabbed him over and over again until she savaged muscle and flesh and bathed in the blood splattering her. He tried to slap her hands away, but she moved too fast.

A blow to her temple left her dazed, and her vision blurred, but while a ringing sounded in her head, she remained focused on her task… complete destruction.

As she worked, all the wonderful memories she'd believed she held with this man ran through her head. All the fake laughter, the kisses, the stolen moments on beaches or beneath the trees bombarded her. *All* of it was nothing but manipulation and lies.

And then the awful emptiness after *he* told her that he'd died —the tears, the heartbreak. *All* of it was nothing but lies. *All* of it was because of this man's inability to handle that she'd turned him down.

He would *pay* for that.

CHAPTER EIGHTY-SIX

AN AWFUL, inhuman sound filled the room. It took her far too long to realize it was coming from *her*, but she couldn't stop it as she plunged her dagger in and out of this *monster*.

Fabian fumbled weakly for her hand. His attempts to stop her were growing increasingly useless as his bloodstained fingers slid across her slippery arms. He succeeded in gripping her wrist, but he was too weak, and she moved too relentlessly for him to do anything more than hold on as she tore him apart.

He sagged against her, too drained to stand alone, but she didn't stop. She couldn't stop, not even when she cut him open enough for his insides to spill around her.

The floor became so slippery neither of them could stand any more, and they went down in a tumbled heap, with her on the bottom. Those awful sounds continued from her as she flipped him over, straddled his chest, lifted the knife over her head, and plunged it into his cold, dead heart.

His hands fumbled at her face, and his fingers ran over her eyes, momentarily blinding her, but she didn't let it distract her while she carved open his chest. His breath rattled as she plunged her hand inside the cavity to grasp the organ within.

She'd expected to encounter a shriveled, dried-up, blackened heart to match his soul, but it was warm as it beat against her. Lifting her head, Kaylia met his eyes and smiled at the terror shining in them.

"Rot in Hell."

With those final words, she tore the organ free and crushed it in her hand. When it stopped beating, she opened her fingers and let it fall to the ground.

As soon as the life extinguished from Fabian's eyes, a rush of relief and something more washed over her. The thunder of blood in her ears faded as the red haze coating her eyes lifted.

Shock and disgust filled her as she gazed at what she'd done. The blood coating her dripped from her hair and ran down her arms in rivulets that pooled on the floor.

Fabian had deserved to die, and she was glad he was dead, but she hadn't recognized herself as she attacked him. She didn't know the woman who had killed with such remorseless brutality and devastating effect.

And now, it was over.

The man she'd once believed herself helplessly in love with, the man she'd agreed to bind her life to, and who had manipulated and used her, was dead. He was once the love of her life, and even if it wasn't real, she could recall the intensity of those fake emotions.

Though she was glad he was dead, a part of her remained torn about it. She hated that part more than the blood and guts surrounding her. Her shoulders hunched forward as a sob lodged in her throat.

"Easy." Brokk knelt beside her and rested his hand on her shoulder. "It's okay."

She lifted her head to look at him; the concern in his gaze was nearly her undoing as tears filled her eyes. When he wiped some of the bloody hair off her forehead, his tender touch brought some warmth back to her chilled body, and she threw herself into his arms.

Kaylia clung to him as he enveloped her in a strong embrace. Even covered in blood too, Brokk's inherent smell pushed away the awful, cloying stench of the liquid.

Her fingers dug into his neck, and she hugged him closer. She craved his strength, his nearness, and the stability he brought to a life spiraling beyond her control. His presence pushed through her distress to ground her in what was important... him... *them*.

"I'm here." His hands ran over her hair while comforting her. "Always."

Kaylia stifled a sniffle; this wasn't the time to break down. She could do that later, but she had to keep it together and learn what happened to the others. Forcing her eyes open, she blinked away the blood coating her lashes as she brought the tavern back into focus.

Twenty feet away, Cole and Lexi stood beside each other as they surveyed the wreckage. He had his arm around her waist while she leaned against his side.

To their left stood Varo with his head bowed. They were all bloodied but uninjured.

Scattered around them were the remnants of the warlocks and their allies who'd tried to trap them. No one had survived.

Orin, Sahira, and the dwarf knelt at the side of the lycan bartender who had transformed back into a man. Sahira assured him he'd be all right; they would take him to Dragonia and help him.

Kaylia closed her eyes and buried her face in Brokk's neck. "Take me home."

"I will."

When he lifted her into his arms, she curled against his chest as Lexi opened a portal into Dragonia. Brokk was her home, but she was eager to return to the realm of the dragons, where they could *finally* start their life together without Fabian hanging over their heads.

CHAPTER EIGHTY-SEVEN

As the water fell around her, blood ran down the drain in rivulets that turned the water pink while Brokk tenderly washed her hair. Kaylia didn't know what to say as Fabian's blood streamed down the drain; she'd thought she'd be relieved the abhorrent man was dead, but she was still too astonished over her actions to feel much of anything else.

Brokk grasped her shoulders as he carefully turned her in the water until she was staring at his chest again. The starburst scar over his heart remained, as did the lashings from the ophidians' whips, but he was still perfect.

He'd released the magic covering some of his ciphers to reveal them all again. The black markings had ceased being their sickly grayish hue and were now a vibrant, healthy black.

She traced the markings on his chest and down to his waist as she marveled at their beauty and *him*. He trusted her with the secret of his markings and often revealed them to her when they were alone.

That knowledge penetrated the haze of numbness clinging to her since they'd left the human realm. "What I did—"

"Was necessary," he interrupted.

"I went far beyond necessary. I butchered a man."

Brokk grasped her chin and tilted her head up until their eyes locked. "It was necessary for *you*. It's what you needed to help heal. Besides, you were far kinder to him than I would have been. If you hadn't killed him, I'd still be cutting pieces off him."

"I was out of control."

"We're all occasionally out of control, but few have endured what you did at the hands of that monster. Don't feel guilt or remorse for what you did to him; he didn't feel it for you."

With that, he caressed the healing cut under her chin. It had stopped bleeding and was mostly closed, but she still winced as she recalled the repulsive feel of Fabian's arms around her. It had been so familiar yet so *wrong*.

Despite the heat of the water, she shivered as she stepped closer to Brokk. She needed to rid herself of the memory of Fabian, and only he could do that for her.

She slid her arms around Brokk's waist and pressed closer as she rested her head on his chest, over his heart. The familiar, well-loved thump was a relaxing beat that called to her as her heart matched the rhythm.

His warmth and the sense of rightness that came from touching him washed away Fabian's wrongness as Brokk pulled her closer. His presence comforted her, and the joy swelling in her heart confirmed *he* was the only man she'd ever loved. The only one she'd *ever* love.

As the water ran over them and her hands stroked his back, the feel of his chest and ridged abs aroused her. He could shut out Fabian and the world, and she yearned for that so badly.

Turning her head, she kissed away the water running down him as she closed her eyes and savored his scent while tasting the saltiness of his skin. This man she'd loathed when they first met was all she ever wanted and more.

"Kaylia." He bent to kiss her forehead. "What do you need from me?"

"You. I just need *you*. You're more than I could have dreamed for. You helped break through the potion's hold on me by making me love you before I ever drank the antidote. You helped heal me, and I plan to move on."

While she talked, her hand slid down the edged contours of his abs to grasp his stiffening cock. She relished the sound of his breath sucking in.

When she met his eyes again, their aqua blue had grown darker with passion, but concern shone in them.

"I want to forget Fabian, and even if that's impossible to do forever, you can make it happen for a little bit," she said.

"We don't—"

She silenced whatever he was about to say with a kiss. Rising onto her toes, she draped her arms around his neck as the kiss deepened.

The taste of him, so familiar and welcome on her tongue, made her groan. Memories of this awful day and the horror of the past few months faded as his hands slid down to cup her ass.

A tingle raced up her spine when the rigid evidence of his erection prodded her belly. Electricity ran up and down her arms, causing her hair to stand on end as every part of her focused on him and the escape he provided.

She bit his lower lip as she sought more. Normally, she loved his teasing touch and the way he stoked the fires of her desire, but now she was desperate to have him inside her as they became one against the world.

His fangs lengthened when she bit his lip again, letting him know what she sought from him. When he nipped her, he licked away the blood that formed on her lip.

Her fingers tangled in his hair, and she pulled him closer as he lifted her. Locking her legs around his waist, Kaylia wiggled against him until she found the head of his shaft and slid herself onto it.

She gasped as he stretched and filled her; her hands tightened in his hair, and the air sizzled and popped around them when her magic seeped out to mingle with it. The water poured down over them as her head tipped back, and she cried out in ecstasy.

Everything about him was *right*; everything about *them* was wondrous, and she never wanted it to end. Not only did he make the rest of the realms disappear, but he filled their small part of them with pleasure and love.

He lowered his head to lick her nipple before sinking his fangs into her breast. The bliss that came from nourishing him swiftly replaced the fleeting pain.

Her heels dug into his ass as she rode him faster, and their love for each other consumed them.

CHAPTER EIGHTY-EIGHT

Over the next two weeks, Lexi worked with the others to put the finishing touches on her dress and plans for the wedding while keeping the realms running as smoothly as possible. It wasn't always easy, considering many immortals could be pretty bitchy if they didn't get their way, but it was worth it.

When her wedding day finally arrived, she could barely believe it and kept waiting for something to go wrong. It had taken them so long to *finally* get here, but soon, she'd marry Cole, and they'd start a new phase of their lives together.

Barely able to contain her excitement, she shifted from foot to foot as she walked with her bridesmaids to where they'd meet the rest of the wedding party. All around her, the beautiful gardens she'd helped bring back to life teemed with color.

The branches of the trees surrounding them arced downward; she could almost stretch her hand up to touch one of the boughs that would make a perfect seat. The red and orange leaves filling the trees burned brightly in the setting sun.

She'd chosen this section not just for the large clearing up ahead that provided enough room for all their guests but because of these sweeping, beautiful trees. Their leaves hung down from the branches, creating a soft curtain that brushed her skin when she moved.

Music filled the air as birds flitted from one branch to another. Maybe it was just her, but the multicolored avians seemed to be singing louder today, and their song was beautiful.

All the dragons of the realm had come out for this, not only to ensure she stayed safe but also because they were excited to watch the ceremony. The sun glinting off their bodies illuminated their brilliant colors as they dove and rolled through the sky.

Her first wedding dress was beautiful, but the brownies had created a masterpiece with this one. The bodice was ivory with a sweetheart neckline, but the strands of orange and red interweaving the skirt and off-the-shoulder bell sleeves made it appear as if parts of the dress caught fire when she moved.

Her bouquet of red and orange flowers matched her dress. Sahira and Kaylia had pulled her hair back and secured it with the beautiful dragon headpiece that belonged to the arach before her. It was now hers... something she was still getting used to.

They'd styled her hair so that curls fell past her shoulders to her back. Interwoven throughout the curls were small white flowers.

When they rounded the corner, her dad, Orin, Brokk, Varo, and Maverick came into view. Her dad's eyes widened before tears bloomed in them, and the others grinned.

Her dad rested his hand over his heart as she stopped beside him. "You look beautiful."

"Thank you."

"Are you nervous?"

The others stared expectantly at her when he asked this question, and she grinned at him. "I'm too excited for that."

He beamed back at her as the music started playing from where all their guests and Cole waited ahead but the bend in the pathway kept them obstructed from view. When her dad held out his arm, she slid hers into it. He locked it against his side before bending to kiss her cheek.

Orin, Brokk, Varo, and Maverick all came closer; she'd seen all the women throughout the morning and day but hadn't spoken with any of the men yet. They'd been too busy with Cole.

"You look beautiful, little sis," Orin said.

"Did you ever see us ending up here when we first met?" she asked.

"When *we* first met?" He chuckled as he shook his head. "Oh, no. I thought we'd end up trying to kill each other."

She looked at where Sahira waited in her steel gray bridesmaid dress with flowing sleeves that made it look like she wore a cape from certain angles. The halter neckline emphasized her figure.

When Lexi shifted her attention back to Orin, her smile remained, but an edge entered her tone. "I still might try it."

He kissed her temple. "I'm glad to have you in the family."

"I'm glad to be part of the family."

After Orin walked away to claim Sahira's arm, Brokk, Varo, and Maverick strolled over to kiss her on the temple and welcome her to the family. When the music changed, it was their cue to start the procession.

Maverick and Elsa walked down the pathway together, around the bend in the trees, and vanished. Varo and Pip went next, with Pip carrying a small bouquet and her dress skirt.

The brownie hadn't quite known what to do with the fancy dress, but she'd happily agreed to be Lexi's bridesmaid when she asked. They'd grown close over the weeks of working together, and while the other brownies had all settled into their new realm with their families, Pip was often in Dragonia.

She'd broken free of the Cursed Realm only to discover she was the last living member of her family. Her mother, father, and the rest of her relatives all perished while Pip was gone.

At first, Lexi believed Pip was focused on her dress, which

was why she stayed in the palace so often. Now, she thought it was too painful for the brownie to see everyone else reunited with their families while she had no one.

Recently, Puth had agreed to let her remain living here so she could be the brownies' delegate in Dragonia. Lexi and Cole had given her a room in the palace, designed it with smaller furnishings to make her comfortable, and welcomed Pip as the newest member of their growing family.

Brokk and Kaylia followed Varo and Pip, and Sahira hugged her before she went next with Orin. A minute passed before the music changed again, signaling it was her time to go.

CHAPTER EIGHTY-NINE

It wasn't the traditional wedding march Lexi had grown accustomed to while growing up in the human realm. It was a mix of the dark faes' musical instrument, the ocraba, and the beautiful song of pixies that mingled perfectly with the birds' melody.

Her father squeezed her hand, drawing her attention to him. "I never knew it was possible to be this happy and sad all at once. I don't know where my baby went, but you grew into a beautiful young woman, Andi, and I'm so proud of you. We're not related by blood, but you are my daughter. My heart."

Lexi blinked away the tears stinging her eyes. "And you are my dad; I wouldn't be here without the strength you instilled in me."

He sniffled while wiping the tears from his eyes. Lexi rose onto her toes to kiss his cheek. "I love you, Daddy."

A choked sob escaped him before he suppressed it. His attention was drawn away from her as Astarot, Belindo, and Nithe trotted into view, pushing and shoving against each other while they jostled for position.

Strapped to their backs were baskets full of white flower petals. When Lexi made a clicking noise with her tongue, their heads turned toward her, and their faces stretched into grins.

Astarot was the first to reach her, and though he was the size of a small car now, he still considered himself a lap dog as he brushed against them, demanding attention. Lexi laughed as she petted him before turning her attention to his sisters.

They still weren't good at flying as their bodies had grown faster than their wings, but they lifted off the ground a little to show their joy before settling down again. They emitted small, cooing sounds, and Belindo released a small burst of fire that caused smoke to spiral out of her nostrils.

Not to be outdone, her siblings also showed off this developing skill while continuing to circle for attention. Some flower petals fell from their baskets, but Lexi didn't stop the young dragons; they were too happy to stop.

"Enough." Her dad waved his hand as he shooed them away. "It's time to go."

Looking more than a little disgruntled with him, they shifted their attention to Lexi, who laughed while rubbing Nithe's head. "Go on now. We'll play later."

They perked up at her words and, pushing once more against each other, shuffled to the head of the pathway. Once there, they each took a mouthful of petals and cast them onto the flat, gray stones Lexi and her father would traverse.

"Ready?" her dad asked.

"Yes."

When the trio of young dragons disappeared, she and her dad followed them to the bend in the trail and around the corner. When the two of them turned the corner, the large crowd came into view, and they all rose from the white chairs set out on either side of the path. And there were *so* many immortals in those chairs.

This wasn't the small, quiet wedding she'd anticipated, but

none of that mattered as her eyes locked on Cole. Her breath caught, and her heart smashed against her ribs as she grinned from ear to ear. His smile might have been bigger than hers.

She forgot about the numerous immortals watching them as she almost dropped her dad's arm and ran to Cole. Sensing this, her dad squeezed her fingers, bringing her back to him and the crowd.

Her smile didn't lessen as she focused on Cole while moving past the different species packing the seats. Pixies fluttered from the branches sweeping over her head while they sang.

Their colorful dust floated around her to speckle the pathway. It caught the sinking sun and reflected it in a beautiful array of colors that made her dress come alive.

Murmurs and gasps ran through the crowd, but she barely heard any of it as her eyes remained locked on Cole's. He stood on the intricately carved wooden stage the dwarves had created for them.

He looked so handsome in his black fae tunic with silver embossed on the sleeves. A vine-like pattern ran around the edges at the bottom of his sleeves and the bottom of the tunic. A pair of formfitting, black fae pants emphasized his muscular thighs and taut ass.

His black hair was brushed back from his face to accentuate the handsome planes of his face and Persian blue eyes. A neatly trimmed, short beard lined his square jaw.

He'd never looked more handsome to her, and she was sure she wasn't the only one here practically drooling over him, but he was *hers*. And after this, everyone in all the realms would know it for sure.

As they neared the front row of chairs and immortals, she saw Zeth and his family, along with Firth, Mira, and some other merfolk. Yamala and Cela sat on the opposite side of the aisle, and, watching from above, were Gibborim and his sister, Banba.

She also spotted Ryker with Leland and other witches, but he was the only amsirah in attendance. His future king hadn't decided what he planned to do about pledging fealty to her, but she was glad to see the amsirah general.

Skog and the dwarves sat in the front row with the brownies. Unicorns, sasquatch, phoenixes, and other assorted creatures stood within the trees or perched in their branches.

As her father led her up the steps, Cole moved forward to take her hand. Warmth spread through her when they connected, and her heart raced as their gazes locked. Nothing in all the realms would ever keep them apart again; she'd make sure of it.

They moved toward the archway the dwarves built. The dragons and wolves etching the delicate wooden frame symbolized her and Cole's joining.

Once they stood beneath the arch, the music stopped. Even the birds ceased singing as the last bit of pixie dust floated to the ground.

Cole leaned forward to kiss her cheek. "You're so beautiful."

She turned her head into his as it became just them… even if hundreds of immortals surrounded them. "You're looking very handsome."

He kissed her cheek. "I love you."

Tears of joy formed in her eyes as their gazes locked. Alina cleared her throat, drawing their attention to the dragon perched in the garden behind the stage.

When they were in place, Alina started speaking. Lexi's heart raced, and she couldn't tear her eyes away from Cole, who held both her hands.

Alina spoke of love, faithfulness, friendship, and cherishing each other, but it was all a blur. When the dragon got to the point where she asked if they took each other as husband and wife, Lexi and Cole responded, but she barely remembered doing so; she was too busy trying not to dance around.

And then, when Alina *finally* pronounced them husband and wife, cheers erupted from the crowd, and the dragons roared as

Cole swept his arms around her waist. He plucked her off the ground and pinned her against his chest.

Lexi was laughing and crying as she draped her arms around his neck. They grinned at each other before her husband kissed her.

CHAPTER NINETY

KAYLIA SMILED as Brokk spun her around the open area of the garden where the reception was taking place. The party was still in full swing as music and laughter filled the air, and overhead, the dragons rolled, dipped, and played while their fire lit the night.

Lexi and Cole had disappeared a few minutes ago, but that didn't dampen the celebration. Beneath the glow of the lights strung from the trees, all different species of immortals danced and mingled with each other.

It was miraculous to behold, and her heart swelled with pride over the fact they'd helped accomplish it. There were still so many obstacles ahead of them, and any number of threats lurking in the realms, but they'd united so many.

Despite her joy over everything they'd accomplished, exhaustion weighed heavily as her eyelids drooped. She was ready to call it a night so she could crawl into her bed, bury herself under the blankets, and *sleep*.

Exhaustion had become a constant companion lately. Some-how, she'd managed to get through the past week despite dragging herself through most afternoons. She'd drunk countless energy potions, but nothing worked.

She'd blamed her weariness on the events of the past months catching up with her but started to worry it might be something more. Immortals didn't get sick or diseases, but they did feel the effects of spells and potions, and she'd been poisoned once without realizing it.

Kaylia liked to think she was too powerful for someone to do such a thing again, but she hadn't thought they could do it before, either. Fabian had proven her wrong.

This morning, when an awful bout of nausea hit her and she was throwing up in the bathroom while Brokk was out with Cole, she *finally* understood what was wrong with her. In the beginning, shock left her sitting on the bathroom floor with her head spinning, but then joy rose to replace it, and she found herself laughing through tears while stroking her belly.

She was dying to tell someone but had managed to keep her secret. This was Lexi and Cole's special day, the one they'd been denied for months, and they deserved for it to be *all* about them.

Kaylia had done everything she could to ensure this day was perfect for them, and everything had gone according to plan. It had been a beautiful day, and the married couple's joy was palpable.

Now, the newlyweds were gone, and she smiled at Brokk as he twirled her again. The anti-nausea potion she'd taken this morning had worked throughout the day, but now her stomach lurched, and when she reclaimed his hands, she gulped back the bile in her throat.

Something must have shown on her face as Brokk's smile vanished. "Are you okay?"

Kaylia swallowed again before trusting herself to speak. "I'm fine but ready to call it a night. Let's go for a walk; I need some fresh air."

The concern didn't leave his eyes as he took her hand and led her through the crowd of immortals. Together, they strolled further into the garden. The noise of the party dissipated, and without the lights, the moon and the dragon's fire illuminated their steps.

She inhaled the fresh air and tilted her head back to take in the stars and moon. Gradually, her newest wave of nausea dissipated, the sweat beading on her forehead dried up, and she once again felt confident she wouldn't throw up all over Brokk.

"The dragons are happy," Brokk commented.

"We're all happy."

He pulled her close against his side. "Yes, we are, and I have you to thank for most of it."

Kaylia smiled, but uneasiness tugged at her. They'd never discussed having children together or a future. They loved each other, and she assumed they would remain together, but she had no idea how he would react to learning she was pregnant.

CHAPTER NINETY-ONE

WHEN THEY RETURNED from Doomed Valley, they both started taking birth control potions again. This meant he wasn't expecting to have a child anytime soon, even if he'd told her he'd like to be a father during one of their many conversations in the dungeon.

That didn't mean he wanted a child now. They were both still healing from what happened to them, and nightmares continued to plague them, but together, they could do anything.

Kaylia's hand instinctively went to her stomach and the tiny life nestled inside. She wanted the best for her child and would do anything to protect it, even if Brokk decided he wasn't ready for this.

Why are you even thinking that? This is Brokk! He's a good man who loves me deeply.

Maybe he wasn't planning on having a baby right now, but while he might be shocked about her news, he wouldn't be angry. And he wouldn't abandon them.

A snow-white owl landed in the tree above them. She ruffled her feathers before settling in to watch them with her golden eyes.

Kaylia smiled when she saw her and lifted her arm. Ursula flew down to perch on her; she rubbed her soft head against Kaylia's cheek before taking to the sky again.

Her familiar had finally returned last week. Kaylia had been so excited to see her, and they'd stayed close to each other ever since.

"She's beautiful," Brokk murmured.

"She is," Kaylia agreed.

He kissed her cheek. "Like her witch."

Kaylia smiled at him, but before she lost herself in his beautiful eyes, she looked away again. She'd kept her secret all day, but he deserved to know he would be a father. Plus, he'd figure it out soon enough. It wasn't a secret that kept for long.

"Brokk…."

When he looked down at her, the smile slid from his face as worry replaced it. "What's wrong?"

"I love you."

He grinned at her. "I love you too."

Unable to put it off anymore, she blurted, "I'm pregnant."

His eyes widened, and he stopped walking. For a few seconds, he stood and stared at her before a big grin lit his face. He released a shout of joy, seized her hips, lifted her off the ground, and spun her around.

Kaylia almost laughed at his happiness, but the spinning caused her stomach to lurch again. She was pretty sure she turned green as he suddenly set her down.

"I'm so sorry," he said as he clasped her cheeks. "Are you okay?"

She pressed one hand to her mouth while holding the other up to him. Swallowing back her nausea, she managed a nod.

When she was sure she wouldn't throw up on him, she smiled again. "I'm okay. Are *you* okay?"

With care, he pulled her closer and hugged her against his

chest. "I'm better than okay. I've never been this happy before. A baby... *our* baby!"

Kaylia blinked away her tears while resting her fingers against his cheek. She hadn't thought she could love him any more than she already did; she'd been wrong.

"When did this happen?" he asked.

"In the dungeon."

He bent to kiss her forehead before speaking. "Something wonderful came out of that place."

Kaylia rested her hand over his heart. "*Two* wonderful things came out of that place... our love and this child."

"I want to marry you. I planned to ask you after the wedding, so it's not because of the baby. I—"

She placed her finger against his lips as her heart soared; it was what she wanted too, but... "Not until after the baby is born. Since this child is already a piece of us and here in its own way, I want the baby to be at the wedding."

He caressed her cheek with his thumb. "That's a perfect plan."

Kaylia wrapped her arms around his neck, and they kissed again. She couldn't recall when she'd ever been happier as the dragons bellowed and Brokk's hand cradled her stomach.

She'd never dreamed feeling this full of joy and love was possible, but Brokk made it so. His love had broken through the effects of Fabian's potion.

It freed her from a trap she'd never known ensnared her. It had given her life, happiness, and a future she'd stopped dreaming about when she'd believed Fabian died.

Now, she would build a life and family with the man who'd shown her what real, true love was. She looked forward to every day they would spend with each other and with the babe growing inside her.

She'd found the paradise she'd once dreamed about with

Brokk in the dungeon, and it was better than anything she ever could have imagined.

CHAPTER NINETY-TWO

SAHIRA FLUNG her arms out as she twirled at the edge of one of the garden's pools. The cooling air caressed her bare skin and sent tingles of power across her body.

Located deep within the garden and tucked beneath the boughs of weeping trees, the secluded spot was one she and Orin liked to visit when they needed time away from the palace and she craved nature. It had become one of her favorite places, and they'd never encountered anyone else here.

Standing in the shadows of one of the large trees, she felt Orin's black eyes on her and the lust he radiated, but he didn't come to her. Dancing together all night had left him on edge and voracious; she'd been sure he would pounce on her as soon as they arrived, but he remained unmoving.

Above, the dragons released more fire before breaking away to sweep over the land and back toward the mountains. They'd finally decided to call it a night.

The moon was sinking lower in the sky. Before she and Orin came here, many of the guests had already retreated to their rooms or realms, depending on whether they'd chosen to stay in Dragonia.

Closing her eyes, Sahira stopped twirling and kept her arms high while she basked in the energy flowing from the earth beneath her bare feet. It was all perfect, and she got to share it with the man she loved.

Lowering her arms, she looked toward Orin and tilted her head. His black hair and eyes blended in with the night, but she saw the ravenous gleam in his eyes while he watched her.

He was magnificent, powerful, lethal, and *hers*. And while he hadn't pounced yet, the power crackling around her and the hunger of his gaze had awakened an answering desire in her.

She relished the cool air moving across her skin as she sauntered toward him with a deliberate sway of her hips. He wasn't the only hungry one, and as she drew closer, he emerged from the shadows.

She expected him to lift her off the ground and take her beneath the trees as he'd done before. Her heart thundered, and her mouth went dry in anticipation as her nipples hardened.

Instead of sweeping her into his arms, he stopped a few feet away from her. For the first time, she saw something on Orin's face that she'd never considered possible… nervousness.

Before she could question what was wrong, he went to one knee. Sahira stopped dead, and her mouth parted when he held out an open ring box to her.

"I told you that I'd ask," he said.

Her wide eyes went from the red stone set on a delicate band, to him, and back again. A burst of white in the center of the stone reminded her of a star. It was beautiful and meant for *her*.

Then, she gathered her wits enough to realize he hadn't asked her anything… which was just like him. She grinned, planted a hand on her hip, and stuck it out. "Ask me what?"

She loved him more than she'd ever believed possible, but she enjoyed torturing him. He deserved it sometimes.

He laughed, and his eyes sparkled. "Will you marry me, Enchantress?"

Sahira half laughed and half cried as she flung herself into his arms. Her agreement was barely coherent as she kissed his face repeatedly.

Somehow, he understood she was happy to marry him as he slid the ring on her finger. She clasped his cheeks and kissed him as he brought her to the ground beneath the trees... like she'd wanted.

CHAPTER NINETY-THREE

WHATEVER JOY RYKER managed to experience during the wedding and reception vanished the second he returned to his father's castle. The freshly built, much-too-large monstrosity was not the castle he grew up in.

All that remained of that castle was a destroyed heap of picked-over rubble that had helped build this much larger counterpart. While much of the realm had struggled under the burden of the ghoul war and Leo's subsequent capture, his father somehow flourished.

But that wasn't surprising; his father always had a way of coming out on top... like pond scum.

Ryker still hadn't gotten used to the size of this place, the echoing slap of his steps against the stone, and the countless new rooms. He doubted he ever would, as he didn't spend much time here.

This wasn't his home, and his father wasn't a man he wished to see daily. If he had his way, they'd never see each other again. But as much as he loathed the man who helped create him, he'd been raised with a sense of duty and had a responsibility to this realm.

He hated his father, but this realm was his home. Even if he felt completely out of place here after the war and his imprisonment, he wouldn't leave.

He would if he could, but he'd promised Leo that if something ever happened to him, Ryker would look over Tempest and those who resided in it. That promise came before Leo's capture and after an especially brutal day on the battlefield against the ghouls.

They'd lost many soldiers that day and almost lost Leo too. Neither of them spoke while they sipped wine near the crackling fire in Leo's tent.

A white bandage covered the gaping wound in Leo's chest. Before Leo was bandaged, Ryker could see his king's heart beating.

He didn't know what Leo pondered, but Ryker spent most of that time replaying the events of the day and all the many things he could have done differently. And how bad it could have been if they'd lost their king.

Hindsight was worthless, considering it was over and couldn't be changed, but he couldn't stop beating himself up over it. They'd lost too many good men and women that day, and he was their general; he should have saved them.

But none of them had seen the ambush coming, and for that, they all paid. They'd removed the two arrows he'd taken to his back and chest, but they still wept blood.

However, he was alive, which was more than he could say for dozens of others.

He didn't know how much time passed before Leo spoke. "Promise me that if something happens to me, you'll look over Tempest and its citizens."

"Nothing will happen to you."

Leo's brown eyes were haunted and shadowed when they met Ryker's, and, looking back, Ryker wondered if his friend knew his time was coming to an end.

"My brother is an idiot," Leo stated. "I should have had children, but it was always something for the future."

"You still have plenty of time for that."

A sad smile tugged at the corner of Leo's mouth before he shifted his attention back to the fire. "Perhaps. If it doesn't happen though, *you* are the one I would choose to rule Tempest."

"I'm not a ruler, Leo."

"You rule over these soldiers with expertise and heart; my brother would see them as expendable pawns to help win this war, but you don't."

"Neither do you."

Leo sipped his wine before speaking again. "No, I don't."

And that weighed heavily on him. So many of those they lost that day were young and starting lives that were cut too short.

Ryker knew Leo would far prefer to end this war, but the ghoul king refused to negotiate, and Leo wouldn't concede any of Tempest to him; he couldn't. They couldn't live with ghouls in their land; *no one* would be safe then.

If Leo agreed to let the ghouls have a small piece of land, they would one day want more and come for it. Nothing ever sated their voracious appetites.

No, Leo couldn't turn away from this war, but neither of them wanted to fight it.

"Promise me, Ryker." Leo didn't look at him again, but his voice was urgent as he spoke. "Promise me you'll watch over Tempest and its citizens."

"I promise."

But he would have promised Leo anything; not only was he a good man and a just ruler but also Ryker's best friend and the father figure he'd been denied. He'd never expected to fail his hero or watch him die.

How Ryker would uphold that promise made over a year ago, he had no idea, as Leo's brother, Ivan, had never liked him, and the feeling was mutual. It wasn't something either of them hid.

Ryker had been Leo's advisor and right-hand man; Ivan wouldn't allow that to continue with him, and Ryker didn't want it to. He'd prefer to have nothing to do with Ivan, his promise, this land, and especially his father.

From what he'd seen of Tempest since returning, the land had been broken by the war... but then, so had he. Ryker had no idea how to help the land and its citizens heal when every day was a struggle for him.

Maybe he'd find a way to uphold his promise one day, but it wouldn't be today, tomorrow, or the next day. He'd waged wars, escaped the ophidians' dungeon, survived Doomed Valley, and watched Leo die; he didn't have it in him to care about anyone else in this realm.

For now, he'd prefer to be left the fuck alone.

CHAPTER NINETY-FOUR

As Ryker strode down the main hall, past the banquet room, solar, and doors leading to his father's aviary where his prized falcons were kept, his feet thudded against the gray stone floor. He was almost to the staircase leading to the second, third, fourth, and fifth floor—which was only the four towers of the palace—when his father's voice stopped him.

"Ryker."

He froze with his hand on the banister and his shoulders back, even as a part of him inwardly cringed away from the ice in his father's tone. It had been centuries since his father took a whip to him, but the man could still make him feel like a child again, cowering from his blows and trying not to cry because that only made the beatings worse.

Lockes didn't cry, or at least that's what his father told him as he lashed him repeatedly. They took the abuse and grew stronger from it; if he didn't become stronger, his father would break him.

And if his father broke him, he'd kill him. Ryker did not doubt it.

There had been many times when he'd believed he would

break, but that day never came. Instead, he grew tired of the beatings and stood there, staring at his father while the man lashed him.

He refused to look away from his father's gaze while the whip fell, welting his skin and slicing it open. Even when blood broke free to slide down his chest, he didn't look away.

He didn't so much as grunt as the whip cracked through the air and connected with his flesh. Sweat beaded his forehead and upper lip as the whip flew more rapidly through the air, and his father's eyes glistened with determination.

At the time, Ryker was nineteen and still not fully grown, but that was the last time his father beat him. Sweating and his shoulders heaving as he panted for breath, his father finally gave up on whipping him.

It wasn't as much fun to whip someone who didn't beg for mercy.

He also suspected he'd scared his father that day... and the duke should be scared. Ryker would have protected this realm from the ghouls, but he'd gladly toss his father to the flesh-eating atrocities if they knocked on the door.

"Where have you been?" his father demanded.

Ryker turned to face the man. He kept his expression impassive as he searched the face he'd grown to hate... a face far too similar to *his* for his liking, though there were differences.

His father's hair was dark blond to Ryker's darker brown, and his eyes were a pale green to Ryker's silver. He'd grown taller than his father years ago; he had broader shoulders and more muscle.

Even after his time in the ophidian dungeon, he had a good thirty pounds on the man. As a lightning bearer, he also possessed more power, and they both knew it.

Ryker would never outright kill his father, but they both knew he wouldn't go out of his way to save him either. He couldn't say the same about this man; if it somehow benefited him, he'd kill Ryker.

The duke most likely hadn't done so already because he had no other sons. There was no benefit to having his only heir destroyed... at least not yet.

Who knew what the future held?

"Since when do you care where I've been?" Ryker inquired.

When his father's eyes narrowed, Ryker braced his legs apart. He wasn't a child anymore; if his father struck him, he would strike back. He didn't give a shit if it was wrong or not.

"You've spent far too much time gallivanting after that fool king. It's time you return to your duties. I will not tolerate you taking off whenever you please anymore. Some things must be dealt with here in Tempest."

Ryker didn't ask his father how he'd stop him from going anywhere. They both knew the Duke of Locksley would fail to physically restrain him.

"There was a war going on, in case you forgot, Father." Ryker kept his tone as bored as possible while replying.

"Of course I didn't forget!" his father snapped. "I could never forget those filthy cretins in *our* land, but the war ended over a year ago."

"I was trying to rescue our king from captivity."

"And failing."

Ryker didn't know what his father saw on his face, but he knew the fury building inside him must have been evident, as the duke stepped away. There was so much Ryker wanted to say, but he refused to give this man the satisfaction of breaking into a tirade.

And while his hands fisted, he didn't lash out. That was his father's way, not his, and he refused to be anything like this man.

"You will stay here and take your rightful place as my heir again. You *will* perform your duties, or so help me, I'll toss you out on your ass... with *nothing*," his father said.

His mother had left him plenty of money after she died, but it was nothing compared to the duke's wealth.

Ryker lifted an eyebrow at his father. "I've spent the past two years sleeping outside, trying to survive a war, making my way through Doomed Valley, imprisoned and tortured by monsters. Do you think I give a *fuck* about your money or this place? I can go without, Father, can you?"

"Is that a threat?"

"It's a question you haven't answered."

They stared at each other as hatred simmered in his father's eyes, but he also saw something he'd never seen in them before… respect. He didn't want this man's respect either.

"Now, if you'll excuse me," Ryker said, "I'm going to rest."

Ryker started to turn away, but his father's next words stopped him. "There are things we must discuss. I expect you in my private solar at five."

Ryker didn't respond as he started up the stairs. That would give him a few hours to sleep before dealing with his father's shit.

He suspected it would be a *big* pile of shit too, as he was fairly certain one of the things his father planned to discuss was overthrowing Ivan. The duke was nothing if not ambitious, and he sought to claim the Tempest throne for himself.

There was a reason his father had built this towering fortress, and it wasn't just to show off his wealth. The duke never could have pulled off such a coup if Leo still lived, but he might be able to get enough support to overthrow Ivan.

While Leo, universally loved and powerful, would have been impossible to overthrow, Ivan was not so loved or powerful. Most considered Ivan a greedy fool, and he'd never done anything to prove himself any different.

It was only a matter of time before his father confirmed what Ryker already suspected of his plans, and once he did, war would come to Tempest again. Ryker would have to figure out which side he was on when it happened... or if he was going to be bothered with *more* war and political bullshit.

If he did have to make a choice, he didn't know what it would be. Would he side with a greedy, incompetent king or the man he loathed with every fiber of his being?

CHAPTER NINETY-FIVE

LEXI LAUGHED as Cole spun her around the great hall of the dark fae palace. Above them, stars shifted across the night sky, playing over the ceiling. The moon rose and fell as he spun her again, and while no music played, they made their own song together.

After leaving their reception, he'd brought her here, to the place where he first laid eyes on her. Their lives together had started on that night, though he never could have imagined what was to come.

He'd been so naïve about her back then, but now he knew she was the stars and moon. She was the light that chased away the shadows… *his* shadows.

She was the love that made him stronger and the woman he'd spend the rest of his days cherishing. When he pulled her close again and settled his hands on her ass, she smiled, and his heart warmed as they moved together.

It had been a beautiful day, celebrated with friends and family, but he'd craved this time alone with her. She rested her hand against his chest before placing her head there too.

Her beautiful dress caught the light of the night sky above

them and reflected its glow in a wave of fire. "This was the most amazing day," she murmured.

"One of many, *many* more to come," he vowed.

Rising onto her toes, she cupped his cheek and kissed him. He'd planned to keep dancing, but he was never one to deny her.

"Are you ready for bed?" he asked.

"Only if we don't go to sleep."

He chuckled as he clasped her hand and strolled out of the ballroom. The hallway was deserted when they stepped into it; he'd told all the servants to retire for the night so he and Lexi could be alone... something they so rarely were.

His pace picked up a little as they neared the stairs. He had something special planned for her once they got to his room, and he couldn't wait to get there.

They were almost to the steps when Lexi stopped. She tugged on his hand, pulling him back as she tried to open a door. Her face scrunched up when the knob didn't budge beneath her hand.

"What are you doing?" he asked.

"I was curious to see if the palace would *finally* reveal its secrets to the queen of the arach and the queen of the dark fae."

Cole laughed. "This palace never gives up its secrets."

"I guess not, but I had many secrets too, and still have more. Maybe one day I'll figure out the rest of my arach abilities."

He pulled her into his arms again. "You will, and I can't wait to discover what they are."

When Lexi's hand slid down to cup his cock, he knew they weren't going to make it to his room before consummating their marriage, and he was perfectly happy with that.

EPILOGUE

Three months later

LEXI SMILED as she stared down the table to where Cole sat at the other end. Brokk, Kaylia, Varo, Maverick, her dad, and Skog were gathered on one side of the table while Orin, Sahira, Elsa, Zeth, and Zeth's wife sat on the other. On top of the table near Cole, Pip, Loth, and Fath were gathered close together.

Lexi's heart swelled with joy as she gazed at the immortals she loved so dearly. They'd all become more than friends. They were her family, and she cherished them.

It had only been her, her dad, and Sahira for so many years. Then, for a little while, they believed her dad was dead, and it was only her and her aunt. Even during that dark time, her home was filled with love, but lonelier.

Now, many loved ones were gathered around, and that didn't include the dragons who guarded the land. Occasionally, one of them would swoop down to peer into the windows and reassure themselves she was okay before flying away again.

Never in a million years could she have imagined *this* was where her life would lead and that her family would grow so large. The responsibility of ruling the realms was still overwhelming, but she loved everything about the life they'd all sacrificed to achieve, and she looked forward to seeing everything it had to offer.

Tomorrow, Sahira and Orin would marry. Her aunt had insisted on a small, simple wedding with only her closest friends and family.

The ceremony would take place in the Gloaming, and Orin's mother, stepfather, and sister planned to attend. Sahira's mother would not be there. She hadn't bothered to reach out to the woman, and Lexi didn't blame her; not all bridges could be mended.

When Kaylia started to rise, Brokk quickly stood from his seat and placed a hand on her back. "What do you need? I'll get it for you."

Kaylia rolled her eyes before patting his chest. "I have to go to the bathroom... again. Sit. Relax. *Please*."

"Oh." Brokk sank back onto his chair. "Okay."

Kaylia kissed his cheek before turning away. When she did so, her dress emphasized the small bump beginning to show.

Lexi smiled at that bump; she couldn't wait to meet the baby, who was a sign of so many promising things to come. Just yesterday, she'd watched as Sahira and Elsa used a divining stone to learn the sex of the baby.

They held the stone over Kaylia's belly and watched as it spun before landing near her heart. Brokk whooped with joy when he learned it was a girl.

Cole, Varo, and Orin slapped him on the back and congratulated him while they started bantering about names. The soon-to-be parents hadn't settled on one yet.

Though Lexi had never been happier, things weren't perfect, and they never would be. Any number of threats could be brewing out there, but here, in this room, it was as close to perfect as it could get.

When Kaylia returned to the table, Cole lifted his drink in a toast. "To family."

"To family," everyone else said.

Their goblets clinked together over the middle of the table before they lowered them to sip their drinks. The happy drone of conversation returned as Astarot poked his head through the window.

The siblings had finally mastered flying and loved to show off their new skill. He was still small enough to squeeze halfway through the window, and he did so to nuzzle Lexi. She smiled as she rubbed his cheek before kissing his nose.

"Go play," she told him.

He snorted a trail of smoke at her before retreating. Over the table, Lexi met Cole's eyes again; his smile caused her heart to leap with joy.

No, things weren't perfect, but together they'd built a life full of love. And one day, when she was ready, they would add their own children to their growing family.

∾

Read on for an excerpt from *A Tempest of Shadows* Book 1 in the brand new Tempest of Shadows series, or download now and continue reading: brendakdavies.com/TSwb

Stay in touch on updates, sales, and new releases by joining to the mailing list: brendakdavies.com/ESBKDNews

Visit the Erica Stevens/Brenda K. Davies Book Club on Facebook for exclusive giveaways and all things book related. Come join the fun: brendakdavies.com/ESBKDBookClub

SNEAK PEEK
A TEMPEST OF SHADOWS, TEMPEST OF SHADOWS BOOK 1

Ellery

I DUCKED LOWER on the tree branch as the rattle of carriage wheels along the dirt road drew my attention. It had only been a matter of time before one came along, but my legs were starting to ache, and my right foot had gone to sleep from the time I'd spent in the tree… waiting.

"Maybe you shouldn't, Lery," Scarlet whispered as the clattering carriage grew closer.

"We've been in this tree for a good hour with nothing coming by; why not this one?"

Scarlet's gaze went to the approaching carriage, but I didn't look back. I'd seen all I needed to… its golden color, large size, two horses at the lead, and driver screamed wealth.

And taking some of that wealth was why we were here.

Scarlet released her grip on the branch and moved closer to the tree trunk. "I don't know."

"You get cold feet before every robbery."

"Because one day it's going to be the death of you, and I'm terrified of that."

I waved my hand absently at her. This wasn't the first time Scarlet grew anxious about what was to come, and it wouldn't be the last.

I should probably be more nervous, but once I saw that coach, my focus became on what I needed to do and not all the *many* ways it could all go wrong. If allowed that to happen then I'd never succeed, and I wasn't about to fail... too many depended on me for that to happen.

The chest strapped to the top of that carriage could feed many in The Hollows for at least a month, if not more. Whoever was in that carriage most likely had plenty of money to spare and, if they didn't, then that was too bad for them.

My callous attitude should probably bother me more, but ever since Ivan took over the kingdom and started draining it dry, I didn't have the luxury to feel bad about things. Whoever was in that carriage was one family compared to the hundreds of starving ones in The Hollows.

All I had to do was picture the hungry kids with their gaunt cheekbones, hollow bellies, and sad faces and any trepidation I felt over what I was doing vanished. I'd get that chest full of money, and I'd help put food in those tiny bellies, smiles back on their sweet faces, and damn the consequences.

I shifted on the branch, checked the rope tied to the bough above me, and made sure my knife was securely strapped to my side. While I worked, the beat of the hooves and rattle of the wheels told me the carriage was drawing closer.

I smiled as I swung my bow off my shoulders along with my quiver. Reluctantly, I handed it over to my best friend, Scarlet.

I was good with a knife, though I much preferred my bow, but it was a lot easier to jump onto a moving carriage without a bow and quiver strapped to my back. It also added more weight, and I needed to be as light footed as possible to get in and out of this without anyone knowing.

Scarlet slid the bow and quiver onto her back. Her brown eyes were full of concern as she glanced from the carriage to me; she understood why I did this, but she hated it. However, she'd stand by me, just as she'd always done, and as I'd always done for her.

"It's going to be okay," I assured her.

The shadows from the branches surrounding us played across Scarlet's pretty face as her mouth pursed. On the trees, the buds were starting to unfurl to reveal the fresh leaves they hid within. After a long winter, spring was finally creeping in, but I wished there were more leaves to offer thicker coverage.

Despite the mostly barren trees, I didn't worry about the driver seeing us; we were too far up for anyone to pay attention and most who traveled through the Revenant Woods kept their gazes on the road. Some of the creatures residing here had a way of jumping onto the road to scare the horses.

From behind me, something howled. The sound caused the hair on my arms to rise, but there were far scarier things in the world than the creatures within this forest.

I preferred to take my chances with the creatures in the Revenant Woods than some of the leaders of our realm. The monsters seeking to eat me were far more predictable.

The rattle of the carriage wheels picked up, and I looked back as the driver used his reins to urge the horses faster. Bracing myself on the limb, I rose a little to grasp the bough above before gripping the rope.

I gave it a small tug as, behind me, Scarlet sighed. "Don't get yourself killed."

"It's not my day to die."

"Oh good, arrogance. That will help."

I bit back a smile as I focused on my target. The carriage was nearly to me when I gripped the rope in both hands, gave it a tug, and swung out over the dirt road.

~

Ellery

THERE WAS a reason I'd chosen this branch and, just as I was about to let go, that reason helped me out when the carriage clattered over a rut just as I released the rope. My added weight to the vehicle was barely detectable as the carriage bounced into the air before crashing to the ground.

The impact nearly knocked me off the back before I grasped the metal ladder leading to the top of the *very* expensive rig. Gripping the cool metal in both hands, I remained low as I steadied myself on the back of the rig.

When I felt secure enough, I stayed away from the back window and used the ladder to pull me up as I rose onto my tiptoes to peer over the top of the carriage. Luckily for me, the driver's seat was below the top of the carriage, and I couldn't see him from here… which meant that if he turned around for some reason, he couldn't see me either.

I did, however, get a great view of the chest tied with a leather strap to the top of the carriage. I tapped the knife against my side to reassure myself it was still there before I climbed to the top of the carriage.

With the silence and speed I'd developed over years of running through the woods and training with my father, I moved swiftly across the top of the carriage while remaining crouched low. The jingle of the horse's harnesses filled the air and their hooves beat out a rapid rhythm against the ground as we progressed around a familiar bend.

I had plenty of time before I had to get off again, and I reminded myself of this as I forced myself not to rush. I'd only make a mistake if I did, and everything was going well.

Kneeling beside the chest, I pulled my knife free and wrapped my legs around the large chest to keep it in place while

I sliced the leather strap. I tied the ends of the strap together to keep them from falling free.

When I finished, I gathered the chest against my belly and scooted backward until I reached the end of the carriage. I swung my legs over the edge and, hugging the chest tight, slid down to drop onto the back ledge again.

Back where I started, I set the chest on the small platform. I was about to leap off the carriage and race into the woods when a noise from inside caught my attention.

I froze while I waited for someone or something to start shouting at me. I'd hate to do it, especially since I knew there was a *lot* in here, but I'd throw the chest at them and run. They'd be too distracted with recouping their wealth to follow me.

As seconds passed and still nothing happened but the noises continued, I frowned as I tried to place those sounds. *What is going on in there?*

Taking a deep breath, I peeked around the window. It was a mistake, I should have jumped off and run, but curiosity got the best of me, and like the cat, I was going to end up dead and worse, since we were in the Revenant Woods, I'd return as a ghost to haunt these trees.

Knowing that still didn't stop me from peering into the carriage. When I spotted the large male within, my stomach sank as I realized how *big* of a mistake I'd made by choosing *this* carriage.

That cat had gotten off lucky.

～

**Download *A Tempest of Shadows* and continue reading:
brendakdavies.com/TSwb**

～

Stay in touch on updates, sales, and new releases by joining to the mailing list: brendakdavies.com/ESBKDNews

Visit the Erica Stevens/Brenda K. Davies Book Club on Facebook for exclusive giveaways and all things book related. Come join the fun: brendakdavies.com/ESBKDBookClub

FIND THE AUTHOR

Brenda K. Davies Mailing List:
brendakdavies.com/News

Facebook: brendakdavies.com/BKDfb

Brenda K. Davies Book Club:
brendakdavies.com/BKDBooks

Instagram: brendakdavies.com/BKDInsta
Twitter: brendakdavies.com/BKDTweet
Website: www.brendakdavies.com

ALSO FROM THE AUTHOR

Books written under the pen name
Brenda K. Davies

The Vampire Awakenings Series

Awakened (Book 1)

Destined (Book 2)

Untamed (Book 3)

Enraptured (Book 4)

Undone (Book 5)

Fractured (Book 6)

Ravaged (Book 7)

Consumed (Book 8)

Unforeseen (Book 9)

Forsaken (Book 10)

Relentless (Book 11)

Legacy (Book 12)

The Alliance Series

Eternally Bound (Book 1)

Bound by Vengeance (Book 2)

Bound by Darkness (Book 3)

Bound by Passion (Book 4)

Bound by Torment (Book 5)

Bound by Danger (Book 6)

Bound by Deception (Book 7)

Bound by Fate (Book 8)

Bound by Blood (Book 9)

Bound by Love (Book 10)

The Road to Hell Series

Good Intentions (Book 1)

Carved (Book 2)

The Road (Book 3)

Into Hell (Book 4)

Hell on Earth (Book 5)

Into the Abyss (Book 6)

Kiss of Death (Book 7)

Edge of the Darkness (Book 8)

The Shadow Realms

Shadows of Fire (Book 1)

Shadows of Discovery (Book 2)

Shadows of Betrayal (Book 3)

Shadows of Fury (Book 4)

Shadows of Destiny (Book 5)

Shadows of Light (Book 6)

Wicked Curses (Book 7)

Sinful Curses (Book 8)

Gilded Curses (Book 9)

Whispers of Ruin (Book 10)

Secrets of Ruin (Book 11)

Tempest of Shadows

A Tempest of Shadows (Book 1)

A Tempest of Thieves (Book 2)

A Tempest of Revelations (Book 3)

A Tempest of Intrigue (Book 4)

A Tempest of Chaos (Book 5)

Historical Romance

A Stolen Heart

Books written under the pen name
Erica Stevens

The Coven Series

Nightmares (Book 1)

The Maze (Book 2)

Dream Walker (Book 3)

The Captive Series

Captured (Book 1)

Renegade (Book 2)

Refugee (Book 3)

Salvation (Book 4)

Redemption (Book 5)

Vengeance (Book 6)

Unbound (Book 7)

Broken (Book 8 - Prequel)

The Kindred Series

Kindred (Book 1)

Ashes (Book 2)

Kindled (Book 3)

Inferno (Book 4)

Phoenix Rising (Book 5)

The Fire & Ice Series

Frost Burn (Book 1)

Arctic Fire (Book 2)

Scorched Ice (Book 3)

The Ravening Series

The Ravening (Book 1)

Taken Over (Book 2)

Reclamation (Book 3)

The Survivor Chronicles

The Upheaval (Book 1)

The Divide (Book 2)

The Forsaken (Book 3)

The Risen (Book 4)

ABOUT THE AUTHOR

Brenda K. Davies is the USA Today Bestselling author of the Vampire Awakening Series, Alliance Series, Road to Hell Series, Hell on Earth Series, The Shadow Realms Series, A Tempest of Shadows Series, and historical romantic fiction. She also writes under the pen name, Erica Stevens. When not out with friends and family, she can be found at home with her husband, son, and pets.

9 798320 585727